THE CALAMITY

JENNIFER MILLIKIN

Copyright © 2021 by Jennifer Millikin
All rights reserved.

This book or any portion thereof
may not be reproduced or used in any manner whatsoever
without the express written permission of the publisher
except for the use of brief quotations in a book review. This book is a
work of fiction. Names, characters, and incidents are products of the
author's imagination or are used fictitiously. Any resemblance to
actual events, or locales, or persons, living or dead, is entirely
coincidental.
JNM, LLC

ISBN: 978-1-7371790-7-8
www.jennifermillikinwrites.com
Cover by Okay Creations
Editing by My Brother's Editor
Proofreading by Sisters Get Lit.erary Author Services

ALSO BY JENNIFER MILLIKIN

Hayden Family Series

The Patriot

The Maverick

The Outlaw

Standalone

Pre-order Here For The Cake - releases May 2nd, 2024

Better Than Most

The Least Amount Of Awful

Return To You

One Good Thing

Beyond The Pale

Good On Paper

The Day He Went Away

Full of Fire

The Time Series

Our Finest Hour - Optioned for TV/Film!

Magic Minutes

The Lifetime of A Second

For all the women who grew up being told they were too loud, too sassy, too bossy. It was never about you.

PROLOGUE
BEAU

Twenty-Two Years Ago

My love,
I spend a lot of time looking up at the sky at night. It steals my breath away. It seems impossible so many stars exist out there. Sometimes they seem close, like I could reach out and touch them, and others, far away.
A bit like you.
For not much longer, I hope.
Meet me tomorrow, nine a.m. at the barn.
Yours,
Me

The slip of paper is pale pink and lined. It smells of her. I fold it in half, using two fingernails to make a sharp crease.

Today will be a hard day. One I thoroughly deserve, a day I've brought upon myself.

My children sit at the table, eating breakfast. I don't know that I can refer to them as *children* anymore. They are twelve, fifteen, and seventeen. The oldest, Wes, is practically a man. He dreams of the military, of taking down bad guys. He carries with him the same spark of indignation I felt when I was younger.

Now the only indignation I feel is pointed inward. I couldn't be more disappointed in my weakness if I tried.

"Good morning," my wife says, walking up to the breakfast table. She nibbles at the corner of a piece of buttered toast. It's all she can stomach right now. Her voice is pleasant, because we're in front of our boys.

I've damaged our marriage.

We were broken before, but not irretrievably so.

For the first time, I wish for better friends. The kind of friends I could confide in. If I'd had that, maybe I'd have known how normal it was to ride the swells of a long-term marriage. The crisis of life and age wouldn't have seemed so pressing. Maybe, if I'd had someone to talk to about it all, they'd have chuckled knowingly and promised me Juliette and I were not a special case, but the same as everyone else. He'd have assured me that long-term marriage is a bit like being on a boat in a hurricane. Just strap yourself to the boat and hold on.

I don't have friends like that. I'm not a man who confesses my feelings and fears. It would make me weak, not to myself, but to others. Of all the gifts my last name has given me, it has removed some opportunities as well. One of which is to fully trust anybody besides my family. I have to operate under the impression that anything I say to someone not bearing the last name of Hayden can and will be used against me.

It is precisely why my affair can never be known by a single soul.

Juliette suspected. By the time I confessed, she'd already convinced herself.

We're fighting for our marriage. I didn't realize how much I loved her, or the life we've built, until it was in jeopardy. Now it's all I think about.

When I looked into her eyes and told her the truth, I understood I'd become half the man I thought I was. But I'm going to get back there. I'm going to be the man she chose. I will never, ever hurt her again.

I reach for her now, curl my finger and run a knuckle along her forearm. She watches my finger, and her lip quivers. She reaches for me, and I brace myself for her to brush me away. She hooks a finger around mine and holds it there. Her gaze lifts, finding my own.

There is love there. Hurt and pain, fury and devastation. But so much love. That is what we will cling to as we rebuild our relationship from rubble.

"Boys," Juliette says, her voice clear as a bell. Three dark-haired heads swivel toward their mother.

Wes, Warner, and Wyatt. My boys. I swallow the lump in my throat. I love them more than I ever knew it was possible to love. It would break their hearts if they learned what I did to their mother. I pray they never find out.

Juliette's hand splays across her mostly flat stomach. "Your dad and I are having a baby."

* * *

"Hi," she says, stepping out from beside the barn. She releases Lilly, her American quarter horse. Her chestnut coat and charcoal mane are nearly identical to my Arabian, Brutus. He knickers beside me as he greets Lilly. If it hadn't been for twin horses, we may not have ever spoken in the first place. Incredible how the smallest spark can result in a tremendous blaze.

She tucks a lock of hair behind her ear. "I wasn't sure you'd be able to meet me."

She's beautiful, but that's not why I made the worst mistake of my life with her. Affairs are rarely straightforward. So I've learned.

She comes to me, smiling, and tries to put her hands on my shoulders. I flinch away from her. Now that I've come up for air and seen the trail of hurt I've caused, I can't tolerate her touch.

She blinks, confused, her smile dropping a fraction. "What's wrong?"

I glance around, though I know we're alone. Juliette and my mom have gone to town to take the boys to school and run errands. The cowboys are all off to check the cattle. Normally I'd go with them, but I told them I needed to pay taxes. I really do need to pay taxes, but that's besides the point. The only person in the house is my dad, and he can't see us from here.

"Listen," I tell her, keeping my eyes on hers but taking great care not to touch her. "We need to talk."

She balks. I wait, watching as her body freezes, then draws in a long breath. "Talk about what?"

"Us." *There is no us.*

"Did you read my note?" She reaches for me again, undeterred when I attempt to shrug her off. Her fingers dig into my shoulders. I would have to physically push her away now, and I don't want to hurt her. Not any more than I'm about to.

"I read the note. Listen to me, please." I look into her eyes. I feel terrible for the words I haven't yet spoken but must. "We need to end this. Immediately. I'm not leaving my wife."

She rips her body away. Tears fill her eyes. "You said you were going to."

My hands rake through my hair. There is so much for me to feel guilty about, but I think those words might be my biggest regret. They were uttered in the heat of the moment, and I didn't mean them. I never had any intention of leaving Juliette.

"I'm sorry," I tell her, and I mean it. I will be sorry for the rest of my life, for what I've done to both women.

"Sorry?" She laughs at the word, disbelief and fury seeping through. "You're sorry?"

"Yes. Deeply."

Her fist balls at her side. I see it coming, and I allow it. I deserve it. The punch lands on my chest. It's not terribly painful, but it still hurts.

"You motherfucker," she screams, making me thankful I sent the cowboys out. Her hands sail through the air as she yells. "Oh my God." She rubs her face. "Oh my God, oh my God." She lifts her hands and I see her tear-soaked cheeks. "I hate you." She points at her heart. "I was in love with you, Beau. And now I *hate* you."

I reach out a hand, I don't know why. It's hard to see someone in such pain. She smacks it away. "Don't touch me," she yells. "I have to get out of here." She wipes at her eyes and spins toward the horses, pulling herself up.

My response is delayed, my thought process clogged.

"Wait," I yell after her. But she is gone. And she's on the wrong horse.

I climb onto Lilly and click my tongue, squeezing her middle with my legs. She starts forward, and I ease her into a trot. Cynthia looks back, sees me, and I stick out a hand to stop her. Not from leaving, but from what she's about to do.

"Don't," I shout, but it's too late. She has already kicked Brutus's sides to make him go faster.

She doesn't know Brutus came from a place where he was mistreated and kicking him is the worst thing someone can do. He rears back, and Cynthia leans out of the saddle.

"Hold on," I scream, urging Lilly into a gallop.

Brutus twists his body, trying to throw off his rider. Cynthia holds tight, her body too rigid. She is not experienced enough to handle this. He jumps, bucks again, and Cynthia lets go. She glides through the air like a rag doll, landing five feet from Brutus. I arrive a few seconds later, scrambling from Lilly before she's come to a stop. Cynthia's on her side, and I crouch over her, not sure I can move her. I brush her hair back from her face and see it.

The gash.

The blood.

The rock.

I drop to the ground, my hands press to my thighs, and I sway back and forth. There's a sound, it's so loud, and then I understand. It's me. I'm screaming.

Hands grip my shoulders. "Son. Be quiet."

My dad's face blocks out the sun, its rays emanating from his head.

I look up into his eyes. "It was an accident, Dad. An accident."

"I know. I saw it happen. I heard the yelling and I

came out front." He grips my upper arms, a dull pain barely registering as he pulls me to standing. "Go to the homestead. Get inside and don't come out."

"What are you going to do?"

"Take care of it."

It.

It.

It.

Her.

"Dad—"

"Go."

I back away. Brutus is nowhere to be found. I'll never look for him, either. I hope he keeps running and stays gone.

I do what my dad says. I go into my house. I walk into the bedroom I share with my wife. I take off every article of clothing and force myself to meet my own eyes in the mirror.

Then, as hard as I can, I punch myself in the chest. Twice.

1

JESSIE

"I figure if a girl wants to be a legend, she should go ahead and be one."
— Calamity Jane

Present Day

It smells like wood. Rich mahogany. Deep and spicy.

The dean of Arizona State University is late for our meeting. A meeting he called me to, mind you, not one I sought out and certainly not one I willingly agreed to attend. Lack of choice is why I'm here, sitting in this tufted leather seat in front of the gleaming desk, waiting on someone I'd rather not meet face-to-face.

My stomach sank when his assistant, Rosemary, called my cell phone. My first mistake was answering. I should've let it go to voice mail. My second mistake was telling her I was available to meet the dean. I should've said I was back home at the Hayden Cattle Company, bad reception out there on the ranch, *crackle crackle, I think I'm losing you.*

But if I dare to be honest with myself, the real mistake occurred when I did the thing I'm assuming I've been called here for. What I'd really like to know is who told on me? The number one rule of my operation is that nobody is allowed to talk about it. I guess I can't trust anybody in the age of cell phones and instant gratification. Assholes.

The door behind me opens. I sit, my back ramrod straight, and wait for the dean to approach. In my peripheral vision, I see his charcoal-gray slacks, his matching jacket. He rounds his desk and pulls out his chair. His hair is thinning on top, and he has a large mole that matches his skin tone at his hairline beside his ear.

The creaking protest as he settles in his seat is the only sound in the room. He folds his arms in front of himself and leans back. More protests from the chair. "You've been busy, Miss Hayden."

I smile. "My studies keep me very busy."

His lip tugs with a smirk he manages to control. "Right. And your extracurriculars? Do they keep you busy as well?"

"Maintaining a 3.9 GPA makes it nearly impossible for me to have extracurriculars." This little game is... well, to be perfectly honest, it's fun. "Perhaps next year I won't take so many demanding classes."

He nods slowly. "Are you aware it's against university policy to gamble on campus?"

I do my best not to react. I knew this was coming. "I'm not sure what you mean?"

"Miss Hayden, we know you've been operating a weekly poker game from your dorm room."

I palm my chest. "Me?" I'm great at many things, but lying isn't one of them. Like my brother Wyatt, I see rules as flexible. I view outright lying as offensive. It's something I try not to do.

"Dean Mueller," I begin, forming the beginning of my defense, "I am not a woman who goes into anything blindly. I did my research and learned an unlicensed poker game may still be legal if the game is played in a residential building. Hence, it was played in my residence hall." Leaning forward, I remove my palm from my chest and place it on the desk in front of me. "Moreover, I do not profit from hosting the game, and I keep the buy-in very low. All of which makes it acceptable."

It's immediately obvious to me that, while impressed, Dean Mueller is out for blood. The contrite expression in his eyes tells me everything I need to know. An example will be made of me.

My fingers shake, and I slip them under my warm thighs to hide them. The rest of me is still, my back remains straight as I prepare to hear my punishment.

"Miss Hayden, due to offenses that are, quite frankly, illegal in the state of Arizona and punishable by law, I have no choice but to ask you to withdraw from Arizona State and vacate your dorm room immediately."

My stoicism breaks. A gasp slips between my teeth. "Withdraw?" My voice cracks. "From college?" I thought I'd get a slap on the wrist. Be forced to volunteer in some capacity that benefited the campus. "Isn't there something I can do? Volunteer?"

The dean watches me react, then says very simply, "No."

"How about..." What I'm about to say is a risk, but who really cares at this point? "Restitution?"

His eyes squint. "Are you suggesting a bribe?"

"Not at all." I shake my head vigorously. *But also, yes*. "I'm simply suggesting compensation or repayment for the hurt I've caused. Like, maybe I can fund a Gamblers Anonymous club on campus?" I have no idea if that's a thing, but if it's not, I'll make it one.

Dean Mueller shakes his head slowly from side to side. "Withdraw immediately, Miss Hayden." He rises to his feet. "You're lucky I'm giving you the option to do so. If I find you haven't withdrawn by the end of tomorrow afternoon, I will kick you out."

I grab my purse from the floor beside my sandaled feet and wind my arm through the straps. I swallow back my emotion. "Of course," I say. Standing, I step from the desk and make my way to the door. As I grip the handle, the dean says my name and I turn back.

Behind him is a large window overlooking campus, the sun streams in, backlighting him so he looks oddly ethereal. The god residing over this institution, deciding on who stays and who goes. I could fight his decision. Make an appeal. Call my dad, ask the big, bad Beau Hayden to step in and make a donation. It's not that I'm above doing that, but I overheard him when I was home for Jo and Wyatt's wedding. The HCC is struggling, though I wasn't clear on why.

And, at the end of the day, Dean Mueller isn't wrong.

He addresses me now. "Miss Hayden, you're a bright young woman. You have something my mother called 'moxie'. More often than not, that will serve you well.

Every once in a while, it may turn out otherwise. This happens to be one of those times."

I nod and thank him, then slip from the room. Avoiding the eyes of his assistant, I make my way out of the building and into the warm sunshine.

Moxie. The word rolls around in my mouth, balancing precariously on the tip of my tongue, and I tuck it back into my cheek, like a squirrel with an acorn.

My family calls me 'calamity'.

The dean says I have moxie.

I cannot figure out if these are good things to be.

***

"I can't believe you're leaving school. There are only, like, two more months before the semester is over." Lindsay throws herself into the chair at the little table we claimed in the corner of the bar. As upset as she is, I have a sneaking suspicion my roommate is looking forward to having our room to herself. Probably about as much as I'm looking forward to not hiding under the covers with my headphones in every time she and Kurt are fooling around in her bed.

"Why can't they let you finish out the semester, at least?" Jayce, our friend from across the hall, adds to Lindsay's complaining. She wipes a line of sweat from her hairline and grabs a bottle from the ice bucket in the center of the table. She pops the top off the beer and takes a drink.

I do the same, and say, "I was lucky he didn't call the police. There was no way I could argue. He had me over a barrel."

Jayce and Lindsay share a knowing look. "Wouldn't

be the first time a person of authority had you bent over something," Lindsay says, the bottle of beer poised at her lips.

I give her a look, and they laugh. I never should have confessed my other sin to them. Maybe that was my first mistake. Or my hundredth. Depends on how the counting's being done, I suppose.

At this point, maybe I should be happy I only got caught for the gambling, and not for sleeping with my professor.

"Austin is serious about me," I argue, trying to sound like I'm unaffected by their teasing, when in reality it makes me feel prickly. "No matter how we started, he likes me."

Lindsay lifts her hands in surrender. "Fine, fine." The music in the bar switches, and Lindsay's eyebrows shoot up. "I love this song. Come on." She sails from her chair and goes to the dance floor, arms swaying above her head.

Jayce gives me an exasperated look. She doesn't appreciate the country western bar we've brought her to. She's more of a sweaty, techno club kind of girl. I sneak a peek at my phone on our way to join Lindsay.

No missed calls.

I try not to let it bother me, but irritation works its way into me anyway. Austin hasn't returned my calls or texts today. He doesn't know what happened earlier in the dean's office. He doesn't know I'll be going home to my family's ranch.

What if he asks me to stay here with him? Now that I've withdrawn from the university, as quickly as I was told to, I'm no longer a student. We can stop hiding our relationship. We haven't been seeing each other long, just a few months, but this whole situation could be what forces us to have 'the talk'.

I dance with my friends until we're sore and our throats are parched. I tell Lindsay and Jayce I'm going to get us another round and make my way from the packed dance floor to the equally packed bar.

When it's my turn, I order another bucket and smile politely at the couple beside me while I wait. They're seated at the bar, and I watch as they take a shot of Jack Daniels. The woman, a brunette beauty, grimaces at the man. She puts her hand on his chest, the diamond on her ring finger sparkling in the overhead light, and says, "It's still as awful as it was that night." The man laughs and replies, "At least this time you'll accept an open drink from me."

The woman notices me standing there and grins at me. "We're recreating the night we met."

"That's adorable." I smile at the couple. It makes me wish Austin were here.

"This is what you have to look forward to when you're old and married like us," the man says, and his wife laughs. He looks at her and says, "No babies tonight though. We don't need to recreate it precisely."

My jaw drops and the woman playfully smacks his arm. She grins at me. "He's not wrong. We have three kids. That's enough."

The bartender hands over the icy bucket. The wife waves at me while the husband orders another shot, and I walk back to the table.

I want to be that couple one day. I want to have kids and still be in love with my husband.

Now I miss Austin even more. After another hour of dancing, and the depletion of our bucket of beers, I bow out for the night. Lindsay and Jayce give me grief, but I remind them I have a lot on my plate right now.

I tell them I'm going back to the dorm for my final night of sleep there, but I don't. Instead of taking a right, I go left. I walk four blocks, past the darkened stores and late-night restaurants, and into a neighborhood.

I've never been to Austin's house. He has a roommate who teaches communications studies at the west campus, so his place has always been off-limits to us. He's also always busy preparing lessons and grading papers. And, despite the bullshit I gave the dean earlier, I really am busy keeping my 3.9 GPA. And, of course, operating a now-defunct poker ring. Most of our time together was spent in Austin's office, or at cozy little restaurants, and that day trip to Canyon Lake. We had to be careful. But not anymore.

I find the street I'm looking for and cross to the other side. The homes here are small, built in the 1970s, but charming. No master-planned communities in sight.

Technically, Austin didn't tell me where he lives. I saw it on a piece of mail sticking out of his messenger bag in his office last week. It's not my fault it's the easiest address to remember in the history of addresses. *4545 N. 45th Place.* Um, yeah. That's a gimme.

He's going to be thrilled when he hears my news. After he gets over the first part, anyway. I hadn't told him about the gambling. Once he moves past that, and my subsequent withdrawal, he'll be ecstatic. Just last week he whispered in my ear that he wished he could tell the world about us.

Wish granted.

I find the house with the number 4545 on the front.

My shoulders shimmy in anticipation, and I start up the short sidewalk to the front door. A light suddenly shines from a window at the front of the house, momentarily blinding me. My hand lifts to protect my eyes from the surprise glare, and once they adjust, I drop my arm. In the corner of the window, I see a shadow moving back and forth. Instead of going to the door, I creep to the window and peer in.

I smile automatically when I see Austin, but the smile is all wrong. It drops from my face as quickly as it appeared. So lovingly, so carefully, he holds a tiny baby in his arms, rocking the bundle.

This must be his sister's kid. Relief flows through me. He'd told me his sister was having a baby. I bet she's come to visit. Which explains why he didn't answer my calls and texts today. He was busy with his sister and her new baby.

Obviously this is not a good time. I'll stop by again in the morning, in the light of day, when I'm not mildly intoxicated and can make a good impression on his sister.

Just before I turn away from the window, a woman walks into the room and comes to stand beside Austin, arms extended. He hands the baby to her. She touches something on the strap of her nightgown, and one triangle of fabric falls, revealing a humongous breast. I'm all for feeding your baby however you see fit, but something about this scene feels very, very wrong.

As though I have a crystal ball, I see what's going to happen next.

But, just to make sure my heart really gets the full picture, I stick around long enough to watch Austin fondle her breast before the baby latches on. She laughs in this tired but content way, her head tipping back slowly, and he kisses her before walking from the room. She settles into a rocking chair and closes her eyes. The scene would be beautiful if it weren't so nauseating.

I back away from the window and get the hell out of there.

I guess when it rains, it pours.

2

SAWYER

Sixteen Months Ago

If it had been solely up to me, I wouldn't have chosen this house.

I prefer something a little more rustic. Warm oak, worn terra-cotta tile, creamy window treatments blowing in a breeze, and beyond the open window, miles of little more than pine trees and blue skies. Like the house I lived in for a while when I was a kid.

The beachside cottage I shared with my wife was her choice. And I happened to love her smile more than my design preference. There was no chance I'd argue with her, not on that day when she walked out of the black-paned French doors, the corners of her grin stretching toward her ears. Not even the diamond studs in those ears could sparkle as much as her eyes when she reached for my hand.

What kind of man denies his wife her dream home? I bought it. Right there, without a second thought, I turned to the realtor and told her we'd take it. Later, I learned she used the commission to take her recently divorced self on an extravagant beach vacation. Good for her.

I had Brea. And we had this cozy cottage, with its white walls and gray roof tiles and predesigned landscape. We ate alfresco in the evenings, both of us moving in our own lanes in the outdoor kitchen. I manned the grill, she handled the vegetables and salads. We sipped white wine and talked about our workday. We made love on the double chaise lounge, hidden from view by ivy-covered trellises on either side of our yard. Brea winked at me when she had them put in, and I immediately knew her intention. I eventually grew so used to the sound of crashing waves, it became little more than a low-level hum, like soothing background music. We no longer saw the ocean as powerful and mystical, but as a backdrop to our everyday lives.

Until the day it took Brea's body, folded it into its swell, and swallowed her.

Is it common for your wife to swim fully clothed? I wanted to slap the pity from the police officer's face but made a much wiser choice and shook my head. *No.*

Did you ever know your wife to be depressed? He continued on, asking questions that felt more like barbs digging into my cold skin. Maybe they were routine, but they felt intrusive.

The first time I lost the most important woman in my life, I was ten years old. Losing Brea marks the second time my heart has been ripped from my chest, and I'll save the sadness for later. The only way I can remain upright is to push the pain away, locking it deep inside. If I don't, I might just follow my wife into the ocean.

* * *

"I REFUSE TO PUT IT ON THE MARKET." MY WEIGHT presses into my forearms as I lean forward on the dining room table at my dad's house. It's been six months since I've been back to the home I shared with Brea. I hired someone to clean out her half of the closet, her cupboards in the bathroom, her shampoo from the cutout in the shower. A second crew placed most of our belongings in storage. What's left is a skeleton of a home.

My dad has enjoyed having me here, despite the passive-aggressive comments from his wife.

I wouldn't say I've been a good influence on my dad. At first I drank. A lot. Too much. He joined me. When Brea's toxicology report came back, it showed a high blood alcohol level. I was drunk when I read the email.

Her death was ruled an accident, which I already knew. I also knew she'd hate to see me getting wasted every night, so I quit. Cold turkey, for two whole months. I'm back to my usual glass of wine in the evenings.

Across the table, my dad pushes his empty dinner plate back and forth with his fingers. He shakes his head. "You must."

"It's not your decision," I point out. The house is mine.

"Don't let your grief cloud your judgment. That house is already worth double what you paid for it." He points at me. "And you know it."

He's right. I do know it. I know everything there is to know about the housing market. I'm the CEO of Tower Properties, the real estate investment trust my dad and I started ten years ago. Which means I'm very aware the current market isn't going anywhere but up and selling now would keep me from benefiting from its future value. But none of that matters to me. The home I shared with Brea has a value that cannot be counted in dollars.

A loud, metallic sound, perhaps a copper pot slamming down on the counter, comes from the kitchen. Renee's voice, determined and irritable, spits out, "Don't worry about me, I'm just in here working over a hot stove for you."

My dad and I share a quick look before he continues on like we never overheard what's going on in the kitchen. "At least turn it into a rental." His flattened palm slices the air vertically with his adamant statement, but then his stomach rumbles audibly, and we both glance down to the sturdy brown paper bag beside his seat. Its contents will most likely end up being our dinner. My dad's wife insists on cooking but has never actually learned how. Her failed attempts have done nothing to improve her skill.

My fingers flex and curl, and I tuck them under the table in an attempt to hide what I'm feeling. I do not want someone else walking barefoot through my house, placing their feet in the same places Brea's wandered. I do not want them to stand at the farmhouse sink, to push their hands through soapy water and gaze out at the churning blue monster that stole my wife.

My dad eyes me. He sits back. He is not overweight, or thin. He is your typical sixty-year-old, a body slackened by time. He takes a drink of wine, swallows, and says, "You aren't the only one who's experienced loss."

I blow out a heavy breath. I think Brea's death has brought out a lot of his feelings about my mother. The same is true for me.

I should ask him about it. I really should. But I can't. Seeing past my own suffocating grief is an impossible task.

"The way you feel right now..." He looks me over like he's evaluating me, determining if I'm ready for what he's about to say. "It's how I felt when we left Sierra Grande. Like a piece of me had been ripped away."

I blink. I wasn't expecting him to say that. We never talk about the town I called home when I was younger. Sierra Grande, more specifically the Circle B ranch where we lived, is a place I think about more often than I care to admit. The small town, with its quaint High Street and big grassy park, it's eclectic residents who somehow all knew each other, the mercantile that sold the best candy, it's all in my memory as a happy time in my life. It's a shiny, clean memory, and I revisit it frequently.

When we lived there, we were whole. A three-person unit. Except for the very end, when we'd left town like we had fire ants in our underwear.

Just me, my dad, and my mom's ashes. We came to California and spread the ashes in, of all places, the ocean.

My dad couldn't wait to be away from the place where my mom died. The opposite was true for me. All I wanted was to roll out my sleeping bag next to the tree she'd run into, and stay there forever.

"We still have the ranch there," he says, drumming two of his fingers on the table.

"I know. I've seen it in the portfolio."

"I was thinking you should go there and sell it."

I blink, surprised. "You want me to return to Sierra Grande?" The town has always felt off-limits, as verboten as speaking about it.

"It might do you some good. You need a project."

"I'm plenty busy with work," I argue.

He shakes his head. "You need a change of pace. Different scenery. Some time to clear your head."

"The place where Mom died? Are you sure?" He can't be serious. Years and years of avoiding the place, and now he wants to send me there?

He looks away from me.

I did it. I said her name. The one thing we never do. "It's time we sell the ranch," he says gruffly. "There's no point in holding on to it. Keeping it won't bring her back. I didn't set a good example for you when it comes to grief, and it's starting to show."

If the ache in my throat from just the mere thought of my mother is any indication, I'd say he's right about that.

Why now? I want to ask him, but I don't, because I think I know the answer. Brea's passing not only added to the mountain of grief living inside us, but it unearthed the old pain, exposing it to light it hasn't seen in a long time. And, if my dad is feeling anything like I am, it's an old pain longing to be healed. Sometimes the only way forward is back.

For me, anyway. As for my dad, there's no way he can be a part of the sale. If the world was ending, and Sierra Grande was the only town that was going to survive, he would choose death. This will have to fall on my shoulders.

"You should go," he insists. "It'll get you out of town for a while. I remember what it's like. Everywhere you look, you see her."

"Is that why we left so quickly after Mom died?" Every part of this conversation has been like walking across a minefield, yet this question seems like a guaranteed explosion.

I meet his gaze. He's biting his bottom lip, allowing it to slide slowly out from between his teeth. It feels like forever has passed when he finally speaks, and all he has to say is, "Yes."

I wait for more, but it doesn't arrive.

Renee walks out, frowning. "I burned dinner," she announces, taking my dad's wine and finishing it. I keep my grimace on the inside. This woman is my mother's opposite. Why did my dad choose her? How did he ever fall in love with her?

In the end, I take my dad's advice. I locate a realtor in Sierra Grande, list the property, then pack some bags and head to the last place I can remember feeling truly happy before I met Brea.

It's also the place that broke my ten-year-old heart.

3

JESSIE

Present Day

Austin has called three times today. I've sent him to voice mail every time. I'd like to answer and give him a piece of my mind, but I don't think I can. Not without crying. And the last thing I want to do is show him how hurt I am.

I woke up this morning, exhausted from a night of bad sleep, and fully in the knowledge that tonight, I'll get the kind of sleep only found when I'm home on the ranch. Then I packed up my room and loaded my car, driving west and then north toward home.

Suddenly I can't wait to get there. I turned off the interstate ten minutes ago, passing the small sign declaring Sierra Grande in fifteen miles, and the words below it, *Home to the Hayden Cattle Company.*

The Hayden Cattle Company. My family's legacy, a four-generation source of infinite pride and the largest cattle ranch in Arizona. It's an institution in the small but rapidly growing town of Sierra Grande. Every time I come home, there are new roads, new stores, new restaurants. The townspeople grumble about the growth, and they're quick to point a finger toward the culprit.

The Haydens.

My family doesn't care. We're used to being blamed for things. Broad shoulders carry wide loads.

Besides, Sierra Grande needed the new life my sisters-in-law breathed into this place. To say my brothers married up would be an understatement. First there was Dakota, who showed up and knocked my oldest brother, Wes, on his reclusive ass. She bought a parcel of Hayden land, developed it into what has quickly become the best restaurant, wedding venue, and once a month local vendors market in central Arizona. It brought tourists to our town, and their spending money, too. The old grumps in this town didn't mind that too much, because they benefited from the influx of money. Last month she was featured in Arizona's Best magazine, and I made sure to show every one of my friends the article.

And then came Tenley. And her movie. And her movie star status. Followed by curious people stopping in town, hoping to catch a glimpse of the retired-for-now actress who found true love with a handsome cowboy. Also known as my second oldest brother, Warner. Arguably the nicest of my three brothers.

The real uproar came when one of Sierra Grande's own, longtime resident Jo Shelton, bought an abandoned ranch and transformed it into a therapy camp for troubled youth. My other brother, Wyatt, helped her. They fell in love, because *of course* they did.

There's a lot to love about Wyatt. He's my favorite brother, Wes and Warner know it, and I'm pretty sure they don't give two shits. All four of us Hayden siblings know that at the end of the day, no matter who likes who better, there isn't a single thing we wouldn't do for one another. That declaration's not empty, either. We've had more than a few opportunities to make it true.

And yet, as much as I'm looking forward to getting home to the HCC, I find myself letting off the gas pedal, making a right turn instead of staying on the road that will lead me up in elevation and take me home. I haven't quite figured out how I'm going to tell my parents about what happened at school. Stopping for lunch at the diner on High Street will give me just a little more time to figure out what to say. Or not say.

As if my hometown is welcoming me back, I find an open parking spot right in front of the diner. I've been gone for three months, but I already know exactly what I'm about to smell when I open that metal and glass door with the *No shirt, no shoes, no problem* sign. For the record, they don't mean it. Plenty have tried.

Fried onions. Oil. Cinnamon. I step inside, inhaling deeply. A familiar, melodious voice sails across the wooden chairs and plastic countertops.

"As I live and breathe, it's my favorite Hayden." Cherilyn, a woman who's as much a fixture in this town as the HCC, waves me over. "Come sit, honey. This booth has your name on it." She smacks an empty, Formica-topped table.

I make my way over and step into her fleshy, open arms. A sudden lump forms in my throat. I've done a good job pushing away thoughts of what I saw at

Austin's house, but Cherilyn's embrace forces it from behind the curtain.

Once again, I catapult it back to the recesses of my mind and step out of her arms. I smile at her and slide into the booth. "How have you been, Cherilyn?"

"Same as always," she answers, winking at me. "Expanding waistlines and making friends."

I laugh, and the lump in my throat disappears. "I guess I came to the right place, then."

"Patty melt, half fries/half onion rings, Oreo milkshake?"

My salivary glands kick in. "Yes, please. Phoenix has thousands of places to eat, but nothing is better than this diner."

Cherilyn barks a loud laugh. "Something tells me there'd be people willing to argue about that if they overheard you." She touches my chin affectionately. "But thank you."

She walks away. I lean back, resting my head on the fake leather covering the back of the booth, and close my eyes. Cherilyn's cheerful voice floats around the room as she talks with other tables. It comforts me in a way that doesn't make total sense.

Three years ago, I couldn't wait to go to college, but as time went on, I realized how much I didn't know what I wanted to do. Lindsay's laser focus made it even more stark of a realization for me. I have no doubt she will be the journalist she's always dreamed of being. She nabbed a summer internship with one of Arizona's biggest news stations and talks incessantly about how she can't wait to meet a certain female news anchor she's been idolizing for years. I envy her determination, her knowledge of what she wants.

I have none of that. All I really know is how much I love this town. The ranch where I grew up. My family. I don't have grand plans the way other people do. Not that any of that matters anyway. The dean did me a solid by allowing me to withdraw as opposed to kicking me out, so at least my transcripts won't bear that mark.

Despite that show of kindness, the fact remains. I'm twenty-one years old, and where most of my peers are gearing up for their first steps onto career paths, I've been knocked on my ass on the sidelines.

I take a deep breath, determined not to feel sorry for myself. My lungs are full of air when goose bumps ripple across my forearms, even though it's not cold in here. I look down at the tiny, taut hairs, and around the room for the source of the sudden chill. There's no obvious reason for this feeling, but my gaze lands on a man fitting his tall frame onto a stool at the eat-in counter.

He wears a suit. Fancy leather sneakers. He shrugs off his navy-blue jacket and carefully folds it in half, draping it across one thigh. His crisp, white shirt stretches over an expansive upper back. He is large, well-built, and oddly reminds me of my brothers. If they'd ever wear a suit, that is, which none of them do. He turns his head, revealing his profile, and all thoughts of my brothers vanish. This man is strikingly handsome, with a strong jaw and a perfectly straight nose. He's completely out of place. Maybe his Porsche broke down as he was passing through.

Cherilyn approaches him, exchanging pleasantries. He isn't overly friendly, but he's not rude. Reserved. Something about their exchange seems comfortable, as if she knows him. *Interesting.*

She pivots, grabbing my lunch from the window, then sets an ice water in front of the mystery man. When she drops off my plate, I ask as casually as I can muster, "Who's the suit at the counter?"

She glances over her shoulder, then back to me. "That would be Sawyer Bennett."

I sneak a peek at him, admiring the way the fabric of his shirt molds to the dips and rises of his upper arms. I look back to Cherilyn. "Why do I feel like I know that last name?" It's ringing a bell in an off-hand way.

"His family lived here way back when. Before you were born. Bennett is the B in Circle B. Also known as the previous name of your newest sister-in-law's ranch."

I nod slowly. This is getting more interesting with every unearthed detail. "Why is he back?"

Cherilyn shrugs. "He came back a while ago to sell the ranch, but he started buying up other properties too. He's some kind of real estate guy. He was buttoned up when he arrived, but I've been wearing him down." She gives me a pointed look and ducks her chin at me. "He has some ties to you."

My eyebrows cinch. "How's that?"

"He invested in Jo's ranch when she needed cash."

"Ohhh..." I knew there'd been an investor, I just didn't know who. When I hear the word *investor,* my mind conjures up an old guy. "That was nice of him," I say, my lips wrapped around the wide straw poking out from my shake.

Cherilyn looks at him again, eyes squinted in suspicion. "I suppose so. Couldn't have been for nothing. I'm sure he gets a percentage of the profits for the cash he fronted."

"As most investors do," I comment, taking a bite of

my burger, and the automatic groan brings Cherilyn's attention back to me. "Do you know how much I love that I can come back here and order this and it's still as good as it was the first time I had it? That constancy makes my heart happy."

"I'm just happy you're happy." Cherilyn taps my nose and walks away to take care of her other tables.

And me? Well, I'd be lying if I said I haven't glanced over at the counter a few times. That man, *Sawyer Bennett*, is hard to look away from. Gorgeous and a mystery? Great combination.

My thumb taps the table as I chew through my food, my mind on my current situation. No school. No Austin. Blank slate, as they say. A chance to rewrite my future.

I don't know a lot about what it will look like, but I know one thing for certain.

It will not be boring.

* * *

I PAUSE AT MY OPEN TRUNK, MY HAND ON MY BAG, drawing in a lungful of air. The smell of the ranch, a scent I wish I could have bottled and taken with me to school, is a caress for my wounded pride. As hard as I'm trying not to think of Austin, it's impossible not to. Especially since he has texted me twice since I left the diner, wanting to know what I'm doing and why I wasn't in class today. I send him one text informing him we are over and not to contact me. He responds wanting to know why, and I ignore it. I plan to ignore every message he ever sends me until the end of time. Now that I know the truth about him, even a single word to him feels wrong.

What a fool. He was married. He must've loved the adrenaline surge of that tightrope he balanced on. How much longer would it have continued if I hadn't found out? I guess I don't have to spend too much time thinking about that.

My head tips back, the ends of my long hair tickling my back, and the sunshine spills over my face. In the distance, a horse whinnies, and I smile. I know that sound. I've missed her, and she's missed me.

Pulling a couple of my smaller bags from my trunk, I haul them over my shoulders and leave my trunk open. I'll have to come back for my other things. I take the steps up to the wide front porch of my childhood home. The homestead is my favorite place to be, aside from my secret spot on the edge of our land, where there's a dry waterfall. In late summer, the monsoons come through and the waterfall runs.

The homestead is large, made of wooden logs and stone in varying shades of gray. It's rustic, and intimidating to people who don't consider it home, and suddenly I'm overcome with relief. But then I remember my parents don't know I've been kicked out of school and I still don't know what to tell them about that. The truth is probably best, considering it's two months before the school year should be finished and *I'm so smart they let me take my finals and finish early* isn't going to work.

I swallow around my nerves and push through into the house. At first it appears empty, not a sound coming from any room as I wander through. But then a loud snore fills a room I've been through already, and I smile as I double back to the living room. Gramps lies on the couch facing the floor-to-ceiling fireplace, fast asleep.

He twitches, and I back away quietly and go to my room to deposit my things.

I'm on my third trip from my car to my room when my mom walks in the back door. She presses her hands to her lower back and arches, grimacing. I watch her pull off thick work gloves, sit down on the bench next to the door, and start on her boots.

I come forward, my shoes making noise on the wood floor. She looks up and startles, halfway through removing her second boot.

"What are you doing here? Are you okay?" She stands and starts for me, still wearing her socks.

"I'm fine, Mom. I promise. I just missed you guys." Not a lie. "Home for a long weekend." Definitely a lie, and not one I really meant to tell. It just slipped out. I start to correct it, thinking maybe it'll be better to make a clean cut, but her reaction stops me.

She pulls me in for a hug, then pushes me back and looks at me. "I'm so glad you're here. I've been missing my girl."

The truth sticks in my throat. Instead I hug her again, inhaling the familiar smells of the ranch that nestle in her hair. My brothers consider my mom to be tough, and she is, but she was different with me. She and my dad tried so long for a girl, and after a few miscarriages, they'd given up. Then one day, surprise! She was older by then and convinced herself it wasn't in the cards for them. Between the fact that I'm the baby of the family, and they never thought they'd have me, I've been allowed to get away with a lot more than my brothers.

Something tells me illegal gambling and being

asked to withdraw from school goes far beyond the shit I pulled when I was younger.

She backs away from our second hug and looks me in the eyes. "Anything else?"

I purse my lips and shake my head. I don't want to see the disappointment on her face. Not yet. I don't want to hear that it's just like me to go and do something like that.

Calamity Jessie.

"Is there anything I can help you with?" I ask.

Mom steps into the little bathroom across the hall and turns on the sink faucet. "Vendor weekend at The Orchard is this weekend. I could use an extra pair of hands making the goat cheese I'm planning to sell."

"Put me to work," I say, taking her place at the sink when she's done washing her hands. She waits for me to finish, and we walk into the kitchen. I get out a colander and the fine cheese cloth, and she pulls out a stock pot and pours in the goats milk.

"How are your goats?" I ask, watching her stir the milk as she tests its temperature with her digital thermometer.

She smiles. "Freddy is so funny. He hates when I pay attention to Daisy. And Delilah does this thing where she..." I nod like I'm listening, but I'm thinking about how her face lights up when she talks about her animals. We used to joke that she loved her goats more than us, and maybe we were really only half kidding. A few years ago there was a barn fire and my mom lost some goats. If it hadn't been for Wes's bravery, (or stupidity, depending on who's talking about it) she would've lost more.

"I'm glad you're enjoying them, Mom."

"I need something now that you're all out of the house. Wes is the only one still living on the HCC. You're at school, and Warner and Wyatt moved out to be with their new families." The thermometer hits one hundred eighty degrees, and she moves the pan from the burner. "Not that I'm complaining. I'd be kicking their asses out if they were as old as they are and still living at home."

I measure out the lemon juice and add it, she stirs, then I add the vinegar and she stirs again. "Okay," she announces, using a dishcloth to wipe a few drops of milk from the counter. "Thirty minutes at rest and then we'll finish up."

"Sounds good, Mom. Anything else I can do?"

"Why don't you go see Hester Prynne? Wyatt rides her to make sure she gets exercise, but she misses you."

"Good idea." I kiss her cheek. "By the way, Gramps is sleeping in the living room."

Mom smirks. "The man sleeps more than he does anything else."

A twinge of worry tugs at me. "Is he healthy?"

Mom tips her head to the side. "That depends on how you define healthy. He's old, honey. His body is tired." She makes a face. "But that mind of his is sharp. I won't tell you what he said last week. His filter is gone."

I chuckle. "Hopefully I can get him to say some bad things in front of me."

Mom shakes her head. "Don't worry, he will. He doesn't give a fuck about anything anymore."

"Mom," I chastise, acting offended by her swear word.

She winks at me. "Just getting you warmed up for Gramps."

I leave her in the kitchen and go to my room to change into jeans. I grip my taller boots on either side, sliding my foot into the supple leather, and curl my toes when they're all the way on. I stand up and look at myself in the full-length mirror.

Tight jeans tucked into my favorite pair of boots, and a T-shirt knotted on the side. This is the person I've been missing, but there's just one more thing I need. I smile at my reflection and grab my purple suede cowboy hat. I fit it over my head and look once more.

Just right.

4

SAWYER

Sometimes, Sierra Grande feels more like a person and less like a landscape. Green lawns, mature trees, the Verde River cutting through the town. Go south and find cactus. Head north and hit the pines. The town nestles between the two, marrying the landscapes. But all that is surface beauty.

Underneath, it's the heart of this place that makes it seem human. The people of the town care about each other. They tell stories about the flood in 1988 when so-and-so's barn washed away and they all came together to rebuild it. Or the time Lucy Wilson's dog went missing, and she was too blind to find it herself, so everyone turned up to help. The story doesn't have a happy ending, unfortunately, but that's not the point.

Sierra Grande's residents act like family. They support each other, show love through action, and aren't afraid to piss each other off.

When I first showed up in town, I assumed I'd be nameless in the crowd, but the waitress at the diner knew me immediately. She took one look at me and said, "There's only one other person I've seen with eyes gray as an angry summer thunderstorm, and I think you're him."

I introduced myself, though I didn't need to. Cherilyn welcomed me back to Sierra Grande, didn't ask me why I'd returned, and didn't say a word about why my dad and I left the way we did. She brought me a piece of pie and that was it. A shred of my reservation about coming back melted away, and I began to understand returning to a place that will undoubtedly hold sadness may also contain hidden joy.

After that, I checked into The Sierra and told them my stay was for an undetermined amount of time. Then I met up with the realtor, and she presented me with the offers for the ranch. I could've sold for more, but money wasn't going to soothe the pain of letting go of the last place I saw my mother. The second I heard of Jo Shelton's plans for the ranch, I knew it should go to her. The realtor, Jericho, argued with me, but I'd shut her down. There was no room for my mind to be changed. Once the deal was finished, Jericho asked me out. I politely declined.

Quickly I realized the town is a gold mine. Exponential growth, but the price for land hasn't gone up much yet. It's the sweetest spot a buyer can find themselves in, and I began taking advantage of it.

Then Jo approached me. She stopped me outside The Bakery on blueberry muffin day, and my heart leaped into my throat. She had the same white-blonde hair as Brea, with the addition of pink tips. They also shared kind eyes and an endearing smile. When she told me she needed an investor, I knew I didn't have a chance. I couldn't say no to a woman who reminded me so much of Brea.

I wouldn't have thought it possible, but Sierra Grande is starting to feel like home. A lot of it is new, so it doesn't hurt as much as I anticipated. There are moments, though, memories that rise to the surface like pieces of a sunken ship. Sometimes I see my mother in an arc of sunlight, stepping from the Merc holding a bag of saltwater taffy. Those moments are when I'm not sure it's good that I'm here, but I suppose it beats being in California and remembering my wife. I've traded new grief for old grief.

On my way to my rented office space, I stop in at the diner to see Cherilyn. I order the same sandwich as always. I watch the same midday news channel. The only difference today is the woman in the booth across the room. I've never seen her before, but Cherilyn addresses her like a long-lost daughter.

When the woman gets up, I avert my gaze. There's a mirror on the wall behind the counter, meant to keep the servers from running into each other as they come around the corner. I use it to look at this woman. She's younger than I thought at first glance. Her cheeks are full, her lips pouty, but it's her eyes that take me by surprise. They hold no trace of naïveté. Wise beyond her years, and determined. In the three seconds time it takes her to pass me, I decide there's no way I want to reckon with a force like her.

It's a damn good thing I'm still in love with my wife, because there was a day when that woman would be just my type.

* * *

SOMETIMES, I DO THIS THING THAT'S PRETTY STUPID. AND here I am, doing it right now.

I park my car in front of Wildflower and get out. It looks nothing like the Circle B from my memories. Jo has changed more than just the name. The entire place has undergone a face-lift. Even the heart of the place has changed. Jo is at its core now, a place my mother once occupied.

I am partial to Jo, not just because she reminds me of Brea, but because she also reminds me of my mom. Considerate and caring, but not a pushover.

I head for the stable, where the stupid thing I'm about to do waits for me.

Wyatt Hayden, Jo's husband, is inside, showing two boys the proper way to brush a horse. Equine therapy is an integral part of the program Jo has created with the help of the psychologist she hired, and Wyatt leads it.

He says hello to me in that short way of his. He's not rude, but he's not over-friendly either. I didn't make it known who I was when I agreed to invest in the ranch, and somehow Wyatt found out. He'd asked me about it, and I explained I came back to the place where I could last remember being happy. It was the truth, and Wyatt accepted it as such. I can still sense a low level of wariness from him though. I think it has more to do with his last name than it does with me. From what I've heard, Hayden's are trained to be suspicious. When you're on top, there are always people who want to bring you down. Considering the Hayden Cattle Company is the largest cattle ranch in Arizona, their fall could be catastrophic. Heavy is the head that wears the crown.

All that aside, I actually like the guy.

"Are you riding today?" Wyatt asks.

"If you don't mind," I answer.

He strides over to a honey-mustard-colored horse. I don't know the breed from sight. I'm still learning. I was lucky enough my riding lessons from when I was a kid came back to me.

"This girl needs some exercise," Wyatt says, grabbing a saddle from the tack and securing it onto her.

I thank him and lead her out into the sunshine. Before I mount, I run two fingers down her muzzle to say hello. When I'm on, I glance up at the main house. Jo stands on the porch. She waves at me, and I wave back.

* * *

THIS IS WHERE THE STUPID PART COMES IN.

If someone caught me riding on HCC property, there'd be trouble. Maybe in the days of the Wild West, a cowboy would shoot me and leave me for dead. In this modern day, they might just kick me off the property.

I have no intention of being caught, because I'd like to keep coming back.

I'm not looking for anything in particular. There'd be no way to discern which tree my mother ran into. But it was here, somewhere along the road from the big house where the Hayden's live to the turnoff into town that my mother took her final breath.

I'm coming down over the ridge between the HCC and Wildflower when movement catches my eye.

A woman in a purple cowgirl hat rides across the flat

portion of the ranch, about a mile from the Hayden home. And she is *flying*.

Hair the color of honey stretches into the air behind her, her body in perfect alignment, and she leans forward slightly. My attention is completely captured by this woman, and I feel oddly dazzled. Maybe it's the abandon with which she rides. Or her complete trust in the animal, and the animal's trust in her. They are a unit, a duo, an extension of one another. I'm almost positive I have never done anything so exhilarating.

She approaches the tree line at full speed. At the last second, she tugs the reins left, and the massive horse shifts sideways, slowing, then disappears into the trees. I wish I would've been able to see more of her features.

A long, heavy breath I didn't know I was holding seeps slowly from my lips. It's a good thing she disappeared from view, because I was beginning to feel hypnotized.

As if her ride has exhausted me, I lean back in the saddle. Rubbing a hand over my forehead, I push my lips together and imagine what a woman like that would be like in person.

I get the feeling she's wild. Audacious. Bold, with a smart mouth. She probably says the word *fuck* like she means it.

The heavy hand of guilt slaps my cheek. It's the first time I've really thought about a woman since Brea died. I see women all the time, I notice when they are physically attractive, but that's the extent of it. Nobody has commanded my attention so thoroughly. Not like the rider, whoever she was.

I close my eyes, just for a moment, and let myself

think a little more about the woman. The guilt is there, of course, but my curiosity overrides it. Maybe she—

"Who are you?"

My eyes rip open. There she is, fifteen feet away. Perched atop her horse, cheekbones carving out defiant lines on either side of her face. Her eyes hold my gaze, and in them I see the shortest glimmer of recognition. I recognize her, too. The woman from the diner. She regards me with haughty suspicion.

I get down off the horse, keeping the reins in my hand as I walk over. Her horse is at eye level with my chin. She gazes out at me, and says, "I asked you a question." Her tone is low but commanding.

"Sawyer Bennett," I answer, trying not to marvel at how beautiful she is. Her eyes, blue like a late afternoon summer sky, regard me with a touch of amusement. A low, uneasy feeling thrums through my stomach.

"I knew that already," she says.

My head dips sideways. "Then why did you ask the question?"

"I wanted to see if you were going to lie."

"I'm not a liar."

"Considering you're riding around on land you must know is not public, excuse me for not believing your loose interpretation of right versus wrong." She grips the bucking roll with two hands and leans forward. "Why are you here?"

I absolutely do not want to tell her the truth, and that claim I made two seconds ago about not being a liar? It goes out the window. "My hunt starts soon. Just glassing the area." I struggle to keep a straight face. I don't even have binoculars to support the fib.

She grunts a disbelieving laugh. "You can't hunt on

Hayden land." She points at me. "And you can't be here right now. You're trespassing."

I smile at her, hoping to soften her a little. "I won't tell if you don't."

She rolls her eyes. "Someone somewhere once told you you're charming and you're still riding that falsehood."

A laugh darts from me. I can't help it. She's as brazen and bold as I thought she'd be. "Are you saying you think I'm charming?" *What am I even doing right now?* That sounded flirtatious. Because it *was*.

"You have seven seconds to explain why you're creeping around on my land." She leans back in the saddle, her T-shirt riding up just enough to show a portion of her creamy skin. "Seven... six..."

I drag my attention back to her countdown. "Did you say this is your land?"

She nods and keeps counting. "Five... four..."

I have no idea what's going to happen when she hits one, but I don't particularly want to find out. I put my hands in the air in an innocent gesture. "Bird-watching."

She halts her countdown and frowns. "Bird-watching?"

I nod.

"I thought you weren't a liar." She forms a circle with her thumb and fingers on her right hand and lifts it to her eye, pretending to peer through. "*Just glassing the area.*" She mimics my lie with an exaggerated voice.

I laugh again. I hadn't imagined her being funny. But the way she's looking at me tells me I should stop laughing and start talking. I point up to a nearby tree. "There's a family of cardinals nesting up there." This is, at long last, the truth. I saw the red bird the last time I came through here, followed by his brown-feathered mate. "Would you like me to point them out?"

She stares down at me. "No. Cardinals are always nesting in these trees this time of year."

I walk closer and extend a hand. "Are you going to introduce yourself? I don't enjoy finding myself at such a disadvantage."

She stares down at my hand. Now that I'm closer to her, I can see how strong her thighs are, how the jeans look like they were poured onto her body. She has a freckle on her lower lip, and a small, silvery scar on her jaw curves down onto her neck. Instead of shaking my hand, she pulls the reins and the horse listens obediently. It walks her away from me, and I find myself yelling after her, something I don't even think about before I say it. "Does your horse have a name? Can I at least know that?"

She stops. The horse doesn't turn, but she twists her upper half to look back at me. "Hester Prynne."

Of course. "Like the character in *The Scarlet Letter*?"

She nods, her hair moving with the motion. "Do you know a different Hester Prynne?"

This small detail tells me so much about her. Except her name. "It fits you," I call out.

Her eyes narrow. "You don't know me."

"Not yet. But I'm about to."

A tiny smile causes one side of her mouth to lift. My heart does a victory dance. My brain flips off my heart. *What the hell am I doing?*

"Good luck with that, Mr. Bennett." She turns, and the horse carries her away.

I press my knuckles to my mouth and watch her go. I

hadn't meant to flirt with her, but it honestly felt impossible not to. Something in her personality calls to mine.

Is it okay? To flirt? To be attracted to someone? With her sitting on her horse in front of me, the answer was a resounding *yes*. But now that she's not here, I feel nothing but guilt for my actions.

Curiosity sits alongside the guilt. Who was that woman?

5

JESSIE

I have to tell them. I can't keep lying about why I'm back home. And there's also that little problem of why I'm not leaving when the weekend's over.

I'll do it tomorrow. Today is about family. My parents called my brothers and asked them to come over for a barbecue since I'm home and they weren't expecting me.

"Jessie, can you run this over to Cowboy House?" My mom walks into my room holding a casserole dish. "I made enchiladas for the cowboys. I didn't think it was very nice for them to have to smell our barbecue and not be invited." She makes a face and shrugs. "Family only."

"Sure, no problem." I set my book down on my bed and take the dish. My mom's eyes fall to all my bags leaning against my dresser. It's not even everything I brought, the rest is still in my car. I could've done a better job keeping the belongings out of sight, but... well, it was kind of on purpose. I was hoping she'd see it all, put two and two together, and then we'd talk. That way, she'd have a head start on her response, and I'd be spared the first part of it.

She points at my things and says sternly. "We're going to talk about that later."

I nod and scoot from the room, happy as hell to have a reason to escape. Unfortunately, I'm trading one place I don't want to be for another. Cowboy House is where all the cowboys stay, and normally it wouldn't be a big deal if I went over there. But last year at the annual cowboy barbecue, I *might* have stayed up shooting whiskey with the cowboys. I *most definitely* ended up making out with one behind a tree, and I do not remember who it was. Oops.

It's the one and only time that happened, and there won't be a repeat. I'm back home for good, which means I can't go scampering off to college after shenanigans like that and act like it never happened.

It's time for me to stop relying on my status as the baby of the family and step up. When I caught Sawyer Bennett on our property yesterday afternoon, adrenaline wasn't the only feeling surging through me. I also recognized the clean relief brought about by a swift and clear truth.

My land. That's what I'd said to him, and I meant it. The HCC is mine, and I felt a parental instinct to protect it.

I knock on the door of the long, low-slung building. It's similar to the place at Jo's ranch where the campers sleep, but Cowboy House bears the HCC logo on the front.

"Come in," someone yells.

I pull back the screen door and prop it open with my hip, then open the door and walk inside. There's a living room and kitchen, which is where I'm standing now, that splits the structure in half. On either side of the common area are short hallways with bedrooms, two cowboys to a room. Wes says it reminds him of Army barracks.

Josh glances up from his seat at the old wooden table, a *Bass Master* magazine lying open. He hustles to his feet when he sees it's me. "Miss Jessie, I didn't realize you were home."

I duck my chin in greeting. Josh is a fixture on the HCC. He's been here since my earliest memory. He's probably only ten years older than Wes, and he's the natural leader of the cowboys. They tend to fall in line when he speaks.

I set the huge glass dish on the cooktop. "You know you don't need to call me 'Miss'." I remove the tin foil cover, letting the scent of enchiladas fill the air. Balling up the foil, I toss it in the trash and say, "My mom made dinner for you guys."

"That was very nice of her."

I spin, my elbows bending and my hands gripping the countertop, and study Josh. He's getting older, and though I used to think of him as handsome, he is less so now. Has he missed out on a traditional lifestyle, marriage and kids, in service to this ranch? Is he, like so many, simply betrothed to the demanding, intoxicating lifestyle?

I'll never ask him, of course, but I'm curious.

"She likes to take care of you guys. You know how she—"

"What. The. Fuck is that smell? Who's eating without me?" Denny comes around the corner, a fistful of towel gripped near his hip bone. He wears nothing but that towel.

I clear my throat and look away.

"Go put on some clothes, Denny," Josh says, displaying his authority.

"I didn't know she was here," Denny grumbles as he recedes down the hall.

"I'm sorry about that, Miss—"

I stop him with a stern look. "I've seen shirtless men before. I've been to the beach." And I'm, you know, twenty-one years old. I'm not a child.

"Right." Josh smiles politely. "But you are the boss's baby sister."

"Right," I repeat. I just love how these men have slotted me into these roles my whole life. Boss's daughter, and now that Wes has taken over the ranch from my dad, the boss's baby sister. "I sure am." I return his polite smile. "Enjoy your dinner. You can bring that dish back whenever you all are done with it." I slide from Cowboy House, kicking up dust as I make my way to the green grass lawn in front of the homestead.

Someday, everyone is going to have to stop seeing me as the little girl who used to run around here barefoot, and start seeing me for the woman I've become.

* * *

WE'RE IN THE BACKYARD AT THE HOMESTEAD, THE LATE afternoon sun tucked behind the tall pines, when Wes and Dakota appear around the side of the house. Wes wraps me in a hug, very familial and a tad reserved. He'd move a mountain for me, but we're not super close. I was only a few years old when he shipped out, and most of my early memories of him include seeing him when he came home for R & R. His wife, however, is a different story. I adore her.

"Jessie, what a nice surprise." Dakota kisses my cheek, her baby bump pressing into me. She's not far along, about fifteen weeks, but she's already bigger than last time. Colt lopes past, going as fast as his almost two-year-old legs can carry him.

I jump in front of him and he startles when he sees me, stopping short and wrapping his arms around my legs. I run my hand through his dark hair, the exact color of Wes's, and he looks up at me. He is his father's son, almost like God pressed a 'Duplicate' button, except for those eyes. A perfect mixture of brown and green, hazel eyes that are clear and bright and full of mischief, just like Dakota's.

"Yeah, I thought it was time to visit." I pick up Colt, holding his wriggling body suspended in the air, and plant a kiss on his forehead. "Hi buddy," I say loudly, wincing as soon as I do it. I set him down and he darts around me. I scrunch up my face and blow out a breath. "I'm sorry," I say to Dakota, opening my eyes. "I know better than that."

She shrugs. "It's okay. It's natural, Wes and I have done it a hundred times. Believe me, if a raised voice is all it takes to make him hear better, his hearing would have repaired itself by now."

"He's a gorgeous child," I comment, watching him zoom past, going the opposite direction. Wyatt's chasing him, making monster sounds that Colt most definitely can't hear, but when he looks back he can see Wyatt's facial expressions and curling fingers lifted on either side of his face. Wyatt pauses on his way past me, kissing my cheek quickly, then continues on after Colt. "Good to see you, baby sister," Wyatt calls before he resumes his monster act.

"Colt's getting cochlear implants soon." Dakota smiles, and it's equal parts happy and sad.

"How do you feel about that?" I take her hand and pull her over a few feet so we can sit down on the outdoor couch.

"Relieved. Nervous. Sad that my baby hasn't been able to hear and has had to face adversity already in life. Annoyed with myself for feeling sorry for him."

I laugh softly. "Conflicted, then?"

Her eyes fill with tears and she palms her burgeoning belly. "Pregnancy hormones don't help." She rubs a circle and points her next words down at her stomach. "Do they, baby girl?"

"May I?" I ask, holding out a flattened hand.

Dakota leans back. "Have at it. Lord knows Wyatt does."

I shake my head, running my hand across the expanse. "For a man who loves children, you'd think they'd have one of their own. Not that Travis isn't Wyatt's," I hurry to add. He's in the process of adopting Jo's fifteen-year-old son. As soon as Wyatt and Jo hit their one-year wedding anniversary, he can make it legal.

Dakota grins. "I happen to know they've been trying."

I gasp excitedly, pulling my lower lip between my teeth and dancing my head around. "The three of you ladies are doing a good job making sure there's a next generation of Hayden's."

"How about you?" Dakota scrutinizes me. "Do you

expect me to believe you're here because you missed everyone so much?"

"Am I that transparent?"

Dakota shakes her head. "No, I'm just that good at reading people."

I take my hand back and Dakota straightens up. "Is it a man?"

I could kiss her for not asking 'Is it a *boy*?'. At least someone around here realizes I'm not fourteen anymore.

"Partially," I answer. "Can you keep a secret?"

"Not if it's going to hurt anybody or require me to lie to Wes."

I grin at her honesty. "All good." I shift forward so we won't be overheard. "I got involved with my professor. And it turns out he was married, but I didn't know it. He didn't wear a ring. There was never an indication."

Dakota blows out a noisy breath. "I'm so sorry. That's awful."

"It... gets... worse..."

Her eyes widen. "How much worse?"

"I ran an underground poker ring from my dorm room. Apparently it was very frowned upon. Someone reported it to the dean, and they kicked me out. Sort of. They suggested I withdraw."

"Jessie," Dakota hisses reproachfully.

"I know." The shock of it all is wearing off, and I'm starting to feel supremely foolish.

"Why did you do that?" She sounds less disappointed in me than my mom is going to, so at least I have that going for me.

"I don't know. It was fun. And I was bored."

"Those aren't good reasons to break the law."

I frown. "You break the law when you speed. What's the difference?"

Dakota groans. "You sound like Wyatt."

"I'll take that as a compliment."

Dakota laughs. "Consider it one. Do your parents know yet?"

"Nope," I answer, popping the 'p' sound. I look over to the grill, where my mom stands beside my dad. "They're going to look at me with disappointment, but also like the situation isn't too shocking." I point back at myself. "Calamity here, remember?"

Dakota scoots closer to me, wrapping her arm around my shoulders and giving me a squeeze. "You're so much more than that. And whatever you go on to do next, you're going to knock it out of the park. I know it."

"Thanks, Dakota."

"I got you, babe." Her mouth opens in an excited '*o*' and she claps once. "Why don't you come to the vendor market tomorrow and help me out? Today was busy, and Sundays are always crazier than Saturdays."

"Hmm..." I pretend to think about it. "Let me check my calendar. Not sure if I'm free. I have a whole lot of *nothing* to attend to."

She laughs and nudges me. "Be ready by ten. You can ride with me and your mom."

I nod my agreement, and then Tenley and Warner arrive, bringing commotion with them. Peyton is on her phone, but Charlie starts running around with Colt, and little Lyla cries like the sky has fallen. My mom takes her from Tenley, and I hear Tenley say they had to wake her up to come here and she's pissed about that. I'm still a bit starstruck by Tenley, I won't lie. I grew up watching her in movies, how could I not be?

I gaze out over the scene, watching Warner greet Wes with a clap on the back. Wyatt approaches and hands each a beer, and they fist-bump. My brothers. Each one unique, but each one a true Hayden man.

My parents, standing together at the grill, my dad's arm around my mom's waist. And Gramps, sitting in a chair, surveying it all.

Yes, I was kicked out of college. Yes, the guy I was seeing turned out to be married.

But I could've gone anywhere.

And I chose to come home, because this place is where my heart is permanently rooted.

6

JESSIE

"Good morning, Jessie." My dad's boots clomp up to the dining room table, and he ruffles my hair.

I give him a playfully rude look and fix my hair. "Hello, Dad."

He comes back a few minutes later with a breakfast burrito. Steam wafts up from his first bite, and I have no idea how he's chewing through such hot food.

"What's on the agenda today before you drive back to school?" He stretches out one leg and grabs his phone, navigating to his news app. He hates reading the news on his phone, but he doesn't have a choice unless he wants to turn on the TV. Newspapers aren't delivered all the way out here.

"I'm going to the vendor market with Mom and Dakota, and then," I pause to collect myself. This is a chance to tell him about school, and I may as well take it. "Dad, I—"

"Dad, did you need me for something?" Wes walks in and looks expectantly at our father, inserting himself into my sentence without an ounce of apology.

"Weren't you just here last night?" I ask irritably.

Wes scowls at me. "Nice to see you so soon too."

"Knock it off," my dad growls. He's not really growling, per se, he just has a voice that sounds like tires spinning through loose gravel and most of what he says sounds like growling. "Josh and Ham came over thirty minutes ago. They said some cows are showing dead eyes."

Wes sighs. His head droops and he grazes his scruffy cheek with his knuckles. "Fuck."

"Agreed."

I look from one man to the other. "What are dead eyes?"

My dad answers. "Eyes that are dull. Sunken."

It's descriptive enough that I can picture it too clearly. My heart twists at the image. "What the hell causes that?"

"Drought," they answer at the same time.

"Drought?"

"Yeah, you know that thing we're in?" Wes makes a face like I am extraordinarily stupid. "Or don't you watch the news at ASU?"

I open my mouth, a heartfelt *fuck off* poised on my tongue, when Wes turns his attention back to my dad. "Last night Wyatt called Jo's ranch a tinderbox." His sentence has additional meaning, one I don't understand. But our dad certainly does.

"Don't even think about it." This time, Dad is actually growling.

I know better than to ask the obvious question. I sit quietly and keep my ears open, hoping to learn through listening.

"I told Wyatt no, Dad. He looked pissed, but he

understood. Once I tell him about the dead eyes, he'll understand even more."

Our dad nods. "Let's go for a ride this morning."

Wes eyes him with uncertainty. "You sure about that?"

"As goddamn sure as I've ever been about anything. You can only count on grass-fed cows staying grass-fed for so long without water."

"What is it you think you'll find out there?" It's my question. I can't help it. I'm dying of curiosity.

Dad gazes at me, his stare intent, as he decides if he's going to share the ranch's woes with me. He takes a bite of his breakfast, chews and swallows, then speaks. "I want to take a look at the land that borders our back pasture. It was purchased a couple years back and nobody ever did anything with it. But as dry as the ground is right now, it makes me think it's more than a lack of rain. Where the hell is the groundwater?"

"What do you think is happening?" Wes asks.

My dad shrugs. "Let me finish my breakfast and we'll go find out."

"Can I come?" Excitement tumbles through me as I think about riding with my dad and Wes.

"No," they answer at the same time, and it's irritating.

The muscles in my face tighten. "Why not?"

"Because I don't know what we're getting into," my dad says, "and I don't want to put you in the middle of it."

"Bullshit," I challenge. "You think I'm too young. Or..." I cock my head to the side. "Is it because I'm a girl?"

"Well, now..." my dad starts.

"Hold on there," Wes begins. Neither one of them

wants to be called out, nor do they want to be guilty of what I've hinted at, but that's too damn bad. It's not my job to tend to their comfort level.

"I don't want to hear it from either one of you." I stand quickly, the chair scraping the wood floor. "It's early, and I have enough time before I'm supposed to leave for the vendor fair. I'm going to get Hester Prynne ready. I'll see you out there."

I stop at the front door to pull on my boots. Gramps sits in the rocking chair in the living room, his eyes closed. I turn the knob, and with one boot out the door an old, creaky voice behind me says, "Give 'em hell."

* * *

"You see what I'm talking about?" My dad nods down at the grass we're riding over.

"It looks more like hay," Wes comments, and I sense defeat in his tone. "Just a little farther and we'll hit the property line."

I know this isn't a pleasure ride, we're doing real 'reconnaissance', as Wes called it, but it's nice to be out here with Wes and my dad. I can't think of a time it's ever been just the three of us.

We approach the property line, as delineated by a wooden fence. I hop down from Hester Prynne and stride forward until my hips are flush with the top of the sun-warped wood. Tenting a hand over my eyes, I gaze out at the vast land. It's lower in elevation, more desert than the HCC. In the far-off distance I see a home, and beyond that large machinery dots the landscape. From here it looks as if Colt dumped his small toys on a field.

I wonder what it is they're doing out here. And I'd really like to know why they need balers.

My dad says something but I don't hear him. I reach for the joint of the fence, disconnecting a rail from the post and tossing it aside.

"What the hell, Jessie?" Wes calls out. "That's private property."

"Don't you want to know why this place neither of you know anything about has balers down there?" I step one leg over the downed portion of fence and turn back to look at my dad and Wes. "I sure as hell do. Tie up my horse, please." Then I step a second leg into the so-called private property.

"Goddammit," I hear Wes grumbling. "We should have made her stay home."

It stings, but I don't show it. Instead I keep walking, but then I remember my dad's not as spry as me, so I stop and wait for them. They tie up all the horses and step over the fence.

We walk in a row, right down through the middle of the fields, so that whoever is in that house will know we don't have any malicious intent. We're purely information seeking.

The closer we get, the more the scene around us shifts in my mind. If what I'm seeing is correct, this isn't good. "Wait." I grab Wes's forearm and he slows. Dad does too.

"What's wrong?" Dad asks as I hurry forward to the first acre of real growth. I yank out a small fistful of what's pushing up through the soil.

"Feel that," I instruct, extending my open palm.

"What is that?" Wes asks.

"Alfalfa," I answer, trying to keep the pride from my

voice. "Alfalfa hay. Meet the reason for your loss of groundwater."

My dad eyes me. "How do you know that?"

"I took agriculture classes at school."

"I thought you were in marketing?"

"I was. But I was supplementing with classes I liked better."

Wes takes what I'm holding, rubbing it between his fingers. "It doesn't feel like hay."

"That's because it has too much moisture in it right now. Also known as *water*. Give it a few hours in the sun and it'll dry out. That"—I point at the balers—"is the reason for those."

"So they're growing hay and baling it?" Wes sighs. "That's not a crime. There's nothing we can do about it."

I can't disagree, as much as I'd like to.

The snapping sound of a screen door pulls all of our gazes to the little house. A man stands, legs wider than his hips, arms crossed and rocking back on his heels. He's young, maybe forty, and for some reason I find that surprising.

"This is private property," he hollers, his tone angry and edged with a challenge.

Wes walks closer, and my dad and I follow. "Hello, sir, my name is Wes Hayden. This is my dad and my sister. We're your neighbors." He gestures in the direction of our ranch. His voice is cordial as can be.

The man squints at us. If friendly had a face, his is the opposite. "Not sure how neighborly it is to trespass."

Wes lifts a flat palm. "No harm meant."

"What do you want?"

Wes continues doing the talking for us. "We were on a ride and thought we'd introduce ourselves. Wanted to make sure you knew we keep lots of sugar around, in case you're in need of a cup sometime."

The man cracks a small smile. "Gee, thanks. I'll keep that in mind."

"You've got quite the operation going here. I didn't know there was a hay farmer right behind me. Makes me wonder why I've been going all the way into town to buy my hay."

The man shakes his head. "You can't buy this hay."

"Why is that?"

"It's not sold here."

"Where is it sold?" Wes's voice continues to sound affable, but I can tell he's doing his damnedest to keep his temper in check.

The farmer gives Wes a long, hard stare. My guess is that Wes would like to smack it off him. "It gets baled and sent to a port in California, then shipped across the ocean."

I make a noise of surprise and indignation. Wes sends me a warning look. He looks back to the man, nodding. "Right, right. What are you going to do come summer? Hay is a thirsty crop and it gets pretty hot."

"That's not a concern. I get plenty of groundwater."

"Is that right?" Wes's voice is tight.

The man's gaze narrows. "Why are you really here?"

"You're taking all the groundwater and not leaving any for us. My cows are pasture-raised, and pretty soon there won't be enough grass for them to eat."

"That's not my problem."

I know Wes is the leader of the HCC and therefore should be the one to speak, but I can't stay silent any longer. "Can you suspend your growing through the summer? That's when we need water the most."

It would be one thing if this guy looked at me with dislike, but he's looking at me like I amuse him. He addresses Wes as if I never even spoke. "Good luck with your herd, neighbor."

He turns and walks inside.

My blood is hot. "We can't let him continue this," I hiss at Wes. "He is essentially exporting water. During a *drought*."

Wes starts the walk back. "There's nothing we can do, Jessie."

"Like hell there isn't," I shout.

"Keep your voice down," my dad hisses. "I don't like that guy and I don't want him hearing you."

"Buy his farm, Wes. Buy him out and take over his water rights."

Wes sets a pace that is too fast, even for me. His head is bent, and he says, "There isn't money for that, Jessie."

"Take out a loan."

"It doesn't work that way," he thunders. He looks back at me and sees the hurt in my eyes. "Sorry," he mutters. To my dad, he says, "I'm going to call Lonestar."

Another comment I don't understand, but it doesn't matter because I'm not its intended recipient. My dad lets out an angry breath. "I hate that fucker."

"He'll give us a fair price, Dad."

"You mean he'll fuck us over the least."

Wes shrugs and doesn't slow. "What else am I supposed to do? Pretty soon, thinning the herd won't be a choice, but a necessity. And I need to sell before everyone else does and there's too much supply and not enough demand."

I speak up. "Maybe we can explore the possibility of expanding what the HCC offers—"

Wes glowers at me. "Quit acting like you know what's going on here."

He lengthens his stride, knowing I can't keep up.

Fine. I slow my pace so that my dad and I can walk comfortably and put space between us and the walking storm cloud in front of us. "Wes is angry." It's a completely unnecessary comment on my part.

"Wes is frustrated, and you keep poking at him."

"Trying to solve a problem is not poking at someone." He doesn't respond, so I ask, "What will happen to the HCC if the drought goes on much longer?"

"We can stay afloat for a while. We might not have enough to buy out that asshole, but we have enough. The real problem is the cows. We can feed them regular feed, but then we'd have to change our entire structure, and all of our branding, to run-of-the-mill beef, and it's not as simple as it sounds. Selling off some cows would be the next logical step. That's what Wes means when he says he'll call Lonestar. It's a ranch in Texas."

It's a punch to the gut. Selling cattle? Thinning the herd? "Dad, I'm sorry."

"We'll get through it, hon. We always do." He looks at me meaningfully. "Hayden's don't run from problems."

I glance away. Sounds like my mom told him about all my bags.

Wes is standing beside his horse when we reach him. His lips form a tense, straight line.

"Son," my dad begins, but Wes shakes his head.

"Don't, Dad. Just don't." He places a foot in Ranger's stirrup and swings his leg over. He looks down at us, and I wish I could erase the fear in my big brother's eyes. I don't think I remember seeing it there before.

"I'm going to figure this out." He turns Ranger around and waits for us to untie our horses and follow him.

Once we're both on our horses, I look over to my dad. The sight of his drooping shoulders steals my breath. Like Wes with fear, I've never seen my dad dejected. The man is a legend, his presence formidable. I've watched him cock an eyebrow and cause my date to junior prom to stammer. It was a power play, through and through, and I acted embarrassed, but secretly I loved it.

There must be some way I can help Wes, and if he's too hardheaded to let me help, I'll do it my own way.

7

JESSIE

This isn't what I was expecting. The last time I came to the vendor market with my mom was last summer when I was home from school. In eight months time, it has grown to be twice as big.

White tent canopies stretch out in long lines, row after row. The chapel where each of my brothers were married sits in the distance. A few hundred yards from that is The Orchard, and the outdoor area dotted with oversized yard games.

Dakota excuses herself to check on the sandwich stand where The Orchard sells lunch to the shoppers. She also told me about three food trucks that should arrive any minute, and not to offend my sister-in-law's restaurant, but I'm definitely looking forward to the Native American fry bread truck.

The vendors are allowed to arrive up to two hours early to begin setting up. Some of them have taken advantage of that, their booths erected and displays organized and inviting. Others walk in double-time to their tents, arms full and pulling wagons. My mom has a fairly easy setup and she's mostly finished, so I take off to help some people who look like there's no way they'll be ready in time.

I stack homemade soap for a sweet old lady, and when I leave her area my hands reek. I stop in to the restroom at The Orchard and wash off the gag-inducing mixture of scents, then head back out and help another woman hang her homemade blankets on wooden ladders. After standing on a real ladder to hang hand-painted pallet signs for someone else, I venture back to my mom.

The market has officially begun. It's slow at first, then increases steadily as the afternoon continues.

I'm making change for a woman and her young granddaughter when, from the corner of my eye, I notice someone join the line.

The woman and her granddaughter leave with their change and their herbed goat cheese log, and I swing my gaze sideways. He's there, at the back of the line, a head taller than the three people in front of him.

My eyebrows lift, acknowledging Sawyer, and a flurry of excitement skitters up my spine. He doesn't smile, but his entire face softens.

"Honey with almond crust," my mom says without looking at me.

I tear my gaze from Sawyer and retrieve the goat cheese, packaging it up in those cute boxes my mom bought. I place a circular sticker that reads *Hayden Goat Cheese* on the seam where the lid tucks into the box. The first time I'd seen the stickers, I'd asked her why she didn't come up with a name that was all her own, nothing to do with the HCC, and she said it's another way of advertising the HCC. She's right, but

I'd felt like she should've done it anyway. It would've been neat to see her have something that was her's only.

I don't look at Sawyer again, fearing I'll lose my focus. But then he's there, standing in front of my mother, and there's nowhere to look but at him.

This is my third time seeing him, but his features still take me by surprise. He carries himself stiffly, hands tucked in his pockets in this stand-offish way, but I sense something underneath it. Like he's waiting, *hoping* someone comes along and tells him it's okay to be himself.

He orders a plain goat cheese, and when I step aside to gather it, he steps with me, mirroring my movement along his side of the table. I can feel my mother's gaze on us. Nobody else was in line behind Sawyer, so there's nothing else to capture her attention right now but he and I.

"I figured out your name," he says, his voice low. It curls into me in a way I'm not ready for. It's too soon. My life is a mess right now. Shouldn't I be focusing on getting everything settled down first before I allow myself to feel attracted to somebody?

I place his order into the box and lift my chin, looking him in the eyes. The table's width is all that separates us, and if I didn't know better, I'd say he's leaning forward. And if I'm being honest, I am too.

"Oh yeah?"

"Jessamyn Hayden."

He looks pleased with himself. "Congratulations, super sleuth," I tease. "I go by Jessie, though."

He snaps. "Damn. Almost."

I take way too long to apply the sticker to the box,

just for the sake of keeping this banter going. "Who was your source?"

"Waylon Guthrie."

I nearly snort my laughter but catch myself in time. "Of course it was. He's the only person who ever calls me Jessamyn."

"It's a lovely name."

"Thank you. I think Jessie suits me better, though."

His gaze skims my face. "It sure does."

It's those sweet words, wrapped up in flirtation and delivered as a compliment, that make me wonder what it would be like if he pressed his lips to mine.

"Jessie, are you going to introduce me to your friend?" My mother's voice railroads into my thoughts.

I take a step back, turning toward her. Sawyer beats me to it, though.

He extends a hand. "Mrs. Hayden, I'm Sawyer Bennett."

Her hand, already halfway to him, stops in mid-air, a good eight inches from his. Her eyes widen, she visibly gulps, then recovers. She shakes his hand quickly, mumbling that it's nice to meet him, and waves over a passerby, offering a sample. They approach, and she treats them like a life preserver.

I look Sawyer over, from the top of his head to exactly where the table cuts off my gaze. When I don't spot what had my mother acting so bizarre, I ask, "Why did she act like that?"

He shrugs and shakes his head. "I honestly have no idea."

He pays for the cheese, and I hand him the box. Our fingers brush, first when he takes the box, and second when we exchange money. The second time, his touch lingers, and I hear his sharp inhale.

"Thank you," he says roughly, turning away.

I watch him walk through the crowd, turning heads as he goes. It's not just his handsome face, or black jeans that are most definitely not Wrangler, that command attention. There's something to the set of his shoulders, the tension along his jaw. He is a man burdened by something.

I tear my gaze away, and into my mother's waiting stare.

* * *

"Did you know Sawyer Bennett was back in town?"

My dad's gaze comes up over the top of his worn hardback novel. *Lonesome Dove*. He removes his wire-rimmed reading glasses, running a hand through his hair as he looks at my mother.

She didn't have a word to say to me after Sawyer walked away from our tent, but based on her question to my father I'd say she didn't need my introduction. It's not surprising to think she knew him from when he used to live at the Circle B, but the real mystery is why she'd have this response.

"Yes," he answers.

My mother's posture is stiff, my father's relaxed. He hasn't moved from the buttery leather chair that enveloped him when he sat down to read. The tic along his jaw tells me just how deceptive his appearance is. Their stare, thick with something I don't understand, causes a boulder to park itself in my stomach.

I think I like Sawyer more than I've let myself

believe. My heart has been keeping secrets from my brain.

"Why didn't you tell me?" There is strain in my mother's tone as she stretches to keep something else from seeping in.

My dad's gaze flickers my way, then back to my mother. "I figured you knew."

I'm losing patience. This conversation, if it could really be called that, uses few words but says much more. None of which I can interpret as anything meaningful.

"Um, hello?" I wave my hand in the air. "What is going on?"

My mom looks my way as if she's just now remembered I'm in the room. "Nothing."

"This is not *nothing*," I respond. "This is something, but I can't figure out what. You went silent after I introduced you to Sawyer, but apparently I didn't need to because you already know him. And now you're here exchanging cryptic dialogue with Dad." My hands are in the air at my sides, palms face up, my eyes wide in an *I'm waiting* stance.

My dad leans forward, uncrossing his legs and placing his book on the table. "Years ago, before you were born, there was bad blood between me and Sawyer's father. He did something pretty shitty, and I retaliated. He eventually left town, and abandoned the Circle B." He stands. "The rest is history." Striding to my mother, he gathers her in his arms and kisses the top of her head.

"It was a hard time," she adds, the side of her head pressed to my dad's chest. "Seeing Sawyer today was a bit of a shock for me, that's all."

It feels like that's not all there is, but I'll take what they're giving. I don't need all the details. What I needed to know was that there isn't anything fundamentally wrong with Sawyer, or me liking Sawyer.

One hurdle cleared.

The second one looms in front of me. Sawyer carries with him an obvious pain, elastic enough to allow him to stretch forward in my direction, but sufficiently tight to keep him bound to the source.

The more interactions I have with him, the more I'm hoping something comes along and takes scissors to it.

8

SAWYER

I LOVE THIS.

Sweat pouring off me in streams, my hair matted to my head, ungentlemanly grunts filling the air. Leon, my trainer, holds the bag for me.

Jab, cross, uppercut, cross, hook.

"Again," Leon barks.

Generally speaking, I don't do well taking orders, but I like Leon. I even respect the guy. So I do it all again.

We finish up, and I capture the strap on my glove with my teeth, ripping apart the Velcro.

"You did good," Leon says, walking beside me to the locker room. "There was a little extra oomph in there today. What was that about?"

I remove my gloves and curl and flex my fingers. "I think you're imagining things."

"Sure, man." Leon chuckles, making sure I know he doesn't believe me. He nods his goodbye and peels off, going in the opposite direction.

I take my time in the shower, thinking over what Leon said.

He is not imagining anything. I've been trying to get a certain female out of my mind since I saw her, and that's a real problem for me. I love Brea, even if she's gone. Emptiness and anguish easily bleed into one another, and I've been immersed in them for so long. They are familiar. Pain is painful, obviously, but it can also be comforting. While it hurts to hold on to Brea, it also keeps her close. I cannot have one without the other.

But then... Jessie. Her bold strength disarms me, and in her presence I feel discomfort. She shakes the hold I have on my heart, the sadness I use to keep the memories of my wife at the forefront of my mind.

Waylon told me her family calls her *Calamity*. The nickname couldn't be more accurate.

What she's doing to my heart and my mind and my soul, the way she's challenging all three simply by virtue of entering my life?

I know, beyond a shadow of a doubt, the results could be calamitous.

* * *

I MAKE MY WAY BACK TO SIERRA GRANDE. LEON'S BOXING gym is located in a nearby town, and though Sierra Grande has a gym, I prefer the physicality of boxing.

I skipped coffee this morning, so I stop at Marigold's on my way to my office. I'm standing in my open passenger door, digging my wallet from my gym bag, when I hear my name. I turn around and watch Jo and

Wyatt approach. Jo smiles wide, so cheery and trusting, but Wyatt is much stingier with his greeting. Per usual.

"Hey, Jo." I give her a wave. "Wyatt," I extend a hand. He shakes it, ducking his chin at me in lieu of actual words.

"What are you up to?" Jo asks.

"I got in a workout at the boxing gym and decided to stop for coffee on my way to work. You?"

She beams. "We were at the high school watching Travis accept an academic award, and we grabbed coffee after."

"Proud parent moment," I respond.

Wyatt touches Jo's forearm and says, "Are you going to tell him about the water situation?"

I train my eyes on Jo. "What water situation?"

Jo sends Wyatt an irritated look. "Everything is fine."

"I know you want to solve the problem by yourself, but everything is not fine, Jo."

I repeat my question. "What water situation?"

Jo lets out an annoyed sigh. "As I'm sure you're well aware, we're in the longest drought in the history of Arizona. Everything at Wildflower is just so... dry." She chuckles, but the sound is empty. "I don't have a better way to describe it. Wyatt is worried about fire."

"I'm not worried," he amends. "I think it's smart to be aware of the possibility, that's all. There are a lot of lives in our hands, and we need to make sure we have plans for all outcomes."

Jo turns to Wyatt, a soft smile curling up one corner of her mouth. "You do a good job loving those kids."

Wyatt shrugs off the compliment, but I see when his hand slips around her waist, the way his fingers curl over her hip.

I remember what that was like. Standing beside Brea at a party, leaning down and nuzzling the top of her head, breathing in the scent of her shampoo. It's something a man does when he adores a woman. A flash of pain stabs my chest.

Wyatt looks at me. "There might be a solution."

"What's that?" I ask.

"Wes, my dad, and my sister went to scope out the farm that backs up to the HCC."

My ears perk up at the mention of Jessie. "What did they find?"

"An alfalfa farm. Sucking up every last drop of water and all of the HCC's allotment. And also Wildflower's. Turns out, the farmer is baling it up and shipping it overseas."

I whistle, long and low.

"Exactly," Wyatt says. "My sister asked him to at least stop during the summer when it's the hottest."

"That was a smart suggestion." Not that I'm surprised. Jessie's intelligence is obvious.

"Yeah, well, he refused. Apparently he's a dickhead." Wyatt says it louder than he probably intended, and a couple old ladies sitting on a bench outside the coffee shop make a show of acting offended.

"Where do I come into this?" I ask, cutting to the chase.

"Buy the operation." Wyatt shoots as straight as I do, which I appreciate.

"That's a big ask," I respond.

"It's a big problem."

I run my tongue along the inside of my lower lip. "I'll think about it."

We say goodbye and part ways.

I grab my coffee and head for my office, running through it all in my head. I had no intentions of buying an alfalfa farm, but then again, it's not the crop I'd be buying. It's the land. The water. If I do this, I'd be helping Wildflower, sure, but it would help the HCC, too.

Something that would make Jessie happy.

Just the thought of that makes the corners of my lips turn up in a smile. I wait for the guilt to plow into the moment, but it doesn't.

I wait a little longer, certain it will arrive belatedly. But it never does.

Instead what I feel is *relief.*

And that confuses me more than anything.

9

JESSIE

I knew this was coming, but now that it's here, I want to run away.

Between yesterday's busy day at the vendor market and my mom's feelings about seeing Sawyer, I evaded the big talk about school.

But not for long. My mother has called me into the living room and asked why I'm still at the ranch. And why I have so many bags in my room.

I square my shoulders and look across the coffee table at my parents, who are both seated on the couch across from me. Taking a deep breath, I say, "I was asked to withdraw from school because they found out I was operating a poker ring."

My mom blinks hard, over and over, until she finally squeezes her eyes closed. My dad stands up, his face contorted into anger.

"Jessamyn Janice Hayden, you'd better be telling me the worst joke of my life."

"I'm not kidding, Dad. I'm sorry."

"You're going back," he thunders. Reaching into his

pocket, he pulls out his phone. "I'm calling the dean right now."

I fold my hands in my lap, but I'm careful to keep eye contact with him. "I am not going back."

His lower lip shakes, and he looks down at my mom for help. They've been married for so long she can read his mind. She says, "You need to get a college degree, Jessie. This is a big mistake."

"Maybe I will in the future, or I'll do it online. Like Warner." I shoot my dad a look as I wait for him to challenge me, but it doesn't come, so I continue. "But this ranch needs me, and I want to be here. I want to work."

My dad sinks back down alongside my mom and tosses his phone on the cushion beside him. "No," he says, the refusal muffled by the hand he holds cupped over his mouth.

"Yes," I reply. I'm far too stubborn to give up so easily.

"Jessie," my mom starts, adopting an on-purpose, calm air. She does this when she's preparing to lay down the law in a peaceful way. I've been the target of this method a hundred times and seen it countless more with my brothers. When it comes to me, she has about a fifty percent success rate.

"Ranching life is hard, hon. It requires a certain type of love and commitment." She glances at my dad. "And maybe even a mild level of insanity."

He doesn't crack a smile.

"I grew up here, Mom. I already know all that."

"You don't know it the way we do, Jessie." Exasperation comes through in her tone. "You were a child during the tougher times. The ranch isn't all fun and games."

"I know that, too," I answer, digging my heels in. "I also know you're in trouble now, and I can help."

"Wes is going to handle it," my father says harshly.

"All by himself?" My eyebrows lift. "He's going to single-handedly deliver water to every blade of grass on Hayden land?"

"We have employees, Jessie. Cowboys. They help Wes every day."

"Wes lost his second-in-command when Warner went to teach. Wyatt didn't want the position. As far as I can tell, it's still empty."

My dad scrunches up his face. "Are you telling me you want the job?" But he's not asking a question, not really anyway. He's incredulous.

"I realize I'm your last choice. You've already gone down the line of all your other children."

"You've been away at college."

"I'm here now," I grit out. My hold on my temper is becoming tenuous.

"Absolutely not." My dad's voice is deep and rich, a final answer.

And I do not accept.

"Last I checked, my last name is Hayden. That makes me as good as any of my brothers at being a leader on this ranch. I learned to walk on Hayden soil just like my brothers. I learned to shoot here, just like they did, and I'll bet every breath I have left in this world that I'm a better shot." My hair has fallen in my face as my head shook with the vehemency of my words, and I tuck it back behind both ears.

My mom sighs and shakes her head. "It's not—"

A thought slams into me and I cut her off. "You never even thought of me during all this, have you?" My gaze flies from her to my dad. "Warner vacates his position, it's not filled by Wyatt, and you don't even think about your fourth child? You want to make sure this ranch is run by Haydens, well, guess what?" I point back at myself. "You've got one. Right here. I have ideas for days, I could bring so much to this place. You need to diversify. Your entire livelihood is based on cattle, but if you—"

My dad's head is shaking before his mouth opens, so I beat him to his sentence.

"Let me guess. I'm young. I'm a woman, and to date, a woman has never been in a position of leadership on this ranch."

"No," my dad storms. His flattened palm smacks the table, sending a thunderous wave through the room. "It's because you're not ranch material. Yes, you're young, but you've always been impetuous. You make unwise choices, like running a gambling ring in your dorm room. You are a liability, and that"—he points a stiff finger across the table at me, and it feels like a physical assault even though it's nowhere near touching me—"is why you've never been considered for stepping into Warner's spot."

I can take a lot. Negative opinions roll off me like a bead of sweat in the blazing summer sun. But this? It stings.

The fire inside me has been snuffed out. I'm done with this conversation. My hand taps my knee as I think about what to do next, and very quickly I settle on an idea. "I'm going to move into Warner's cabin for the time being while I figure out my next steps."

"Jessie, I didn't mean..." My dad's words fizzle out.

"Yes, you did." I stand. "And that's okay. You told the

truth." I lick my lips, gathering my courage. "So here's my truth. I love this land as much as Wes. As much as any of you. And maybe I've lived my life in a way others view as impulsive. But I can't think of anyone you'd hire to help Wes who would bleed for this ranch. I'm a Hayden too, and there's nothing I wouldn't do to keep this ranch going. What weighs more? A handful of bad choices, or my commitment to the hundred plus years of Hayden blood, sweat, and tears that saturate this land?" I start to turn away but turn back for a quick second and point up at the family crest above the mantel on the fireplace. "*Legacy. Loyalty. Honor.* Who else embodies all three values? I don't want an answer, Dad. I already know it. The real question is if you do."

I go to my room, the very same room I used as a nursery. The walls have seen three different colors of paint, but they are the same walls I looked at through newborn eyes.

I begin repacking what I unpacked when I arrived. The living room is empty when I pass back through, arms full of my belongings. I load up my car and drive to Warner's place.

When I arrive, I realize I don't have a key, so I leave everything on the covered porch and return to the homestead. When I enter my room, there is a single gold house key on the end of my dresser. I don't need to ask what it unlocks, or who put it there. It could only have been my mother.

With the key safely tucked in my back pocket, I load up more of my things from my bedroom. I don't have boxes, so I make do with old backpacks and tote bags. I even strip my sheets from my bed, so I won't have to deal with it when I get back to Warner's.

I need to stop thinking of it as Warner's house. Now, it's mine. I'm taking it over. A land grab. If I have to, I'll plant a flag in the front yard.

The key slides in the lock, and I open the door with my foot, propping it open and picking up two bags. I step in, standing in the foyer and looking around. Warner didn't take much furniture with him, just a few items here and there. Tenley had wanted to start over together, and they'd gone to Phoenix to pick out all new furniture. I'd met them for lunch when they were in between stores.

I walk through the house and into the master bedroom. Warner's furniture is still there, minus his collection of books. While I'm in here, I remove the sheets from the bed and toss them on the ground in a heap.

In the living room, I remove a painting from the wall and go back out to the porch, returning with my favorite picture.

"There," I say proudly to the empty room. I stand back and gaze upon the charcoal drawing of a much younger me perched on Hester Prynne. My mother snapped the picture of me, my head tipped up, my cowgirl hat poised just so on my head. I look confident and sublimely happy. Wyatt took the photo and had it made into the charcoal drawing for Christmas. It has always been my favorite gift.

"Now I'm home," I whisper. "Jessie's cabin."

* * *

I SPEND THE NEXT WEEK MAKING THE CABIN INTO MY OWN. New throw pillows and blankets, some cheap wall hangings, and candles that make this place smell more floral than I'd prefer. Beggars can't be choosers, and there wasn't a huge selection, so I bought them anyway.

I've seen my mom and dad almost every day, and Wes too. Wes hasn't even asked why I'm still at the ranch instead of going back to school, which either means he doesn't give two shits or he's that preoccupied. My dad offers me terse nods and grumbles, and my mom swears she's never seen him so stressed out. It worries her, and me too. After his heart attack a few years ago, stress is the last thing he needs. At this point, I'm trying to stay out of his way and help my mom as much as possible with the hundreds of chores she has on the ranch. I like helping her, but taking care of goats and making goat cheese are not where I'm meant to be. I want to be in the saddle. I want to manage operations.

Yesterday I watched Wes and the cowboys ride out to lead the cows to a new pasture, hoping to find better grass. I kept imagining I was out there too, and that daydream is still in my head, even now, while I'm rearranging my clothes in the closet. My phone in my back pocket begins to vibrate, and that breaks into my thoughts.

Marlowe, according to the flashing screen.

"Hello, best friend," I greet, cradling the phone between my shoulder and my ear so I can use both my hands.

"Did you come home last weekend and not tell me?" Her accusatory tone holds thinly veiled hurt.

"It's not like it sounds, I promise. I was going to call you tomorrow." I've been avoiding calling her. It's not like I have good news to share. I grab the phone before my neck starts to hurt from the awkward angle. "I have a lot to tell you."

"Is everything okay?" Her tone shifts to concern. I picture her sliding around the 'M' she wears on a gold chain around her neck.

"I think so?" I don't know why it comes out as a question, except that I'm not certain if everything really is okay. It all feels very fluid right now, my life a sloshing liquid where only two weeks ago it was a solid. "Do you want to meet for a drink?"

"You mean this weekend? You're coming back already?"

"I'm still here." I reach up on tiptoe to place a sweatshirt on the top shelf of the closet. "And stop making that face."

"I'm not making a face."

"You are most definitely squeezing your eyebrows together."

She exhales laughter. "You're good."

"So, how about that drink and I'll tell you everything? I'm free tonight." Actually, I'm free every night for the foreseeable future.

"How about the Bar N?"

I wrinkle my nose. I'm surprised she has suggested it. Sierra Grande has better to offer than the ramshackle barn someone had the bright idea to convert into a bar. Apparently the conversion used up their entire store of creativity, because the best name they could come up with is as unimaginative as it comes. It's like naming a dog *Dog*.

"Why there?" I ask, not wanting to offend my best friend since we were twelve. "How about The Chute?"

"I went there last weekend."

"Well, I've never been. I turned twenty-one last month, and this is the first time I've been back." Not that I didn't try my fake ID out at the busiest bar in town. The bartenders were strict, and after they told Wyatt about me trying to get in, I decided not to push my luck.

We make a plan and I hang up. Drinks at Bar N, and more drinks and food at the Chute. Before I get ready to meet Marlowe, I go for a walk. The first thing I see when I step out the front door is Wyatt's old cabin. It's a quarter mile away, and empty. He moved out to Wildflower to help Jo run the place. I'm happy as hell for him. If anybody deserved to find their true love, it was him. He waited years to feel as good as he does with Jo.

I look up as I walk, studying the swaying pines, the wind whispering through them. They are skinny, and so tall. In one, I see a mess of twigs, a female cardinal sitting in the center. It reminds me of Sawyer Bennett. I'd like to see him again soon, but I'm not sure how to make that happen.

As I watch, a scarlet male cardinal flies in, settling on the rim of the nest. Chirping begins, the female welcoming him home. I watch for another moment, then turn back and go to my new home so I can get ready to see Marlowe.

* * *

I'VE LEFT EARLY ENOUGH TO PICK UP MARLOWE'S FAVORITE flowers. Her love language is gifts, and getting flowers makes her happy. It doesn't matter who they're from. I'm more of an acts-of-service person. I once told Marlowe, *You can skip buying me a birthday present, but I expect you to help me bury a body.* She reminded me that she's the mayor's daughter and has to keep her hands clean. *No worries*, I told her, *because I have three brothers and a dad who know places a body will never be found.*

Again, *kidding*. But also, not really. Marlowe looked terrified.

I check my makeup in the rearview, running the tip of my finger just under my lower lip to wipe a lip gloss smudge. I look back at the road and slow for a curve. Once I'm around the bend, I spot a truck ahead. It's parked in the road, a jack placed under the underside to keep it upright. There are two men, one putting on a new tire while the other one rolls the presumably flat tire and tosses it in the truck bed. There isn't room in the road for me to pass them, because they decided to change their tire in the middle of the road. I slow to a crawl as I reach them, and through the front windshield, I spy a gun rack in the back window. And two guns in the rack. Not hugely shocking, considering they are both wearing camouflage shirts.

I stop. Their eyes are trained on me, and it feels like I'm supposed to greet them in some way. Everything about them screams they're preparing to hunt on my land, and I know for damn sure they weren't headed to the HCC for a social call.

I roll down my window. "How's it going?" I'm very careful to keep my voice even. Strong. No trace of feminine lilt. It's an epic shame I feel the need to do this.

"Almost finished," the tire changer says, eyeing me. "What are you doing out here?"

"Probably not the same thing as you."

He guffaws. "Not unless you're hunting." His eyes travel as low as they can go, which isn't too far because I'm sitting in a fucking car, but his intention is made clear, and isn't that all he really wanted? "I'm starting to wish you were the game."

My skin prickles. Every cell in my body works together to restrain my sharp tongue. "This is private property. You can't hunt here."

"I'm sure it's fine, sweetheart." It's the other one talking. He looks exactly like the tire changer. Mediocre.

"It's not fine. This is my land. You need to get off it."

Both men give me slow, lazy looks. The tire changer steps on the jack and lets down the truck. "Did you hear that?" He glances at his friend. "This is her land."

His friend laughs. "What are you going to do about it? Get out of that car and kick our asses?"

Clearly they both know I'm not getting out of my car. I might be impulsive and impetuous, but I have a strong sense of self-preservation. I reach for my phone and bring up my contacts, then press the phone to my ear.

"Hi, Sheriff Monroe. This is Jessie Hayden. Two hunters are trespassing on the HCC about three miles up the turnoff from town, and they refuse to leave." I pause, keeping my gaze trained on the men who are now gaping at me. "Great. See you soon."

I hang up, but I keep my phone in my hand. Just in case. "He's on his way. Feel free to stick around if you'd like an introduction."

It happens so fast. The tire changer sprints toward me, and I fumble for the button to roll up the window. Time slows down, each millisecond quantifiable as the sound of the window rolling up becomes deafening. He reaches me, raising a hand as if to backhand me, but there is too much glass between us now. "Cunt," he spits at me, before he gets in his truck and charges around me, spinning and creating a circle of dust. My fists ball and my heart pounds as I wait for the dusty cloud to settle, praying to God they won't be there when it clears.

They are gone. My exhale is long and loud.

My shaking hand shifts into drive, thinking over what just happened, and my idea to place a phone call.

Perhaps it would be a good idea to put Sheriff Monroe's cell phone number in my phone. Just in case.

I'm sure Wyatt has it.

10

JESSIE

By the time I reach Bar N, I've pushed the hunters out of my mind. All I want is a drink, and lucky for me, I'm in the right place.

It's no fun ordering a drink here, now that I can do so legally. I've been sneaking into this place for two years, using a fake ID in the most flagrant of ways. The bartender, Paula, knew exactly who I was and that I was not of legal drinking age. But, like my ID stated, I was Bailey Johnson, a fresh-faced twenty-two-year-old from Ohio.

"Hi Paula. Can I have a vodka soda, please?"

She nods. Her head is partially shaven, and she has the unshaven part flipped over her head and pinned back with an elaborate barrette. "I have to ID you."

I hand over my real ID. The slight uptick of her eyebrows is my only confirmation of just how fake she always knew my previous ID was. Paula hands me my drink and I hand her cash, then head for my best friend.

Marlowe sits at a far table, her back to the entrance. She stands and her eyes light up when she sees me. She weaves through tables and chairs, arms open and her purse out on the table. This isn't the kind of place where you need to worry about your belongings. It's just as likely the person at the neighboring table is also your real neighbor. So, unless you're an inconsiderate asshole who blares loud music in the middle of the night or refuses to trim your lawn, your personal belongings are safe.

"Hey, lovely lady," Marlowe croons, wrapping me in a hug.

I smile into her wavy brown hair. "Hey there."

She gives me an extra squeeze and I try to keep my drink from spilling over. We settle down at the table and she sips her beer. "Tell me everything," she instructs, pointing the lip of her bottle at me when she's finished drinking from it. "Don't leave anything out."

So I do. She already knew I was seeing Austin, and she's almost as shocked to learn he's a husband and a father as I was.

"I don't understand how a person can be so duplicitous. It's hard enough to live one life, who wants the headache of juggling two?" She makes a face. "Are you going to tell the wife?"

I poke at the ice in my drink with the tiny red straw Paula included. "What's the point?"

Marlowe's nose wrinkles. She looks disappointed in me. "You have a duty to save her from a man who, let's be honest here, is very likely to be a serial philanderer. No offense," she adds.

"None taken. I know I'm not special." It stings a little, this tiny truth. My ego would prefer it if I were just so irresistible Austin couldn't help but stray, but it's far more likely the thrill was the drug.

Marlowe gives me a look. "You know that's not what I meant. Of course you're special. I just don't believe you're the last."

My next thought is icky, and it makes the corners of my lips turn down. "Maybe I wasn't the first either." It's the first time since I caught Austin that I actually feel sad. I didn't love him, but I did like him. We had a good thing going. I shrug off the bad feeling. "Doesn't matter. It's over now. Onward and upward." At those words, Sawyer's image pokes into my mind. I open my mouth to mention him, but Marlowe is already speaking.

"Hear, hear," she bellows playfully, tapping the bottom of her bottle against the bottom of my glass. "You'll have to confront him eventually though. I mean, you *are* in his class."

I make a bare-teeth face and shake my head. "Not anymore." The whole story spills out, and various expressions flit across Marlowe's face as the story progresses.

"Jessie..." My name is spoken as an exasperation.

"I know," I sigh. "It was stupid."

Marlowe's head tips to the side. "It was actually really smart. But very foolish."

A reluctant smile lifts one corner of my mouth. "It was fun. Until I got in trouble for it, anyway."

"What's next for you?"

"Trying to talk my parents into letting me work on the HCC."

Marlowe's eyes widen and her lips purse. She knows all about my feelings when it comes to the way my family views me. "How's that going?"

"Not so well." I roll my eyes. "And the most upsetting part is that they need my help." I lean forward on my forearms. "Real help. The drought is going to drown them"—I wince—"bad choice of words. The drought is going to kill them slowly. They have to start using that land for other purposes." I sit back roughly in my seat, trying to tame the fire reigniting in my heart.

"Have you talked to Wes?"

"He'll take my dad's side."

"You don't know that."

I tap the top of her hand. "Don't defend him just because you had a crush on him before he was married."

She laughs. "He wasn't the one I had a crush on."

I gasp. "You've never admitted to liking one of my brothers."

"Why do you think I was always driving all the way out there to see you?"

"I kind of thought it was for my excellent choice in old-school country music."

"That helped," she says, shrugging one shoulder.

"Which brother?"

Her chin whips back and forth. "Definitely not telling."

"They're married now, what does it matter?"

"You'd never let me forget it."

"True."

I go to Paula and get us one more round, and after that we decide we're more than ready for the curly fries at the Chute.

It's only a few blocks away, so we walk. The music reaches us long before we arrive at the front doors. Marlowe bumps her shoulder into mine. We walk into a roomful of bodies. Music from a few different speakers rains down over everyone. Vintage signs decorate the wooden walls, and the bar is near the back. We head there first, and I order for both of us.

The bartender asks for our IDs, and I hand it over. He looks at it, glances at me, and does this two more times.

"What?" I ask.

He shakes his head disbelievingly. "This is the best fake I've ever seen."

I frown. "That's because it's real."

He snorts. "Okay, sure."

Now I'm annoyed. "It is."

"No offense, but—"

"I really hate when people say that. You clearly know you're about to offend me, so you're already defending yourself." My arms cross and I wait for him to respond.

He swallows in this big way, as if to make sure I know how annoyed he is, but can't really tell me because he wants to keep his job. "I went to school with Wyatt. I remember when you tagged around him like a puppy. You were a *baby*. There's no way you're twenty-one."

My fingers curl into a fist around my purse strap. Everyone else in the world is aging, why wouldn't I be too? "Do the math," I say, at the same time a deeply male voice from down the bar says, "Why don't you call him?"

I know that voice. It makes my shoulders curl in a fraction, and my stomach clench.

I lean over the bar and peer down. Two seats over, with a basket of curly fries and a half-empty glass of red wine, sits Sawyer. He leans on one elbow, his thumb rubbing his upper lip, and his gaze settles over me.

I tear my eyes from him so I can look at the

bartender. "You could call him. Or you could just believe me because I'm telling the truth."

The bartender scrutinizes me, and it takes all I have not to flip him the middle finger. This is ridiculous. Then he grabs a glass and starts making my drink. When he sets it down on the beverage napkin in front of me, he has an air about him, like he's done me a big favor and expects me to feel grateful.

I'd rather swing my foot up at the apex of his thighs.

I raise my glass in the air, catching Sawyer's gaze, and nod at him. He responds with a lift of his wine, a chin dip of his own. And there's a little something extra, an intensity in his eyes, a bob of his Adam's apple on his clean-shaven throat. I swallow and break our gaze, in time to see the bartender give Marlowe her drink without any grief.

She places an order for fries, then turns back to me wearing an apologetic look. "I'm sorry," she mouths.

"You're the mayor's daughter," I gripe. "Of all people he should be carding and not believing, it's you."

She winds an arm around mine. "Sorry about your luck. You're just too famous for your own good."

"Infamous, you mean." I brush the scowl off my face. "How's Brix?" I ask, to change the subject. Brixton is the last name of a guy we grew up with. He goes by Brix, and he and Marlowe began seeing each other a few months ago.

She shrugs. "He's okay, I suppose."

"Don't sound so excited."

She smiles around her straw. "He's boring. And I don't want to date a guy from town."

"That means you'll have to actually move out of town in order to accomplish that," I point out, reaching over the bar and snagging a slice of lime from a container of cut fruit.

Marlowe blows out a noisy breath. "I'm aware."

Our fries arrive and we keep chatting, moving from her dad's plans for reelection to her sister's new baby. I keep my attention on Marlowe, which is a job in itself because all I want to do is peek over at Sawyer. I have no idea if he's still there, because the people between us are big, burly guys, but I haven't seen him stand up to leave, so I'm guessing that means he's there.

Marlowe yawns hugely and waves her hand. "Sorry," she apologizes, yawning again as she says the word. "I just hit a wall." She grabs the folded check off the bar. "Let me get this. You can get next time."

She pays, and I pointedly ignore the bartender when he tries to make eye contact with me. I don't know what he wants, but I do know I'm not interested.

We push back from the bar, and I get the chance to look over for Sawyer. His seat is empty. Everything has been cleared from his place. Disappointment fills me, as if I've lost something.

I'm steps away from the exit when a hand wraps around my elbow, pulling me back gently. I look down at the hand, the long, masculine fingers curled around me, skin to skin. My flesh prickles, heat rushing in where he touches me.

My gaze lifts, his gray eyes like a magnet. We're closer than we've ever been. Goose bumps ripple over me, head to toe. I don't believe in love at first sight, but this? It's *something*.

"Are you leaving?" His voice is low, urgent.

"It would appear so," I say softly, my tongue darting out to moisten my lips.

"Jess-ie?" Marlowe's voice lifts on the second syllable. "You coming?"

I look at my best friend, her eyebrows drawn in confused curiosity.

"Stay." The quiet word slides from Sawyer, draping over me.

"I'm going to stick around here," I answer her. She gives Sawyer a long once-over, then nods slowly. "I'll talk to you later."

Sawyer steps back, his hand falls away, and he motions back toward the bar.

I was right when I thought of him as a magnet, but that's not all he is. There's something in him, like a vein running through sinew, that reminds me of a predator.

This attraction feels primal. Raw.

This is the first time I've ever found myself wanting to be prey.

* * *

I LEAD US OVER TO A BOOTH, PURPOSEFULLY CHOOSING the one out of eyesight of the bartender. He clearly knows who I am, and I'd rather not be gossiped about if I can help it.

Sawyer peels off to grab another round and returns a few minutes later carrying drinks. He slides a vodka soda my way, and I thank him.

Using large, strong hands, he pushes up the sleeves of his long-sleeve shirt. The fabric bunches at the dip in muscle near his elbows. He doesn't speak, but his eyes are on mine, and his thick, dark-fringed lashes sweep over his skin with a long blink. "I'm sorry about what happened to you earlier." He points at the bar.

I glance over, my annoyance flaring. "Has anybody ever given you that much trouble when you tried to order a drink?"

He rubs his chin as he considers my question. "I don't believe so."

"It's bullshit." Anger creeps into my voice, probably more than I should really feel about that situation. I'm mad at the hunters, for treating me like they did. At my dad, for not allowing me to work on the HCC.

Sawyer's eyebrows lift. "Is that all that's upsetting you tonight?"

My hair falls into my face when I shake my head, so I gather it and lay it over my shoulder. I tell him about my dad first, and then the hunters. His jaw tightens during my second story, one of his hands curling into a fist.

"I'm sorry I wasn't there to help you out." He relaxes. "At least I was around to help with the asshole bartender."

My eyebrows wiggle. "You weren't that helpful, if I'm being honest."

Sawyer grips his chest. "You wound me."

A smile pulls at my mouth. "The truth hurts sometimes."

Sawyer places two fingers on the base of his wineglass, turning circles and making the red liquid swirl. "You say it like you know."

"Unfortunately, yes." Austin's light brown hair and nerdish vibe runs through my mind.

Sawyer leans forward, those stormy eyes capturing me again. "Tell me more."

"What do you want to know?"

"Who hurt you with the truth?"

This is all feeling very heavy suddenly, but he's asking, and I believe Sawyer has some truths of his own to share. Maybe if I tell him mine, he'll tell me his.

"Why should I trust you?" I ask. It still feels like I should put up some sort of fight.

"I haven't given you a reason not to." His voice is deep, rumbling across the table like a mini earthquake.

I like that answer. I like the idea of earning something simply by not having broken it yet.

"I was in college up until a few days ago. I was seeing my professor. And I caught him. Red-handed." Sawyer's eyes widen in anticipation of my next words. "With his wife."

Sawyer blinks. "I thought I knew the ending to that sentence. Turns out, I didn't."

My laugh is hollow. "For what it's worth, I didn't know he was married." I picture Austin handing a tiny, bundled baby over to his wife. "Or that he had a new baby."

Sawyer sucks in a breath. "Sometimes people aren't who they present themselves to be. What did he have to say for himself?"

I shrug, acting like I don't care, but the truth is that it hurts. "I didn't confront him. Just a text to tell him it's over and not to contact me."

"Has he called?"

I nod. "Many times. I let it go to voice mail."

"I'd say he deserves the silent treatment."

"And more. But I'm too tired to dole out punishment. Emotionally," I add, when I see him check his watch. "Physically, I'm just fine. Enjoying my drink." I tip my head and smile at him. "Why did you come to Sierra Grande?"

"I needed a change of scenery."

I smirk. "Like pine trees on a mountainside with cardinals?"

He breathes a short laugh. "Yes."

"Tell me why you were really on HCC property, Sawyer. I trusted you with my truth. It's your turn to trust me with yours."

His smile recedes. The side of his thumb taps the table. When his gaze finds mine, I see insurmountable pain rising like a swell. "My mom was in a car accident on the road that leads out to the HCC. I don't know exactly where it happened, so sometimes I ride around and look. I..." His chin moves back and forth quickly. "I don't know what I'm looking for. All evidence is long gone. Maybe I'm hoping for a feeling, like a gut instinct." He huffs an empty laugh. "Maybe I'm looking for some kind of other-earthly event, like she's reaching out to me from wherever it is people go when they die." He shrugs. "So, there you have it. Trespassing for a good reason."

I reach out, brushing my fingers over his forearm. "I'm really sorry that happened to you, Sawyer." I don't know what else to say. I've never even heard of a car accident so close to the HCC, let alone one that resulted in death.

"I really know how to bring down the mood, huh?" His empty chuckle floats in the air between us.

I wave away his words. "Do you want to talk more about your mom? I'm a great listener."

He shakes his head, and I watch the emotion in his eyes fade. It's as if he has closed a curtain. The tension in his cheeks loosens, and the pain in his features dissipates. It makes me wonder when he got so good at pushing it all away.

He looks down at my hand, still poised on his arm. It's difficult to decipher what he's feeling in this moment. Should I move my hand? Am I making him uncomfortable?

"I should probably leave," he says quietly.

My lips turn down and I take my hand back.

He pushes his empty glass to the back of the booth and winks. "It's almost ten. I'll turn into a pumpkin if I'm not back in my room by then."

"You're staying at The Sierra?"

He nods.

"That sounds depressing."

"Thanks," he deadpans. I laugh.

"I just mean it sounds cramped. I need wide open spaces. If I had to look out that window onto High Street every day..." My voice trails off. I don't know how to finish that sentence.

Sawyer regards me with raised eyebrows, waiting. When it's clear I've got nothing to say, he stands. The music changes, the beat slowing. "How about one dance?" He offers me a hand. "And then I'll leave."

"One dance," I agree, sliding from my side of the booth. I wag a finger at him. "Don't get handsy." What a joke. If his hands drifted, I'd do nothing to return them to their proper place.

"No wandering hands here, I assure you."

Sawyer leads me onto the dance floor. He lifts my hand, twirling me in a slow circle, before placing it on his shoulder. I adjust my arm, wrapping it loosely around his upper back. He grips my other hand and brings it into his chest.

He smells like soap and cologne, and something else I can't describe. My head falls against his chest, and he takes a long, slow, deep breath. My head shifts with the movement.

We sway to the music, and I close my eyes. His hand, still on my upper back, begins to move. It's only his thumb at first, gliding over my skin. But then all his other fingers join, and it becomes a caress.

I relax into him, letting him hold me. In all the craziness of recent events, he feels safe. Solid and strong. I'm in the arms of a *man*. Not the coward who cheated on his wife while she was carrying their child.

I'm not prepared for how much I like it.

The song ends. *Too soon*, I think. What I say is, "Thank you for the dance, Sawyer."

I leave him before he can leave me. I stop at the booth to grab my purse and make my way out of the Chute.

11

SAWYER

Conrad McCafferty. That's the name of the alfalfa farmer. He's a son of a bitch, too.

It's a hasty designation to make, seeing as how I've only known him for approximately thirty seconds, but it feels spot on.

He stepped from his front porch the moment I pulled in. He's younger than I expected. In my head, I envisioned him as an old man. He has a full head of brown hair, but it's cut close and doesn't look right, as if he told the barber to use a four and they accidentally used a two.

He's tall, but overweight, his face resembling something of a ferret. From somewhere in the house, I hear gunshots, voices, military-like commands, and realize it's a video game.

"Can I help you?" he says, with a look that says help is the last thing he'd like to provide me.

Might as well cut right to it. "I'm here to make an offer on your property."

"I'm not interested."

"Why not? You haven't heard my terms yet."

He eyes me suspiciously. "Does this have anything to do with my so-called neighbors coming by?"

"I don't know who you're talking about."

"The Haydens came here and tried to throw their weight around. I hate when people like that think they should get what they want just because of who they are."

I hate when people use more than their share of water and the downstream effect means other people don't have enough.

I nod and shrug like I'm clueless. "I have nothing to do with them." And why would they be so-called? Their land butts up against his. Pretty sure that makes them neighbors. "I own a real estate investment trust called Tower Properties. I came to Sierra Grande less than a year ago, and I've been buying properties and investing."

"I don't want to move," he says, crossing his arms like he's settling in for an argument.

"Why not? You're all alone out here." I gesture around the place. "There are plenty of ladies in town who'd love to date you. Or men, if that's your preference. Point is, you'll make enough to buy yourself a nice place in town and then swim in the rest if you want to."

He looks behind me, directing his gaze to the house across from his. His eyes sweep down the road, to all the other houses.

It's an odd setup. His house is the oldest, his property the largest by far. The rest of the homes are nearly identical to one another, little cookie cutters with yards a fraction the size of his. My guess is a home developer came in and developed around the farm.

"You don't need to worry about my social life." He

scratches his forearm and glances once more across the street. "I like it here."

"Can I give you my card? You can call me after you think it over. I've written the price I'm willing to pay on the back of the card." I take the card from my pocket, offering it up like I'm giving a morsel of food to a wild animal. He ventures out from the porch to take it from me.

"I'll be in touch," I say, backing away. I get in my car and reverse out of his driveway. Across from Conrad's house, a woman stands in a front yard. Two kids run around her legs, and she lifts her hand and waves at Conrad. He smiles and ducks his head, his hands in his pockets.

I shift into drive, leaving the farm, but my thoughts are stranded behind me.

A few minutes with Conrad was enough time to get a bad feeling about the guy. I don't want to jump to conclusions, but something about him is unsettling. I'd like to know more about him, but given how defensive he is, that's not going to be easy.

My hand scrapes my jaw and I scratch at the growth from a skipped day of shaving, my mind rolling over ways I can learn about Conrad.

Then I remember.

* * *

I CLIMB THE STAIRS TO THE FRONT PORCH. THE DOOR IS wide open, the bottom of it held in place by some kind of lift, and the person I came here to talk to uses a drill to screw in the new strike plates.

I wait for the high-pitched sound to cease, then ask, "How did you know my background?"

Wyatt looks over at me and sets down the power tool. I climb the stairs so we're on even ground. He crosses his arms, eyebrows raised, and evaluates me, deciding if he should tell me the truth. A sigh escapes his lips as he peers back into the house, then back to me and leans his head in closer. "There's a kid in town who is too tech savvy for his own good. Luckily, that aligns with my goals most of the time."

A twinge of irritation flares. "You had him look into me?"

"Possibly. But you piqued his curiosity all by yourself with that fancy-ass car of yours and the way you dress."

I look down at my navy slacks and pressed shirt. I didn't intend to keep who I was a secret when I came to Sierra Grande, but I didn't feel much like advertising it either.

He continues. "You stick out like a sore thumb, my friend."

I frown, and he chuckles. Enough talking about how poorly a job I've done of assimilating. At least I can ride a damn horse. "Can you connect me with this kid?"

"Why?"

"That alfalfa farmer. He doesn't want to sell, but I think I can wear him down. Besides, something is weird out there. He's not a farmer, not by any means."

His eyebrows lift patronizingly. "You can spot a farmer?"

"Does a farmer sit on his ass all day and play *Call of Duty*?"

Wyatt quiets, pinching his lower lip as he thinks. He pulls out his phone and sends me the contact. My mind races, trying to think of excuses for needing Jessie's number, but I can't come up with any. I can't ask him for it outright. Given the way he acts about everything else, I can only imagine how protective he is of his little sister.

"Tell him I gave you his number. And do not, under any circumstance, call him El Capitan." Wyatt rolls his eyes. "He's trying to make it a thing."

I nod. "Got it. What *is* his name?"

"Eldridge Farley."

I whistle low. "If that was my name, I'd shoot for El Capitan also."

Wyatt laughs. A genuine laugh, and I feel proud of myself. " If that were my name," he says, "I'd even go for Seymour Butts."

Jo comes up behind Wyatt and gives us both a disapproving look. "Keep your voices down. High school boys love stupid nicknames like that, and I don't need there to be a contest as to who can say the dumbest nickname of all."

Wyatt winks at her. "Who said anything about a nickname?"

She makes a face at him and swats his arm. To me, she asks, "Everything all good?"

I nod and tuck my hands in the pockets of my pants. "Question, Jo. Do you think I need new clothes?"

She widens her eyes in Wyatt's direction. "Seriously?"

He lifts his hands like he's innocent, but I answer before he can. "He didn't say anything," I assure her. "I just realized I stick out like a sore thumb."

The corner of Wyatt's lip curls into a smile.

Jo looks like she doesn't believe a single word from

my mouth. "I don't think you need new clothes, considering your job. If you worked on a ranch, those nice fabrics wouldn't last a day."

"Duly noted," I nod my head at them. "Thanks, Wyatt. I'll get out of your hair now."

As soon as I leave Wildflower, I call Eldridge Farley. I use his first name when he answers, and he says, "Do not call me by my first name."

"Sorry about that. Wyatt Hayden gave me your info and—"

"You're a friend of Wyatt's?"

"Yes." Based on his tone of voice, I'm not sure that's a good thing to be. Also, identifying myself as a friend might be pushing it, but in this circumstance I'll roll with it.

"He calls me El Capitan."

This makes me laugh. "He told me you'd try that. How about let's settle for Farley?"

"Farley works. What's up?"

I give him Conrad's full name and tell Farley I need something I can use against him. He doesn't agree until I explain why I'm looking for information. "I'm a hacker with a moral compass," he explains. He sounds very proud of himself.

We agree on a price, after he negotiates me higher than I started out, but not as high as I was prepared to go.

I hang up with Farley and head back to my hotel room. Standing at the window, I look down at High Street. It's lunchtime, and the place is filling up. A few different restaurants have opened for business, even in the short time I've been here. Maybe I'll go get lunch somewhere. Jessie was right. These four walls are beginning to close in on me.

* * *

I SETTLE ON THE NEW DELI, SIMPLY BECAUSE THERE'S A line out the door. All these people must have a good reason for waiting in line.

A woman and her antsy kid walk up and stand behind me. I know who she is, though we've never formally met. A person can't live in this town and not know a Hayden. If Jessie hadn't been away at college most of the time I've been here, I'm sure I would've known her. Look how long it took me to meet her once she came back.

The young mom's name is Dakota, I believe. Wes Hayden's wife. I've seen her in town before, and at the local market she puts on at her restaurant, but not Wes. Wyatt tells me he runs the HCC, and I'm guessing the ranch is where he spends a majority of his time.

The child she holds is young, maybe not even two. He wants down. He wants to touch everything. He wants to eat his fingers afterward.

I look back and smile politely at her. She offers me an apologetic smile. "They don't come with an instruction manual," she jokes. Based on the size and shape of her stomach, I'm pretty sure she's pregnant again. Not that I'm going to ask. That's one of those things you don't ask a woman.

"He's not a bother," I assure her. "Just a busy kid."

The child, Colt she called him a minute ago, walks quickly away from her, and is headed straight for the counter. He'll have no trouble sailing under it and getting into the kitchen. She drops her bag and hurries after him. She darts in front of him, then says his name and gives him a disapproving look. She sweeps him off his feet and he struggles against the cage she's formed with her arms.

"I forgot all his toys at home," she explains as she gets back in line. Colt digs his face into her chest.

I look around, then grab an outdated flyer off a bulletin board on the wall. I crumple it up and toss it from hand to hand. "Do you want this ball, buddy?"

He doesn't respond, and Dakota says, "He's hard of hearing. Mostly deaf, actually." She taps his back and he turns slowly, looking up at his mom. It isn't until now I notice the little hearing aid. It's the exact color of his hair. I hand her the makeshift ball and she takes it, then shows it to him. He takes it and crumples it even more in his small grasp. He looks at me.

"Ball," I say, pointing at his hand. Then I press my fingertips from each hand together, palms apart, and sign *ball*. "Ball," I repeat, pointing at the paper in his hand. I do this three more times. His eyes remain fixed on me. He drops the paper and imitates me. It looks nothing like the sign I made, but that's not the point.

Dakota gasps. "Did he just... did you just...?" Tears spring to her eyes. "Oh my gosh."

I smile at the kid. "He's very bright."

The person behind the counter asks me for my order, and a second person steps up to help Dakota.

I'm sitting at a table outside, unwrapping my sandwich, when Dakota approaches with Colt in tow. I push out the empty chair across from me with my foot and motion for her to sit. "Would you like to join me? Most of the seats are taken."

"I was going to take this food home"—she lifts the

bag—"but after what just happened, I'd like to ask you some questions. If you don't mind."

"Please," I say, moving aside and balling up the butcher paper my lunch was wrapped in.

She sits down and plants Colt in her lap. From her bag she produces a small container of apple slices and gives it to him. He begins munching happily. She takes a breath and extends her hand. "I'm Dakota Hayden. And you are?"

"Sawyer Bennett." I go to take her hand to shake, but she snaps her fingers while I'm still reaching.

"I know you. You bought into Jo's ranch. Jo is my sister-in-law."

I nod. "Don't take this to mean I'm a creep, but I know who you are."

She shakes her head and takes a bite of her lunch. "Sometimes I forget my locally infamous last name." She chews, swallows, and asks, "Are you fluent in ASL?"

I have to nod my answer because I'm chewing. I wipe my mouth with a napkin. Before I can speak, she's asking another question.

"Was it hard to learn? Because I've looked into classes for me and Colt, but they are all in Phoenix and it's a two-hour drive there and back, and we'd need to go enough that we could really get the benefit of it. And I really want his dad to do it too, but he works so much there's no way he could." She takes a breath and laughs, embarrassed. "I'm sorry. I'm just so relieved to meet someone who knows ASL."

I chuckle. "It's okay. How long have you known Colt is hard of hearing?"

"For a while. I started realizing he wasn't responding to my voice." Dakota wipes her hands with her napkin and looks down at the top of Colt's head. "We took him to an audiologist in Phoenix, and they confirmed it."

"He's wearing a hearing aid, so I'm guessing his hearing loss is sensorineural?"

"Mixed hearing loss. He's going to get cochlear implants soon." Her lips twist as she speaks and I can tell there's something more she's not saying, something that's upsetting her.

I nod. "Have you begun teaching him sign language?"

"I'm trying," she says. "It's not easy."

"I know," I respond. I remember the classes I took in the evenings, trying to get up to speed as soon as possible. Even as hard as I tried, it took me a long time to become fluent.

"Do you..." she hesitates, nibbling her lower lip. "Do you think you could work with me and Colt? I mean, I'm sure you're really busy. It's just—" she cuts off, and I realize she's crying. "I feel so alone. I want to be able to communicate with my son. And Wes works all the damn time, and I just want him to put his son before that goddamn ranch." Dakota cups a hand to her mouth, eyes wide. "I'm sorry. I'm so embarrassed. It's just pregnancy hormones talking. They're a doozy." She laughs uncomfortably.

"No worries." I finish my sandwich and toss the paper and napkin in the trash nearby. "I'm not a teacher by any means, but I could help you get started."

"Thank you." She strokes Colt's head. As precocious as he was in line inside the deli, he now delivers the same focus to the task of eating.

"It's not a problem. I never get to use sign anymore, so this will be good for me. Keep the language fresh." I don't elaborate about why I ever learned ASL in the first place.

Dakota asks where we should meet, and I tell her I'm staying in a hotel room. We both agree that's probably not the best place to meet. "This town is full of gossipy old ladies with nothing better to do. They'll have the rumor mill churning in an instant, and I don't need that headache."

"One-hundred-percent agree," I say. Drawing the anger of the oldest Hayden brother is the last thing I want. I haven't met him face to face yet, but I've heard stories. Besides, there's a totally different Hayden female that has captured my attention.

"Can you come out to the ranch?" Dakota makes a face like she's worried she's inconveniencing me. "That way, Colt will have all his toys and maybe be more receptive to learning."

I agree again, and she gives me the address. I already know how to get there, thanks to my rides, but I don't tell her that. We decide on a place and time, and she gets up to leave. Her arms are full with Colt and the bag she carries, so I throw her trash out for her.

Before she walks away, she says, "Sawyer, I almost didn't stop here for lunch. I saw the line and I was going to keep on driving. But something in me told me to brave the line with Colt. And I'm so glad I did. I have a feeling everything just changed."

She leaves me with those words, and I wonder if she knows how profound they are. All it took was her one decision, and now someone will help her and her child learn to communicate with each other. All it took was Brea's one decision, and she drowned in the ocean. What decision am I making right now that is affecting the outcome of my life? I'm allowing myself to feel attracted to Jessie, instead of seeing her as nothing more than the opposite sex. Still, I've yet to get her phone number or ask her on a date. Nothing feels tangible right now. In some ways I still feel like I'm floating above it all, a bystander of this life.

But maybe it's happening anyway. Tiny little choices, like tributaries that run into streams, and eventually, converge with mighty rivers.

12

JESSIE

I nudged him.

The alfalfa farmer.

Just a little push in the direction I want him to go.

After Wyatt told me Sawyer tried to buy the farm and the asshole refused, I thought maybe I could influence the outcome.

The mail was delivered today.

Now I'll put on my patience hat and see just how influential I can be.

Quietly, of course. From the sidelines.

God forbid I do anything effectual in the light of day.

13

SAWYER

"We're working on a long-term strategy that will lead to enhancement of unit-holder value. Our team has come up with several ideas, all of which have been thoroughly thought out. Thus begins our presentation."

I lean off camera and yawn silently. Meetings like this are the worst part of my job.

Andre's voice drones on and on, and I struggle to stay awake. Or present, at the very least. It's hard when my bed is only a few feet away. Normally I take calls like this from my office, but I didn't make it out in time today and I got stuck here.

He's halfway through his presentation when my phone vibrates with a text message from an unknown number.

I accept your offer.

I sit up straight, fully at attention. So much for needing Farley to dig up dirt.

I know who the message is from, but just in case I send him a message confirming it's Conrad. He responds in the affirmative. I write my lawyer an email, instructing him to draw up a sale agreement. I have no hope of listening to the rest of this call now, I'm too keyed up.

I text Conrad. *My lawyer is drawing up the papers. I'll have them to you ASAP.*

He responds with his email address, telling me not to try to reach him at the property because he won't be there. He moved out this morning.

What the hell?

The guy refuses to budge, and suddenly he's running? What happened?

"Mr. Bennett, is the connection bad?"

I snap back to the meeting. "It was, but it's better now. Sorry about that."

Andre repeats his last question, I answer, and we spend five more minutes discussing when the next meeting should be. Incredible how much time we waste having meetings about when our next meeting will occur.

I hang up and take a deep breath, then shoot Farley a text telling him to call off his digging. Adrenaline courses through me. It always does when I'm on the cusp of a deal. I shake my arms at my sides, trying to release some of the energy. It's nearly impossible. I'm due at Dakota and Wes's place in a couple hours, and I don't want to show up looking like I just tanked a whole pot of espresso.

If I'm being honest, it's not just energy over an impending deal that has me hyper. I'm hoping I'll be lucky enough to see Jessie while I'm out at the HCC. I was daydreaming during the call with my team, thinking of excuses I could come up with to ask Dakota to call Jessie over. So far I've come up empty.

I decide to go running, which normally I can't stand, but I need to do something with my limbs. A nearby trail winds over the Verde River and into the cottonwoods, and it's just long enough that I can run it and have enough time to shower and change before heading out to the HCC. I switch from my typical dress pants and shirt and into a T-shirt and shorts. I lace up my shoes, slide in my headphones, and head out of the hotel.

I have two voice mails I need to listen to, so I start my run with those. I want to get them out of the way so I can spend the rest of it listening to the kind of music that will keep me running. The first one is my admin, asking if it's okay to buy lunch for the office tomorrow.

The second is from my lawyer, asking for additional details on the sale agreement. I'll call him back when I'm finished with my run. I'm reaching for my phone to switch over to music when I hear it. My own voice, coming through my ears, but the words themselves are Brea's. She'd written me a note and asked me to speak it into my voice mail. One day, it occurred to her she'd never been able to leave a voice mail before, and she wanted to.

I'd forgotten it was there. Or I'd made myself forget, I'm not sure which.

"Hi, Sawyer. This is Brea. Your wife with the nice ass. I just want you to know I love you to the moon and back. One day, I'm going to have your babies."

My voice pauses, and my laughter rumbles into the phone. I hear the smack of a kiss, and then I say, in words that are my own, *"I love you, my wife with the nice ass."*

The voice mail ends. My knees buckle. I make my

way to a cottonwood tree, grabbing its trunk in an attempt to balance, but it's flimsy. So I shake it instead. My eyes are hot, and the tears form.

A hand touches my back and I jump away.

Jessie stands two feet from me, eyes wide. Concern and fear flash through them. "Sawyer, are you okay?"

I rip my gaze from hers, wiping my eyes on the shoulder of my shirt. "I'm fine," I bark.

"You don't seem fine." She adjusts her weight. Her cheeks are pink. Her sports bra and leggings tell me she was running too.

"Why are you so far from home?" The question struggles from my chest. It's hard to think about anything but Brea's words.

"I can't run at the HCC. There aren't any good trails. And it's pretty here."

I sigh and look down at my shoes. I heard her answer, but I'm not really listening to it. "I need to get back," I tell her. I grab my phone and find my music. "See you later," I mutter as the music fills my ears.

She says something, but I can't hear it because the volume is turned up too loud. I might've missed what her lips said, but there's no missing what she communicates with her eyes.

She's worried about me. And curious.

But most of all, I've hurt her feelings.

* * *

DAKOTA TEXTS ME AS I'M TAKING THE TURN FROM SIERRA Grande onto the road that leads to the HCC.

I grab my phone and read the message. Dakota is asking me to go to the main house instead of her place.

She refers to it as the *homestead*. She tells me it'll be the first house I see as soon as I make the turn and drive under the HCC sign. This is useful information, because as often as I've ridden from Wildflower onto HCC land, I've never ventured near the Hayden home.

Will do, I say back, without asking why.

My stomach tightens at the thought of seeing Jessie again. A couple hours ago I was concocting ways to see her, and now I'm rehearsing my apology.

My tires spin over the road, and I scan the sights. One side of the road is grass, more yellow and brittle-looking than it should be, and the other nothing but trees. Somewhere along this road, my mother lost her life, and I don't even know why she was traveling it.

My stomach turns over as I drive on, and I think back to the way the kitchen used to be when Wildflower was the Circle B. My mother had a dish for her coffee creamer in the shape of a cow, and it mooed when tipped. The center of my chest cracks at the memory. Even an aged wound can break a heart anew.

I'm nothing less than grateful when I see my turn ahead. I make the right, going beneath the large metal sign declaring this the *Hayden Cattle Company*.

The unpaved road kicks up dust, so I ease off the gas. The homestead looms in the distance, and the sheer fact I can see it clearly from here speaks to how large it is. Like a river system, there is a road that veers off from here, going left, and a hundred feet up, another road that snakes right. Both roads trail off into the pine trees and disappear.

The homestead grows in size the closer I get. It's made of rich, reddish-brown wood and stone, with big stone columns lining the front. The roof is dark gray, a stone chimney jutting up into the sky. A few trees dot the front yard, and a walkway leads from a makeshift driveway up to a small set of stairs.

Trucks bearing the HCC logo are parked haphazardly out front. I come to a stop and add my SUV to the mix. Like my attire in this town, it looks out of place.

The front door is massive, a knocker in the center I'm positive is meant to look intimidating. It's doing its job. I'm sufficiently intimidated.

I knock three times and wait. The door opens, and there she is, the doorframe dwarfing her.

Not Dakota, like I'd expected, but Jessie. Her hair is damp, framing her face and a little wild, and her eyes are bright. She's heartachingly beautiful.

She grips the door. "Dakota told me you were coming over," she says, slightly out of breath. She shifts her weight and cocks her head. "Are you good?"

The back of my neck heats. "I'm sorry I snapped at you, Jessie. You caught me at a bad moment."

"I gathered that," she says slowly. She steps back to allow me into the house. "Come on in."

I step inside and out of the way of the door as Jessie closes it. She leans against it, looking up at me. She wears a white tank top tucked into tight jeans. Bare feet. Her toenails are painted red. My eyes scan her body slowly, and I know she's watching me. When I make it to her face, I take in her warm, blue eyes, and she waits for me to say something. *I like how you let me drink you in.*

The corner of my mouth pulls away, contrite. "I'm sorry." My voice is low. "I owe you an explanation—"

"You don't owe me anything. But I'll listen if you want to talk about it."

I open my mouth but hear my name from somewhere in the house. Dakota walks into the room. "Sawyer?" She looks from me to Jessie. "I take it from the way you ran from the room when he knocked on the door that I don't need to make introductions?"

I look down at Jessie, my lips coaxed into a smile by this small revelation.

She smirks. "We've met before. I was on a ride. He was coming from Wildflower and we crossed paths."

Dakota nods slowly. "Right. Okay. Well, Sawyer, everyone is this way."

I halt. "Everyone?"

Her lips press together in apology. "I was kind of hoping you could show everyone a few signs. When I told my husband you'd agreed to help us out, he said it'd be great if Colt could communicate with his family. I hope you don't mind."

She looks genuinely worried I'll say no. It must be hell to worry for your child the way Dakota worries for Colt.

"Of course not," I respond, smiling politely. I don't usually feel nervous in front of people, but nerves are bundling in my stomach. Must be the Hayden effect.

Jessie touches my forearm, and my attention swings back to her. Curiosity rages in her eyes.

"I've learned two things about you since I woke up this morning." She holds up a finger. "For one, you know ASL."

My eyebrows lift. "And two?"

"Something hurt you. Way down deep." She taps the center of my chest with two fingers. "In here."

Emotion catches in my throat, snagging on words I should be saying to her. All I can do is swallow the way I feel at the sight of the tenderness in her eyes and the warmth from her touch.

I tear my gaze away. Dakota waits patiently, and when I start in her direction, she peers around me and sets her sights on Jessie. Her eyes communicate something, and I bet Jessie is talking back, using this silent form of conversation.

Dakota shows me into the house, delivering me to the humongous living room. Two leather couches face each other, a table in the center flanked by upholstered armchairs. A mammoth floor-to-ceiling fireplace takes up residence behind one couch, the logs inside unlit.

"Hi, everyone," Dakota waves, collecting the attention of all the people in the room. I recognize Jo, Travis, and Wyatt, along with Beau and Juliette. She introduces me to Wes, who has Colt on his lap. Next up are Warner and Tenley, and I try my best to act like meeting Tenley Roberts (Hayden?) is not a big deal. I meet their kids, too, but make the assumption the older two are from a first marriage. The goings-on in Hollywood were never my thing, but Brea loved Tenley's movies, and I specifically remember her feeling scandalized a while ago when Tenley's boyfriend cheated on her. The last introduction is an older man, and when Dakota calls him Leroy he waves a hand and says, "Call me Gramps. That's been my name for so long, it's how I sign my checks."

Wes snorts. "You don't sign checks."

Wyatt snickers. "Who uses checks anymore?"

"Gramps, when he goes to the grocery store." Warner gets in on it.

All three Hayden boys are met with an old, wrinkled middle finger, and they laugh.

"So," Dakota says loudly, breaking into the exchange. "As you know, Colt has his cochlear implant surgery soon. But even with the implants, he may not gain full hearing capability. Which means we need to consider additional measures to help ensure Colt is able to communicate with us, and us with him. Sawyer Bennett"—she gestures my way, and many pairs of eyes train on me—"has offered to teach me some ASL. And you guys too, since you kind of Hayden'd your way into it." She stares pointedly at Wes.

Tenley and Jo snicker, and Beau's eyebrows pull together. "Hayden'd?"

Dakota nods. "It's when you step into a situation and begin to command it."

He evaluates her. "Is this a bad thing? Or good?"

She dips her head side to side. "That depends on the circumstance."

He scowls good-naturedly. His gaze swings my way, and our eyes lock. The teasing playfulness disappears. Something in him shifts. He places a hand on his wife's thigh. It's the oddest thing, and I can't explain why the room suddenly feels thick.

"What's ASL?" someone asks.

It's instant relief when I pull my awareness from the head of the Hayden family and find the source of the question. Charlie, if I'm remembering correctly, Warner's son. "American Sign Language," I answer.

"How do you know sign language?" It's Warner's oldest, Peyton, asking from her place on the floor beside her brother.

"I knew someone who was completely deaf. It's the only way she communicated." I prepare myself for the searing pain that flashes across my heart every time I refer to Brea in the past tense. It does not show up, and I don't have time to question it.

We start with the basics. I've never taught ASL before, so I'm calling on what I remember from my own classes. For the purpose of the Hayden family, I think it best they learn what Colt will learn first. This means words that will help him ask for what he needs. I start with *sleep, eat, drink, hungry, more, all done, up, and down.*

Dakota and Wes have moved to the floor and sit with Colt, working with him as they learn. I try to keep my attention on all the Haydens, helping as we go, but I'm watching Jessie more. The tip of her tongue presses against the center of her upper lip as she concentrates, and it's the cutest damn thing. Wyatt makes a joke about her habit of doing it, and she gives him the chin flick, a middle finger equivalent. "How's that for signing? Pretty clear communication."

Wes rolls his eyes and Warner fights a smile. Tenley, Jo, and Dakota laugh openly at her. Tenley makes a joke about how the brothers can dish it out but they can't take it, and Jessie tosses her head back in laughter. Her hair cascades down her back, her cheeks full and round, and her eyes are closed. She obviously loves getting a rise out of her brothers.

I like watching her here, in her element. She is the center of gravity, a magnetic force. Everyone in the family is drawn to her, and it's easy to see why.

She is effusive, a light, capable of bringing a smile to someone's face. I know so, because right now, I'm wearing a dopey grin.

The lesson continues, mostly with me calling out the words we've covered and helping the family to remember the corresponding sign. Despite the fact I'm addressing different people, my body is aware of everything Jessie does.

The way she sweeps her hair back from her shoulders, bounces her heels on the ground, and her frown when she gets a sign wrong.

"Try not to feel discouraged if you can't remember, or if certain signs are harder to recall than others. At this point in our lives, our brains are set in their ways. The language center doesn't like to be challenged." This is almost an exact quote from the woman who taught my classes.

After a few more minutes, I decide to wrap it up. There's only so long a person can practice. What they really need to do is use it in real life. Like most things, it's better absorbed in real time.

I nod at Dakota and Wes. "Continue with Colt at every opportunity. He'll pick up these signs quickly. Look how fast he learned *ball*."

I wave at the Hayden family politely, smiling and saying *you're welcome* when they thank me. I go to leave, and Juliette, who's been the quietest of the entire group by far, speaks up.

"Would you like to stay for dinner?"

For some reason, I glance at my watch. As if I have anywhere else to be. It's an excuse for a pause while I gather myself, so I don't show the surprise I feel. Juliette has given me the distinct impression she doesn't care for me.

She nods encouragingly, like she's nudging me on to say I'll stay. "It'll be ready in thirty minutes. I'm sure my boys are ready for happy hour, though." She looks at each son, and they sit up straight when her gaze lands on them.

"Yes," Wes says.

"Why not?" Warner adds.

And then, from Wyatt. "Does a one-legged duck swim in a circle?"

Jo rolls her eyes at him. "It's a good thing you're handsome," she says, and he slings an arm around her and kisses her long and loud, drawing groans from his siblings.

"Enough, enough," Juliette announces, using a hand on Beau's knee to push herself to standing. "Every man for himself. Get your drinks." She disappears, I'm assuming, to the kitchen.

There's a tweak deep down in my heart. My mom loved to cook.

Wyatt brings me a whiskey. "I hope you don't like drinks as fancy as your car, because you're shit out of luck. No pink martinis here."

The guy likes to give me shit, and I don't mind it. A therapist would probably tell me it has something to do with being an only child, and always wishing for a brother. I take the offered glass. "Whiskey works."

In truth, whiskey does not work. For me, it's wine or gin and tonic in the summer. I'd die before telling one of the Hayden brothers that. Jessie sits back, nestled into the couch cushions, watching me with subdued laughter on her face.

I tip my head up at her. "What?" I mouth. My skin prickles, even from this distance, the air between us charged with electricity.

She smiles and shakes her head, eyes squinting. Her eyes fall to the glass I'm holding. "Where's my drink?" she asks, maybe to Wyatt but also to maybe nobody in particular.

"You need to turn twenty-one, Calamity." It's Warner speaking, sitting back down with his own two fingers of whiskey.

"I already have, asshole."

He thumbs over to his two older kids. "Would you mind watching your language?"

"Would you mind not speaking to me in a patriarchal tone? I'd wager a bet that you setting Peyton up to tolerate or expect such from a man is far more damaging than a swear word she's undoubtedly heard countless times."

Warner throws up his hands. "I'm going to sit by the firepit." He leaves, and one by one everyone trickles out.

Wyatt, the last to leave, pats Jessie on the back. "You sure know how to clear a room."

She crosses her arms. "I'm not wrong."

He stops and looks her over. "No. You are not wrong, Cal." He gets her a drink. Not a white wine, like he poured for Tenley and Jo, but a whiskey. He gives it to her with a wink. "You're a badass. Don't forget it."

She takes the glass, and he walks away. Her eyes are on him as he goes. "He's my favorite," she says, when he's gone from sight.

"Do your other brothers know that?"

"Indubitably."

I choke on the amber liquid I've just swallowed. "That's a ten-dollar word."

"I went to college," she says, her joke delivered in a lofty tone. Her eyes slide away, like she's thinking of something.

"What?" I ask.

She shakes her head. "It's nothing." She stands. "Assholes or not, do you want to join my brothers out back?

Wes is good at horseshoes, but that's just because he's quiet while he plays and everyone else talks shit. Keep your mouth shut and it'll throw him for a loop."

"Um, yeah." I nod. "Show me the way."

She walks closer, and I stay still. I'm rooted in place, mesmerized by the swing of her hips in those dark jeans, the dip of her waist in that white tank top. She pauses near me. Her chuckle escapes only one side of her mouth. "What?" she asks, almost shyly. It's not a quality I'd thought Jessie could possess.

"You are very pretty," I say under my breath. I say it like an admittance, though anybody with fully functioning eyes could see it for themselves. What I'd like to say is that her eyes match the color of the ocean at a certain time of day, when the sun hangs low on the horizon. And that her skin is burnished the same way I've seen on surfer girls, proving that California women may not be all that different from Arizona women. The sun kisses them both.

"Why do you say it like it's a bad thing?" She is directly in front of me, her shoulder just inches from my chest.

"You scare me," I admit. It'd be nice if I had some sense of pride, but it seems to have abandoned me.

She swivels, her brave stare full on. "Sawyer Bennett?"

I swallow and nod.

"You scare me, too."

Then she walks out. And what choice do I have but to follow her?

I eat dinner with the Hayden family. I enjoy their company immensely. Too much? The siblings give one another a large helping of shit, but it's clear underneath it all how deeply they love each other. Best wishes to any adversary who decides to come up against the four of them.

During dinner, Wyatt mentions the alfalfa farm. I'm a couple whiskeys deep by then, so I state, "I bought it."

Voices grow quiet. The sound of forks scraping plates is a lone sound in the room. "You bought the alfalfa farm?" Beau asks.

I nod. "My lawyer is drawing up all the papers and we're signing tomorrow. Don't worry," I add, "I'm ceasing operations. Both the HCC and Wildflower will get their rightful share of water."

Beau gets up, going into the pantry off the kitchen. Wes whistles, low and slow.

Wyatt rubs his palms together. "I've been waiting my whole life for this."

Beau returns with a bottle. *Macallan 25*. He carries two glasses. Wyatt's face falls.

"Sawyer." Beau says my name, and nothing else. He pours the whiskey into fresh tumblers, pushing one my way. "I'd like to personally thank you for what you did for the HCC. We may be an inadvertent benefactor, but that doesn't diminish my gratefulness."

I nod, overwhelmed. "Sir," I start, but he interrupts me.

"And thank you, for this afternoon. For coming here, and showing us how to communicate with my grandson." He swallows hard, and I get the feeling I've been let into a secret showing of an emotional Beau Hayden.

"The pleasure is mine, sir."

He sips the whiskey, and I follow suit. I wish I possessed a more refined palette, so I could properly appreciate the taste. He replaces the bottle in the pantry.

Wyatt nudges me. "What the fuck, man? None of us have been allowed to have that shit. He saves it for special occasions."

Jessie places her hands on my shoulders from behind, and it's everything I can do not to tip my head back into her. "Guess you aren't all that special."

He sends her a dirty look, then offers me a hand. "Thank you," he says, shaking my hand. "For making sure Wildflower has what it needs to operate."

I'm overwhelmed. I didn't do anything extraordinary. I did what was decent.

Juliette serves dessert, an ice cream cookie cake she said was Beau's mom's recipe, and we go back outside. The Macallan 25 goes down smooth. So does the next whiskey Wes pours for me. Beau and Juliette go to bed long before we've left the gas fire. The couples peel off, one by one. First it's Warner and Tenley, who have the longest drive home. Next up are Wyatt and Jo, then Wes and Dakota.

Jessie looks at me. She's tired, her blinks long and slow, her eyelashes brushing her skin.

"You're drunk," she says, twisting a key to turn off the firepit.

"No, I'm not." I'm not drunk, per se. But I definitely shouldn't be driving.

She tips her head, considering me. "Can you at least follow me to my cabin?"

I nod. That I can do.

14

JULIETTE

THE PAST WILL ALWAYS COME BACK TO HAUNT YOU.

It's sayings like that, among others, that don't feel real. Until they show up in human form, standing in front of your goat cheese booth and staring longingly at your only daughter.

Sawyer resembles his mother in some ways. He has her full upper lip, bearing a pronounced Cupid's bow. And her long eyelashes. Beyond that, he is his father's son.

"I'm sure that wasn't easy." Beau drifts up behind me in our bathroom, placing his chin on my shoulder. His arms twine around my waist, his gaze searching out mine in the mirror.

Even after all these years, the regret appears instantly. Despite what happened so long ago, my husband is a loyal man. This loyalty extends even to his remorse. He will never be free from it. I have forgiven him. Forgiving himself is a separate beast.

I look back at my husband of almost forty years. Beau's skin bears the markings of stress and time spent under the often brutal Arizona sun. His crows feet and forehead creases have permanent residence on his face. As do mine. It strikes me now, probably because of Sawyer's reemergence in our lives, that our marriage is as weathered as our skin.

"I did what I'd hope someone would do for one of my children if the situation were reversed." I'd been distracted during the entire ASL lesson, considering whether I should invite Sawyer to stay for dinner.

Loosening Beau's grip on my midsection, I turn so we're face to face. "Him being here will create a problem eventually. Did you see the way he looks at Jessie?" My arms encircle his neck and I let him pull me close. He needs to hold me as much as I need to be held by him.

"I'd have to be blind to miss it." Beau's voice falls over me, and a shiver slips down my spine.

Even after all this time, through small transgressions and the most colossal of mistakes, Beau holds my heart.

"How do you feel?" I ask.

He presses his forehead against mine. "Like you're an angel."

I manage a smile. "You're sweet, but that's not what I was referring to."

He takes a breath, the exhale a warm stream of air from his nose. "Like a bomb has been thrown into the center of my family, and I'm waiting for it to go off."

"They'll be okay, you know? If the bomb goes off. Our kids will make it through."

"They shouldn't have to." The regret is gone, replaced by disgust.

I shrug. "It's too late for that." *You shouldn't have done what you did back then*. I don't say it. It won't help the situation. And comments like that don't make me feel better, either.

"Come on." I step from his embrace and he follows me to our bed. We climb in and slide under the covers. He reaches for me, tucking me into his chest.

We made our babies in this room. We've fought and loved, argued and consoled. These walls have seen us through some of our best and worst moments. They will continue to do so.

The seed Beau sowed more than twenty years ago has finally sprouted. What will come of it is anyone's guess. I pray Jessie will not be the hardest hit once the truth comes to light.

In all honesty, how can she not be? After all, Beau's long-deceased mistress's son is all grown up and has set his sights on our daughter.

If that's not poetic justice, I don't know what is.

15

SAWYER

She's trying to be quiet, but I hear her anyway. The soft, muted thud of bare feet padding over hardwood floors. She doesn't approach, and I don't move to peer over the back of the couch. I'd like to see her, though. Her hair is probably messy. Maybe it's tangled up a little in the back, soft snarls she hasn't yet run a brush through. The rustle of fabric floats through the air as she moves. Maybe she wears matching pajamas. Maybe she wears an oversized T-shirt.

It has been a long time since I've heard these sounds. They weren't special, or notable, until they ceased to exist. I didn't know I missed them until right now, listening to Jessie make them.

There's a tug in the center of my chest, a quick pull of the organ I keep locked up tight. I don't want to think about Brea. I don't want to hurt. I want to think about Jessie.

I lie on the couch, listening to the sounds of coffee being prepared, percolating, and brewing. Minutes later, the smell wafts in from the kitchen.

I push up to sitting. The cabin is a wide-open concept, and I can see directly into where Jessie stands. With one hand braced on the edge of the counter, she rises on tiptoe and reaches into a higher cabinet. Her short, pale-yellow nightdress rides up her legs, revealing tan, toned thighs and the bottom swell of her ass.

I blink and look away, a twinge of guilt creeping through me, as if I've seen something not meant for my eyes. Standing, I reach down and grab the blanket I used last night, folding it. The movement grabs Jessie's attention. Our eyes meet, and even from across the room, I sense her discomfort.

"Would you like some coffee?" she asks, her voice strained, motioning to the mugs she has set on the counter.

I nod, rounding the couch and coming closer. "Yes, please." They are my first words of the day, and they sound rough. I clear my throat. Jessie grabs a glass, this time from a cabinet that doesn't require her to stretch, and pours a glass of water for me.

"Thank you," I tell her, drinking half the glass in one gulp.

"You're welcome," she responds. Her gaze was on my neck, but now it lifts to find my eyes. "Are you okay?"

I nod. "I don't usually drink that much, but I'm fine."

Her head shakes. "I was referring to you waking up here. I didn't know how you'd feel about it."

Oh.

She continues. "You just seem... hesitant sometimes. Two steps forward, one back." Her eyes scrunch and her head moves back and forth in quick, tiny motions. "Disregard that. It wasn't a complaint. You have the right to do whatever you need to do." She turns, pouring coffee into two mugs. She adds half and half to hers, and when she extends the carton to me, I wave it away. "No, thank you."

I'm still digesting her most recent comment. I have the right to get through these new feelings for a woman who isn't Brea just as much as Jessie has the right to know about her. If I tell her now, it will dim this moment, maybe even cast its shadow over everything developing between us. How could it not?

I study Jessie's soft curves, the hollow of her throat, the rise and fall of her chest. And I decide not to tell her. Not yet.

She walks to an opening just off the kitchen, and I follow. Through it is a small mudroom, the washer and dryer opposite a bench with a boot tray beneath it. Hooks cling to the wall, but nothing hangs from them. Another door leads outside, and we step out into the early morning air.

Crisp, clean pine. Dirt and sunshine. It's springtime, and the mornings are chilly. Steam rises from our coffee cups, and it transports me back in time, to a place not too far from here, when I was a child and life was good.

Quietly, I inhale everything. The scent of the ranch, the cold air, and the warm memories. I take them all in. It has been so long since I had a morning like this, and just like the soft footfalls of my wife, I didn't know how much I loved it until it was gone.

"It's beautiful out here." I sip the hot black coffee.

Jessie looks up at me. "Do you remember a lot about living at Wildflower? The Circle B, I mean?" A tiny bit of sleep is crusted at the corner of her left eye, and it humanizes her. She is so audacious, so authoritative, that it's easy to think she is some kind of other-worldly warrior princess.

"For a long time I pushed away the memories, but since I've returned to Sierra Grande, some of it has come back." I take a drink. "Something inside me always yearned for these sights. These smells." I gesture out at the landscape. "This feels like where I belong."

"That's how I felt when I moved for college. This ranch means everything to me." She gazes back out to the wall of trees around her home. Her hair isn't messy the way I pictured it when I first heard her moving around. It's wound on top of her head in a bun, and it makes her seem taller than she is. Our shoulders are almost touching, and I feel the movement of air when she lifts her cup to her mouth. "What means everything to you, Sawyer?"

Such a good question. "I'm not sure." When I came here, there was something that meant everything to me. *Someone.* But now I fear something else is beginning to become important. And now that *someone* is slipping away, seeping through the cracks in my fingers.

"I've never been unsure." Jessie looks back to me with that steady, clear-eyed gaze. "The HCC is my first love. It will be my last love."

I nod. I understand singular devotion.

"You have a busy day ahead of you, I'm assuming?" She punctures the heavy conversation with a basic question. "Buying properties and single-handedly saving ranches?"

I nod and grin at her teasing tone. "Yes, I do. Better get to it."

Her mouth opens to speak, but it's interrupted by the cracking of twigs, the heavy steps of boots. Jessie's eyes widen, but she takes a deep breath and squares her shoulders. *Oh shit*. I know what this scene looks like.

Beau and Wes round the corner of the log cabin. Both men stop short when they see us, then continue.

"Hello," I greet them first, trying to sound as innocent as possible.

Wes's mouth forms a hard, straight line. Last night's friendly expression is as absent from his face as the whiskey glass from his hand.

Beau looks from me to Jessie. His expression is impossible for me to read. At this point, he must be thinking I've slept with his daughter. I open my mouth to tell him it's simply a case of having too much to drink last night, but Jessie speaks first.

"I don't appreciate the way either of you are looking at me. I'm an adult." Anger vibrates off her words, her hand motions, maybe even her breath.

Beau's jaw clenches. "Christ, this again? We all know your age, Jessie."

"Do you?" She takes a step toward her dad. Her nightdress swings around her legs. I can't help but admire her, the way she steps up and challenges her dad when she believes he's wrong, and that she doesn't give a shit about what she's wearing.

"Tell me, Dad. When you were twenty-one, did Gramps come to your home and judge you the way you're judging me right now? Or did he pat your back later, a silent congratulation for getting laid?"

Beau pins me with a hard stare as Jessie all but confirms what he assumes, but couldn't be further from the truth. *So much for the inroads I made with him last night.* He looks back at her. "You need to watch your mouth, young lady."

"Why?" Her tone is calmer now, but she is ardent. "Why do you want me to watch my mouth? Because I'm making you uncomfortable?"

Wes rubs the bridge of his nose. "All of this is uncomfortable, Jessie." He looks pointedly at what she's wearing.

"So? You came here to find me. To my home, where I was drinking coffee and enjoying the view with Sawyer. If that makes you uncomfortable, that's not my problem. It's not my job to adjust my behavior to meet your comfort level. Especially not when I'm in my own home."

"This is Warner's place," Beau grumbles.

"Not anymore," Jessie shakes her head. "It's mine." She stares at both men, daring them to continue.

Wes rises to the occasion, staring Jessie down in equal measure. He towers over her, but her aura is such that she is his equal.

"What did you want, Wes? You came here to find me."

He reaches into his back pocket. He unfolds a brightly colored, shiny mailer. "Do you know anything about this?"

Jessie's lips press together. Wes waves the mailer in the air. I can't see what it says, but I damn sure recognize the picture.

"May I see that?" I ask, hand extended.

Wes gives it to me.

"What the..." my voice trails off. It's the alfalfa farmer in what appears to be a mug shot. The large, bold text beside him reads: **This man is a registered sex offender.** Below it is a website address.

Now it makes sense. Why he sold to me suddenly. Why he left town. I turn to Jessie.

"Did you do this?"

Her expression is stoic. "I felt it was my duty to make certain the people who lived near him knew of the risk he posed."

I think back to the woman across the street. Now I'm not sure if he had a crush, or was thinking of something more sinister. My stomach turns at the thought.

"What if he was simply a man who'd had a relationship with a sixteen or seventeen-year-old when he was eighteen?" Wes asks Jessie. "That happens too, you know. And if the girl had a pissed-off dad, and he pressed charges," he shrugs with one shoulder. "Boom. Registered sex offender."

Jessie gathers her hair in one hand, then lets it drop. "Unfortunately, there isn't a way to know the details of the crime, only the address of the offender."

Wes looks at her like he can't believe her words. "You might have ruined his life, Jessie."

She snorts. "Hardly. He'll move somewhere else and register his new address like he's supposed to. And the HCC and Wildflower will get their water again, thanks to Sawyer. Problem solved."

Wes drops the exasperation and smiles begrudgingly. "You're goddamn crazy in the best way, Calamity." He rubs the back of his neck. "Would you mind coming to the homestead this morning? I'd like to hear some of your ideas."

Jessie nods, furtively biting the inside corner of her lip. I think she's trying to hide her excitement.

Wes gives me a sidelong glance. "We'll leave now.

Obviously we assumed you were alone when we came barging in here."

"No problem," Jessie says flippantly, still not taking the opportunity to set the record straight about why I'm here, and I'd love to know why. I'm about to speak up, but think better of it and keep my mouth shut. She must have a reason.

Beau and Wes say an awkward goodbye and leave.

"You sent those mailers out?" I already know she did, but I have to ask again because it's not something I'd ever think to do.

"I sent one to every person who lives on his street."

"And all you did was look him up on that website?"

She nods. "I had a bad feeling about him that day we rode onto his property. Call it women's intuition."

"Incredible." I scratch at the scruff on my jaw. "Why did you let your dad and Wes think we slept together?"

"For one, it's none of their damn business what I do in the privacy of my own home. For two, I don't need to proclaim my innocence. Sleeping with you wouldn't mean I did something bad, so why do I need to ensure they know I didn't do it?"

I rub my chin. "Those are both valid points."

"Thank you very much." She takes my empty mug and walks inside.

I go to the couch that was my bed last night and pull on my socks and shoes. Jessie walks with me to the front door.

I pause at the threshold, looking back at her. Careful to keep my eyes from straying down her body, I say, "Thanks for letting me stay over. Driving would've been a bad idea."

"You're welcome." She holds out her hand. "Give me your phone."

I fish my phone from my pocket and hand it over. She opens a new text message and begins typing.

"What are you doing?"

"Don't interrupt me," she smiles slyly up at me, then looks back down and keeps typing. "I'm very busy right now." She hits send. A muffled ding comes from her purse on the kitchen table.

She hands me back the phone and opens the front door. "Have a great day. I'll see you later."

I squint at her in suspicion on my way through the door, and she gives me a wide smile. "Bye," she says brightly. The door closes.

I shake my head as I make my way down the three stairs and out to my car. Once I'm inside, I pull the phone out and look at my texts, then laugh. She texted herself, saying *Hi, Jessie. It's Sawyer. Dinner tomorrow night? I'll pick you up at seven.*

The response bubbles pop up while I'm reading. Her text appears. *I'm not sure, Sawyer. I feel like you should work a little harder for a date with me.*

I grin and look out to the cabin. Jessie stands in full view in the living room window, watching me. A smile takes over my face, and I begin to type. I try not to think about what to say, and type with my heart.

You're beautiful, intelligent, funny, and sexy. You also make a mean cup of coffee. Would you please do me the honor of having dinner with me?

My finger hovers over the send button. Is it too much? Maybe. Is it how I see her? Yes. I send it, and watch her read it when it comes through. Her eyes widen and she smiles and shimmies her shoulders playfully. She lifts her phone to her mouth and speaks her response. I read her lips, so I'm already grinning when her message pops up.

You sir, have yourself a date.

She winks at me and walks from the window.

I'm feeling a hundred different emotions when I drive along the long road that leads back to town. So much so that I don't think about my mother's car accident at all.

16

JESSIE

I step into my parents' house, toeing off my shoes and leaving them beside the door.

In the living room, a fire blazes in the floor-to-ceiling stone fireplace, the leather couches look as soft and buttery as always, and the framed photos on the walls are the same as they have been for years.

Wes is standing in the kitchen with Dakota when I walk in, and before they see me I overhear her say the words *help* and *ASAP*. Colt is on her hip, one meaty leg slung over her burgeoning stomach.

I'm not sure what I've walked into, but it doesn't feel pleasant.

"Hey, guys," I say, looking back and forth between them. "Just grabbing some coffee," I lie, going to the cabinet for a mug. The heavy silence draws out the four seconds it takes me to fill it up. I back out, saying, "Wes, come talk to me when you're done."

My coffee sloshes in my cup in my haste, and I take a big gulp to avoid spilling. "Damn," I mutter, biting down on my tongue after I burn it.

The Calamity

I walk all the way out of the kitchen and into the dining room. Gramps sits by himself at the head of the table, with a large cup of black coffee and a plate of scrambled eggs. The mailer Wes came to ask me about this morning lies on the table beside his plate.

"Hi, Gramps." I sit down two seats away. "Want some company?"

He grins, his eyes brightening. "Looks to me like you've already answered the question for me."

My hands wrap around my mug. I don't really need a second cup, but what the hell. "It was more of a formality."

Gramps finishes his eggs and doesn't say a word while he drinks his coffee. When his cup is nothing but dregs, he leans back in his seat and trains his clear, wise gaze on me. "How ya doin', little girl?"

I smile at the endearment. "I've probably been better, Gramps. But I've definitely been worse."

"Been there a time or two myself. What's going on?"

"Wes wants to know some of my ideas for the ranch. And I'm happy about that, don't get me wrong." I nibble on the edge of my thumbnail. I've been trying to figure out my feelings since Sawyer left an hour ago. "I want to *work* on the ranch, too, but Wes and Dad are resistant. And it pisses me off."

"Why do you want to work here?"

I take a second to gather my thoughts. I know Gramps has my dad's ear, and he's one of the few people my dad might actually listen to. This is an opportunity to speak my mind without arguing with anybody. "I love this place. This ranch, she's"—uncharacteristic tears prick the backs of my eyes—"woven into my soul. The soil, the trees, the stream that runs alongside pasture eighty-two. The way the grass grows tall at the edge of the backyard, and if you walk through it in late summer, the ladybugs hitch a ride on your clothes. My heart belongs here, and I don't need to travel the world to confirm that."

"Ranching is about a lot more than just fond memories. It's tough work that can break a man," he ducks his chin at me, "or woman, both physically and mentally. Your dad and Wes know this already, and they're trying to protect you."

"I don't need protecting." I point at the mailer on the table next to his empty plate. "That was my work. I got the asshole to scurry away and sell his place."

He sighs slowly, but keeps his lips closed so the sound is low. "You proved you're smart. Not that you needed to. But you're also about as wild as they come, and people's memories are long. They know you as impulsive, a spitfire, and that doesn't fit the mold of cattle rancher."

I frown. "That's limiting."

"Not when your last name is Hayden. You aren't a cowgirl coming here asking for a job. You're the owner's little sister, and the previous owner's daughter. You'll have to work twice as hard and twice as long to show everyone what you're made of."

My chin lifts. "I'm up to the task."

"Jessie?" Wes walks up behind me. He comes around the table and stands next to Gramps. His eyes look tired, and I don't think the wrinkles between his eyebrows have relaxed since I came back home. "I know I asked you to come here, but can we do this later? Today has already been a real bitch, and I'm running out of fucks to give."

I swallow my disappointment. "Do you need an extra hand today?"

He sighs, very much the same way Gramps did, low and slow through closed lips. "No."

"Lie."

A muscle in his jaw twitches. I am probably the last thing he wants to deal with after his tense conversation with Dakota, but that's too damn bad. "You need help, right?" My arms open wide. "Ta-da. Help has arrived."

"We've been over this, Jessie."

"We really haven't, Wes. You've been without a second-in-command since Warner left to teach at the college and—"

"Let me get this straight. You show up here expecting me to make you my second-in-command even though you've never worked on a cattle ranch? Just because of your last name?"

"First of all," I hold up one finger. "Maybe I've never been an official employee, but I grew up here. I know some shit, Wes. I didn't just fall off the back of a turnip truck." I peek at Gramps. He's smiling. Even Wes has cracked a smile.

"That was Grandma's favorite thing to say." His voice has softened. He looks at me a little nicer now, with the eyes of a big brother. "Do you have a second point to make?"

I hold up a second finger. "I don't have expectations. I'm showing up, ready to work. What I know from growing up here isn't the half of what you do, I get that. But I'd like to learn, Wes." My hand comes back down, my palm presses to the table. I keep a steady gaze on his and watch him consider.

"We're spreading manure today." His eyebrows lift, waiting for me to protest or whine.

"Great."

"We need to spray weeds."

"Awesome, hand me a sprayer."

He falls quiet, studying me. I'd like to tell him to knock it off, but I realize I don't have that much leeway right now.

Then Wes, the most intimidating of all my brothers, says, "Go see if Mom has gloves you can borrow."

I keep the grin off my face. Force the excitement from trickling out. Calmly, I push back from the table and stand. As I'm walking from the room, I hear Gramps say to Wes, "There was a time when you'd do whatever it took to have this ranch."

I grab my mom's second set of gloves from the mudroom and return to the table. Gramps is gone.

"All set?" Wes asks.

I nod. "What was Gramps saying when I walked out?"

Wes waves me off. "Never mind him, he's a few bricks shy of a load on a good day."

"Fuck off," Gramps says. He's coming from the kitchen clutching a second cup of coffee.

Wes laughs. Gramps claps him on the back, and Wes does the same, but lightly. Sometimes I forget Wes has had more time with Gramps than any of us kids.

"You two enjoy your day," Gramps says. He shuffles to me, and I kiss his papery cheek.

"Come on," Wes says, walking from the room.

I follow, forcing down my excitement and my nerves.

* * *

Fucking. Hard.

That's what all this work is. Not that I didn't already know that, but *goddamn*. It's only late spring, and still there are rivers of sweat slipping between my breasts. Swamp ass is no longer something Lindsay loudly complained about on our walks across the ASU campus in August. It is officially a very real thing for me.

I eye Wes, just twenty feet away, as he talks to some of the cowboys. Mostly he addresses Josh, who is the unofficial leader of the group. Wes pointedly ignores Troy, not that I blame him, but it makes me laugh. Troy tries, but he's always just a bit shy of the mark.

I've been spraying weeds for what feels like hours and guess what? There are still more weeds. It's like a pie-eating contest where the only prize is more pie. I'm bored out of my skull, and I have something to say. So, in true calamity fashion, I open my mouth.

"Wes, can you come here for a second?"

Wes pauses his sentence, neck swiveling my way. The cowboys stare, mouths pulled into tight lines, as if my interrupting Wes is a big deal. "Yes?" he says, eyebrows lifted on his forehead. He addresses me from where he stands, refusing to do as I've asked and come my way.

"Why am I spraying all these weeds again?"

"Because I can't get much else to grow here besides these damned dandelions, and I can't have the cows eating them."

"Right," I say slowly, setting my sprayer on the ground. One of the cowboys snickers, and I'd love to know who it is so I can knock the shit-eating grin off his face. "So here's the problem. Dandelions indicate poor, compacted soil—"

"No shit."

I glare at Wes but keep going. "Their roots are actually doing the job of breaking up the soil." This is, word for word, what I learned when I was searching the internet this morning. Maybe I am an impulsive spitfire, but I came prepared. "So don't just kill them and move on. Think about this proactively instead of reactively. Yes, you have weeds, but they are doing a job for you. If we eliminate them, we need to replace their function and aerate the soil ourselves."

Wes gives me a long, hard look. "Are you going to be the one to do that? Because I can tell you right now, I don't have a single second to spare."

My shoulders straighten. "I'll do it." Not that I have a clue how to, but I'll figure it out. I'll make a way.

A terse, disingenuous laugh bursts from my brother. He shakes his head and rubs a thumb over his lower lip. "You have all the answers, huh? You haven't worked this land a day in your life, but you arrive here with your head full of grand ideas."

Earlier this morning he'd shown up at my place asking me to come share those ideas with him, and now he's being an ass. His argument with Dakota must have been a doozy. "I grew up here, too, asshole. And just because I'm not the chosen one, the *number one son*, doesn't mean I don't have valuable contributions."

"Like sending out a mailer?"

I send him the dirtiest look I can muster.

"Newsflash, Jessie. Even without that alfalfa choking out the land, we still need a little something from Mother Nature." He points up at the sky. "Rain."

I'm very well aware of that. And unfortunately, water

from above isn't something I can magically produce. Or send mail to.

"The fact remains," I respond, digging in my heels, "that you have it within your abilities to do something about this soil *now*. You do not have to wait for the right weather pattern. Don't just sit back and jaw about how dry it is. Prepare the soil so when it does rain, you're in the best position to benefit from it."

Wes stares me down. I realize I'm overstepping, but I'm not his employee, so technically I can say what I want. His pulse pounds in his neck, and I have no idea what he's thinking. He's so damn good at keeping his emotions in check.

Unlike me. "What do you think?" I press. "I could—"

"We're done." Wes's voice rings out with finality. I want to argue, but I know better. Challenging the ranch boss in front of his subordinates will get me nowhere fast.

I turn away, pointing the nozzle of my sprayer at another dandelion. Yeah, it's a weed. But it has a function. A purpose. It's actually doing some good.

My brother, the de facto head of the Hayden siblings, needs to up his ranching game.

17

SAWYER

"We're shutting down the hotel for the time being while we deal with the problem."

I blanch at the general manager of The Sierra. "You're shutting down the entire hotel?"

He apologizes again. "It's necessary. The termite inspection showed we have an issue, and quite possibly a hazard to our guests' safety. This is not a precaution, Mr. Bennett, but a response to a very real problem." He gestures to the front desk. "Geraldine will be happy to call around and get you set up at one of the other hotels in the area."

I nod curtly. "That won't be necessary, I can make my own arrangements. Thank you." I head upstairs to my room, where, per the manager's instruction, I am to pack all my stuff and vacate the hotel immediately.

As I fold my slacks and pressed button-up shirts, it reminds me of what Wyatt and Jo said about my clothes. Maybe I should do some shopping before my date with Jessie tonight.

I get everything packed and walk out of The Sierra. I

place it all in the back of my car, then use my phone to search for a place to shop. Boutiques dot High Street, but many of them don't carry clothes I'm interested in wearing. I'm not a cowboy, and I don't need to dress like one.

I text Jo, asking her where a guy can get clothes that fall somewhere between Wrangler and business casual. She sends me the name of two stores Wyatt likes, which are perfect. He never looks one-hundred-percent cowboy.

By the time I'm done shopping, I don't have time to check in to a new hotel. I call around, find one place that has a vacancy, and head out to the HCC to pick up Jessie for our date.

I'm nervous as hell. It's been years since I've been on a first date. And I thought I'd never have to go on another one again. Brea was supposed to be my last first.

I drive the same route I drove two days ago, veering off on that dirt road I'd noticed as I drove toward the homestead. At the time I didn't know it was how to get to Jessie's cabin.

I pull up and cut the engine, wiping my sweaty palms on the front of my jeans before climbing out. My heart races, and I take a deep breath. *Should I have brought flowers?* I look around, and when I don't spot any, I vow to get them for our next date.

Next date? Whoa there, buddy. Maybe I need to slow down.

Jessie opens the door before I can knock. "Hi," she says, breathless. "I saw you from the window."

I like how honest she is. She didn't make me wait out front, counting down so she wouldn't look too excited. Nothing with Jessie is manufactured. What I see is what I get. And damn do I like what I see.

A watermelon-pink dress skims her legs, hitting the middle of her thighs. Her shoes lend her a few inches in height, but she's still shorter than me by a good five inches.

"You look beautiful," I tell her. I pretend to hand her a bouquet. "These are the flowers I didn't think to get you until it was too late."

She takes the pretend flowers and scrunches her nose. "I hate roses," she says.

"It's a good thing they're sunflowers," I respond.

She laughs and drops the act. "I like you, Sawyer Bennett." She steps out and closes the door behind herself. "Let's go. Show me a good time."

* * *

"WHERE ARE WE GOING?" JESSIE ASKS, PROPPING HER forearm on the door. She peers over at me expectantly as I navigate my way off her family's land.

I glance at her, then back at the road. I make a left and head toward town. "Do you like French food? There's a place about twenty minutes from town."

"I sure do, and I'm starving, too."

"Perfect."

"So, Sawyer, tell me more about yourself. It's an obligatory first date question."

It's an opening to tell her about Brea, but it feels like terrible timing. "Not much to tell. You know most of it already. I work in real estate. I know how to ride a horse. I like my coffee black."

"Tell me things I don't already know."

I rattle off the first things that come to mind. "My favorite color is navy blue. I hate mint, but love mint ice cream. I'd much rather be hot than cold."

Jessie makes a sound with her lips, letting me know the details I'm sharing aren't cutting it. "I think there's a lot more to you than you let on."

My lips stretch across my face and my eyebrows pull together. "Oh yeah?"

"Mm-hmm," she says, her voice vibrating through my car.

I keep my eyes trained on the road, but the heat of her stare warms my skin.

"I guess you'll have to stick around and see." I dare a glance at her. Her tongue darts out to swipe over her bottom lip.

"Tell me about you," I say, slowing down as I approach a curve. "Why does your family call you Calamity?"

She tucks a curtain of hair behind her shoulder. "They've been calling me Calamity Jessie since I was little. Apparently I was pretty wild, running amok around the ranch." A tiny grin appears on her face. "And I cursed a lot."

"As a child?"

She nods. "That's what I'm told. *Calamity* comes from Calamity Jane."

I look at her, trying to imagine her as a child, chubby-cheeked and cussing like a sailor. Right now, it's impossible. Long, tanned legs extend from her dress, and she fills out the top. She looks too womanly for my brain to envision her as a child.

I force my gaze back to the road. "It doesn't sound like you appreciate the nickname."

"Its synonyms are disaster and tragedy. Would you appreciate that?"

I shake my head slowly. "Can't say that I would."

She grows quiet for a few minutes, looking out her window as we pass the tall pines. We're at the point with the stark transition of tree to scrubby brush, signaling we're exiting Hayden land, when she punctures the silence with a question. "What's the scariest thing you've ever done?"

"I'm doing it right now." The words are out before I have time to think about them.

Jessie's silent. Of all the time I've spent around Jessie's quick wit and smart mouth, her silence is the most unnerving.

"How about you?" I ask, and the light turns green.

We're driving again. She's answering my question, and the moment has passed.

"I do scary things every day."

I chuckle. I can't help it. "You? You appear to be the most unafraid person I've ever met."

"I'm afraid every day. I'm afraid Wes won't let me be a part of the HCC. I'm afraid I'll be forced to find a career I'm only half as passionate about. Yesterday, Wes let me help on the ranch. I tried to tell him something I learned about the soil, and now I fear he'll never let me step foot beyond the backyard at the homestead ever again."

"He didn't want to hear it?"

"Not at all. Even though he's the one who came to me and asked me to tell him my thoughts. He ran out of patience, I think."

"Maybe it'll just take some time for him to warm up to the information."

Jessie sighs. "Gramps told me I have to work twice as hard and twice as long to prove to Wes and the cowboys that I'm serious."

"How do you feel about that?"

"Angry. Like I want to prove myself my own way."

I pull into an open spot in front of the restaurant. Turning to Jessie, I say, "Do me a favor?"

"What's that?"

I lean forward and smile at her. "Give them hell."

She grins. "I intend to."

* * *

"Ughhhhh," Jessie says, a hand to her stomach. "I forgot how rich French food can be."

I laugh at her. "You ate as much as me."

"I know," she wails, "don't remind me. Maybe I'll just take a nap in the trunk while you drive us home." She turns to look at the back seat. "Never mind. Why does it look like everything you own is in your trunk?"

"Because everything I own that's currently in Sierra Grande is in my trunk."

She faces the front again. "Why?"

"The Sierra has termites. I've been kicked out, along with every other guest."

"What?" She gapes at me. "How was that not a topic of conversation at dinner?"

"Pest infestations isn't good dinner conversation."

"Agreed. Where are you going to stay?"

I flip back through my conversation with the person at the hotel I called, trying to recall the name. It was a little kitschy, and very on the nose. "Sleep Easy? Rest Here? Something like that. Everything else was full."

"Sleep Here?" Jessie screeches. "Nope. Absolutely not. You'll trade termites for bedbugs. And then I will want nothing to do with you for approximately ninety days."

"Is that how long it takes to get rid of bedbugs?"

"I don't know. It was a random number."

I laugh. "You're funny."

"You're going to be sorry if you stay there." She snaps her fingers. "You can stay with me. Problem solved."

"Right. Your dad would love that."

"He already thinks we slept together. Who cares? And this way, you can spend time with Colt. Dakota said she asked you to meet with just her and Colt and help him."

Jessie makes a good point. Dakota called me yesterday and asked, telling me she'd pay me to work with him. I have no intention of accepting payment from her, and every intention of helping the little guy out as much as I can.

"See?" Jessie sits back, smiling contentedly. "You're considering it."

"It makes sense. Especially because I can work from anywhere." I'd rented office space because working from the hotel room was depressing. But working from Jessie's cabin? Sounds like paradise.

"Is that your way of saying yes?"

I look over at her. Her eyes are open wide, anticipating my response.

"Yes."

"Yes?"

"Yes."

18

SAWYER

I'M STANDING IN THE DOORWAY, STARING INTO THE bedroom, trying not to let my emotions show on my face. There's no way I can sleep there. My entire body is bigger than the bed.

"That's a twin."

Jessie appraises me, laughter in her eyes. She's standing in the middle of the room, and points a finger at the wall. "Do you prefer the bunk bed in Charlie's old room?"

My gaze narrows at her. I've been a grown man for a long time, but here I am choosing between a teenage girl's former twin bed, and a young boy's old bunk.

"What size is your bed?" I ask.

"King."

I make a *come the fuck on* face, and she smiles. "Four of you could fit in a king, Jessie."

"What are you saying?"

We stare at each other. A showdown. She holds my gaze, steady as can be. "You haven't even kissed me yet. We are not sleeping in the same bed."

You haven't even kissed me... yet. We both know it's coming. How could it not? Given the way my body responds to merely being in the same room as her, it seems a foregone conclusion. And still, there is such distance between knowing it will happen, and putting those thoughts to action.

"I wasn't suggesting I sleep in your bed." I look past her, to the bed better suited for its previous owner. "Can I have new sheets?"

Jessie rolls her eyes and smirks. "Well, yeah. There are fresh linens in the closet."

I pick up the bag at my feet and give it a toss. It sails through the air and lands on the bed. I do the same with the next two. "Home sweet home."

"Good," Jessie says, walking to me. She passes through the doorway, her forearm brushing mine. She lifts up onto tiptoe and presses a peck to my cheek. Her lips are soft, her kiss gentle and fleeting. She pauses near my cheek, her lips hovering, giving me a chance to turn my face. Just an inch or two and my lips could crash to hers. I could hold her in my arms, run my hands through her hair, taste her.

These inches, they feel like miles.

Jessie settles back down on flat feet. "Thank you for dinner. See you in the morning."

* * *

In the morning, I discover Jessie has squat for groceries. We make our way into town.

Our appearance together at the grocery store does not go unnoticed. A woman I don't recognize, but Jessie greets, gives us a lengthy once-over.

"Sheriff Monroe's wife," Jessie whispers when we're far enough away. "Hand to God, she is the biggest busybody in this town. Give it three days, and everyone will know you're staying with me."

"How will she know if nobody tells her?"

"She's a better detective than her husband ever was. A bloodhound, that one."

I glance over at the sheriff's wife. The old woman tears her gaze away from us, and I laugh. "Had to happen at some point, I suppose." Maybe it sounds cavalier, but I actually like the idea of people knowing about me and Jessie. I'm not sure what there is to know, seeing as how last night she reminded me how little kissing we've done so far, which is to say *none*. Still, if people assume we're together, I'd consider it a fortunate misconception. If she has to be associated with someone, I want that person to be me.

"Sure did," Jessie replies, adding tortilla chips to the basket.

"You're not worried this gossip will make it harder for you to get a date in this town?" I look away after I ask the question. I'm fishing. For what, I don't exactly know.

"Sawyer." The way Jessie says my name, all soft and sweet like that, has my breath slamming up my throat. I meet her gaze.

"I'm not going to French restaurants or letting anybody else stay in my home. Does that answer your question?"

She stares back at me. Her baby blue eyes are an endless sea, one I want to swim in. What would it be like to let myself go with her? To have her? To let her have me?

Fuck, I like this woman. She doesn't play games.

And she doesn't deserve any from me. I need to tell her about Brea. She needs to know the reason for my hesitance.

I swallow and nod. "Yes, that answers my question."

Jessie leads us into the next aisle, and when I move for a jar of salsa, she stops me. "I do not allow that salsa in my home."

I raise an eyebrow and point at the different brand beside it. "Nope," she says, with a shake of her head. "This way." She leads me to the produce section, choosing cilantro, a white onion and a head of garlic. Next she grabs canned diced tomatoes and dried red pepper flakes, then turns to me.

"Salsa is the one and only thing I can make, but I make it damn well."

I chuckle. "Far be it for me to change that."

I gather items for dinner, now that I know Jessie doesn't cook, and we check out. The cashier gives us a look as long as the sheriff's wife, but she doesn't say anything. Jessie smiles at her and makes small talk.

I watch her relaxed grin, the ease with which her body moves, how comfortable she feels in her skin. How can someone as young as her be so composed?

I ask her that exact question when we're back in my car.

She shifts, so she's facing me, one leg bent at the knee and propped on the seat. "I like to think I've been living two lives. One as an only child, the other as the baby of four siblings. My brothers are so much older than me that technically I could be considered an only child. So it's like I got the benefits of both birth orders." She bites her lower lip. "And maybe the drawbacks."

Before I can respond, she follows up her answer with a question. "Do you have any siblings?"

My knuckles tap the steering wheel. The closeness of the Hayden siblings makes me miss something I never had.

I shake my head. "I'd always wished for a brother, but no. Only child."

Jessie playfully smacks my shoulder. "I can halfway relate to you."

"And halfway not at all."

"Is the glass half full or half empty?"

"Half empty. Always. Why set yourself up to be disappointed?"

Jessie grins. "I agree. Screw that positive attitude shit."

I smile, and it occurs to me I smile a lot when I'm around her. I like it. I think. I'm not sure. Am I allowed to like it? It's confusing.

I showed up in this town a broken man, and now Jessie, just by virtue of being herself, is picking up the pieces and putting me back together.

"Are you going to start driving?" She sounds impatient. "There are groceries in your car, and it's still a twenty-minute drive back to the ranch."

The ranch.

"Right," I say, reversing from the spot. "Let's get going to the ranch."

I like the way it sounds. Like standing out in the clean morning air, sipping coffee and smelling pine.

Most of all, I like Jessie.

* * *

Whole chicken, washed and patted dry. Butter tucked under the skin. Whole lemons cut in half and nestled in the cavity.

"Can you please grab the roasting pan?" I ask Jessie, who has not stopped reminding me how hungry she is. Even after she prepared her salsa, which admittedly is better than any store-bought salsa I've ever had, she's still hopping around me like a starving baby bird. I'm learning she has a low threshold for hunger.

She slides the roasting pan over to me. I lift the chicken, wrapping the cooking twine around the bird. I use a kitchen knife to cut it, then tie it off.

Jessie leans an elbow on the counter, watching me.

"What?" I ask, as I pick up the chicken and transfer it to the pan.

"I didn't have you pegged as the cooking type."

I frown at her while I wash my hands. "Why not?"

"You're too pretty."

I make a face and wipe my hands on a kitchen towel. "Too pretty?"

She looks me up and down. "Yeah, you know... kind of... precious."

I slide the pan into the oven and close it, turning back to her. My eyebrows lift. "Pretty and precious? Is that how you see me?" If so, this isn't going so well for me.

Her lips purse, slowly releasing. "You're very put together. You just seem like someone who has dinner cooked for him. Or ordered. Not someone who stands in front of a hot stove."

I nod slowly. "I don't think you're complimenting me."

She chuckles. "I'm not, I guess. But I'm not insulting you either, at least I don't mean it that way."

"I'm not insulted."

"Good."

"I would like for you to see me differently, though." I exhale silently, trying to release some of the nervousness I feel on the inside.

Her head tips, her hair cascading through the air like a waterfall. "How would you like for me to see you?" Her voice is deeper, throatier.

My hands tuck into my pockets. "As a man."

She swallows audibly. "I'm very well aware you're a man, Sawyer." Her lips peel apart, a small gap appearing between them, and she drags in a breath.

Fuck.

She's waiting for me to make the first move. Bold, brave, ebullient Jessie wants me to come to her. And I want to. I really, really do. But just like last night, the longer I wait, the more the inches grow into miles.

Now it's been quiet for too long, and there's no coming back from it. I don't know what to say. "Wine," I blurt out, remembering the bottle we put in the freezer when we got back. I take it out and pour two glasses. The outside of the glasses immediately clouds with the frosty temperature. She takes one off the counter. She looks... annoyed. *Join the club. I'm irritated with myself too.*

"Cheers," I say, holding up my glass.

"To?"

I pause, glass aloft, thinking. "To Hotel Jessie."

She laughs and drinks.

"It's going to be an hour or so before the chicken is ready, and I need to get started on the rice. Do you"—I glance outside to where we stood a few days ago when Beau and Wes walked up—"want to relax outside? It's nice right now."

"Good idea." Jessie grabs her phone and walks out back. She settles into a chair and draws her legs into herself. She opens her phone, and I can't see clearly from here but it looks like she's reading something.

I'm toasting the dry rice when my dad calls.

"Hi, Dad," I say, holding the phone between my lifted shoulder and my bent head. I add the rice to the boiling water, then turn it down to a simmer and cover it with a lid.

"How's it going out there?" he asks. We talk every few weeks, and this is always his first question. He knows I've been buying property, but I haven't fully explained to him how much I like Sierra Grande.

I rest a hip against the counter and look out the window where Jessie sits. The sun grows dark, amber-hued like her hair. The trees block the view of the horizon, but the sky above is beginning to purple on one side, arcing across the expanse like veins.

"Well," I answer, knowing it won't be enough. "I met someone."

"Oh yeah?" he asks, his tone cautious. He knows firsthand how shaky the path to moving on can be. "Tell me about your someone."

"Her name is Jessie Hayden, and she's—"

"Hayden?" The jovial tone has disappeared.

"Yes," I say slowly. "Why?"

"Nothing. Nothing. I need to go. Renee is calling me."

"Dad—"

"Bye, Son. Take care." He hangs up. I place my phone back in my pocket. The conversation, or lack thereof, gnaws at me. His reaction must have something to do with my mom, and where she died. So close to Hayden land, practically right on it. I've thought of it nearly every time I've traveled that road, including when I took Jessie on a date last night, and today when we went to town for groceries. But is there more? Does my dad have a bigger reason to be spooked by the Hayden name?

I stare at my phone, thumb poised to dial him, but movement through the window catches my eyes.

Jessie stands. She tosses her phone down on the chair and strides opposite the house. She walks closer to the trees, bending low. She gathers a handful of dirt and watches it slip through her fingers, then rubs her thumb against two fingers. What is she thinking about?

Jessie stands up straight and looks at the sky with determination, the final rays of sunlight washing over her. She has the spirit of an unbroken horse, but there's also something tender about her. A rawhide exterior hiding silk.

Something about her last name upset my dad. And I'd love to know what the hell that was about.

I call him back. It rings and rings, then goes to voice mail. I hang up.

19

JESSIE

When Marlowe calls and demands to know about these rumors she's been hearing in town, I'm not sure what to say.

I tried the truth, but now she's yelling at me. "There is no part of my brain that can comprehend how you allowed him to move in with you."

I've defended it so many times already I'm getting sick of it. To Greta, when I was picking up blueberry muffins yesterday. *Yes, it's okay, I'm old enough to have a man living with me.* To Maia, when I was grabbing some items at the Merc. *I don't care that our dads were adversaries.* Even old Waylon Guthrie, who, I'd like to point out, was three sheets to the wind when he stumbled up to me asking about me 'living in sin' with a Bennett. *Your alcohol vapors are offensive, don't breathe on me.* Living in a small town can have its disadvantages.

"And," Marlowe continues, "why am I hearing about this from someone other than you? That hurts."

"I know," I whisper, pouring my coffee. The door to Sawyer's room was closed when I passed by a few minutes ago, so I'm assuming he's still asleep. "Hang on," I whisper, dropping my phone in the pocket of my oversized cardigan. I add creamer to my coffee, grab an apple, then go outside.

"I'm back," I tell Marlowe, settling into a chair.

"Great. I can resume yelling at you."

"No, you cannot. The Sierra had a termite problem—"

"I'm aware. They have to tear down and rebuild."

"That's awful." My heart goes out to the couple who own the place. "Sawyer staying here is temporary. Besides, it was either my cabin or Sleep Here."

"Ew. Go clean out your mouth."

"Exactly."

"How's the sex?"

I tuck my legs up into my chest and use an arm to keep them in place. "We're not sleeping together."

"Why not? You sound disappointed, by the way."

"That's because I *am* disappointed. We haven't even kissed yet."

"And yet he's living with you?"

"You already know the answer to that."

"Have you thought about the fact your dads hated each other back in the day?"

I'm starting to regret telling her about that. When I'd called to tell her Sawyer and I were going on a date, I'd also included what I'd learned from my parents after the vendor market. I should've known she'd tuck it away for use in a future argument.

A black hawk lands at the top of a pine, perching there as his neck swivels. He's hunting. "Hardly at all," I answer Marlowe, my eyes on the predatory bird. "My parents don't care."

"What does Sawyer think about it?"

I sigh and look back down at the base of the trees. "I don't know if he knows."

"You haven't talked about it?" she screeches, and I pull the phone away from my head. I wait a few seconds, then bring it back to my ear.

"I'm afraid to. With Sawyer, I have to tread lightly. Something happened to him, somewhere along the way. I can see it in his eyes. He wants to kiss me, but he stops himself."

"You know, that's something you could ask him about too. Your communication skills are lacking." Her tone is dry.

"I don't want to scare him off." I like Sawyer enough that I'll take what I can get from him, for now at least. I won't be patient forever, but I have the capacity to wait a little longer.

"Ri-ght. Can I be honest with you?"

"Were you not being honest this whole time?"

She ignores my question. "You have a tendency to run at life head-on, with your heart leading. You love out loud, and you do big things for the people lucky enough to be loved by you. But," she hesitates, and I think this is where she's about to be painfully honest with me. "I think maybe you've fucked up this time. The Bennetts lived here a long time ago, but they left town suddenly and without explanation. Don't you think there's something more to the story than just bad blood between your dads?"

"I don't know. Maybe," I concede, even though I don't want to. "Have you ever heard that you shouldn't go looking, because you might not like what you'll find?"

"God, you really are Beau Hayden's daughter."

Her playful complaint makes me laugh. "What's done is done, Marlowe. I'm not going to kick him out. I like him, and I like who I am when I'm with him. He lets me be the person I'm trying to become. You know how important that is to me."

"Yes, I do. And I'm happy you've found someone who can do that for you. I don't think you would've ever found that by looking in the Sierra Grande dating pool."

"Definitely not. I need to keep moving forward now. Starting with talking my brother into letting me help on the ranch. I'm not in school anymore, and I don't have a job. If I don't contribute in some way, I'll go crazy out here."

As much as I love this cabin, with its stone columns so much like the homestead and the trees that surround the place, I can't be here all day. I need something to do. I need to work on the ranch the way I want to. I've been reading and researching every spare minute, and I have a lot of value to add to this place.

"I know, Jessie. I know. You love that ranch to the point of absurdity."

I chuckle softly. Whether it was meant as an insult or a compliment, I'm taking it like a compliment.

We say goodbye and I place the phone back into my pocket. I finish my coffee and go inside.

Sawyer stands at the counter. I watch his profile as he drinks a glass of water. His throat undulates with each gulp, and I wish I could trail my fingers over the stubble darkening his skin. Maybe wind around and push my hand into his silky, dark hair. He is shirtless, wearing only a pair of snug-fitting sweatpants. A sheen of sweat covers his back.

I don't know how to identify by name all the

different back muscles, but I know that on Sawyer, they are developed. Big, curved, rising high and dipping low. He is all male, all sexy, all tempting. And so damn closed off.

I could force the conversation and communicate the way Marlowe thinks we should. Ask him to tell me his reservations and move our attraction out into the open. But I get the feeling Sawyer needs to sift through whatever it is on his own. His timeline differs from mine, and I want to respect that.

"Hello," I say, tearing my gaze away. I walk to the sink, placing my coffee cup inside.

"Good morning," he answers. His voice is warm.

I turn to meet his eyes. Sweat beads at his hairline. It helps to distract me from looking at his chest. "Why are you sweaty?" I ask.

"Working out in the living room. I came out here and saw you were on the phone, so I did a quick circuit. I have a session with my trainer today and I like to do a few things to help warm up my muscles and get the blood flowing."

I nod, thinking about all the parts of him where blood could flow. To distract myself, I turn to the fridge and get out everything I need to make breakfast. "Do you work out at the gym in town?"

"There's a boxing gym in Brighton. I like to go there."

"Hmm," I answer, popping bread into the toaster. So that's how he gets all those well-defined muscles. Boxing.

"Have you ever tried it?" Sawyer moves to the fridge, grabbing a carton of eggs.

"No," I answer, peering down into the toaster at the hot, red coils.

He reaches for a bowl and begins cracking eggs. It's my chance to peek at his abs, and I take it.

Oh, yes. Just like I thought. Rows upon rows of abs. There're no way fingertips, or a tongue for that matter, could glide easily over that. Those are *rutted* abs, the kind that make for a rough path downward. The best kind.

Pop! The top of the toast peeks up. I grab it, wincing at the heat, and drop it on a plate.

"What are you up to today?" Sawyer pours the egg mixture into a pan. He's speaking so casually, it's like he doesn't realize he's half naked.

I spread butter on my toast and take a bite. "I'm going to the homestead to force Wes to let me work on the ranch."

Sawyer looks at me while he stirs the eggs. "Doesn't seem to me that Wes has spent much time being forced into anything."

I frown, not because I disagree, but because I know he's right. "I know what I'm up against."

His eyes warm the longer he looks at me. "Do you know what you are?"

I swallow and sigh. "Headstrong. Inflexible. Obstinate. Stubborn." I tick the characteristics off on my fingers, then drop my hand.

He shakes his head. "Those are all basically synonyms of the same word. And I think you might be some of those things, to a degree." He smiles, but I watch him with cautious eyes. I don't know where this is going.

"But isn't determination just varying degrees of stubbornness? Someone might call you headstrong, but someone else might say you're *driven*. Are you obstinate, or *tenacious*?" He grabs a plate and slides his eggs onto it. "It's two sides to the same coin. All I'm saying is that I've never met a person as determined, driven, and tenacious as you. And if you've spent your whole life hearing you're headstrong, inflexible, obstinate, and stubborn, let me be the first to flip the coin over for you."

Oh. My heart. Maybe all the things I'm so known for are actually good.

Sawyer walks toward me, the plate in his left hand, and reaches out with his right. My breath halts in my throat. Is this it? The moment he finally grabs me and kisses the breath from my lungs?

His hand sails forward, toward my hip. The hip I have pressed to the drawer. The drawer containing the silverware.

Sawyer jiggles the drawer and it moves against me. "Are you guarding the forks? Is there a password?"

I step aside. "No password," I mumble, grabbing my second piece of toast. "Thanks for saying all that nice stuff about me. Wish me luck with Wes." I turn around and walk from the room, taking all my patience with me.

* * *

I CAME TO THE HOMESTEAD LOOKING FOR WES, BUT I encountered my parents first and decided to let them know about Sawyer staying with me. They haven't been to town in a few days, so I know they haven't been informed by the rumor mill. I have no idea if they're going to show up to my cabin unexpectedly, or worse, see Sawyer around my place and assume he's a trespasser.

"You've done what?" My dad tips his ear closer to me, like he's heard me incorrectly.

"I asked Sawyer to move in with me. He needed a place to stay. The Sierra—"

"I know about The Sierra. Are you trying to tell me there was no other place in Sierra Grande for a person to stay?"

"Not really. He probably could've rented an apartment or something, but he needed a place right away. I have plenty of space, and I like him. So I asked if he wanted to stay."

"Usually you date for a while before you move in together." My mom rubs a hand over her eyes.

"We're not even dating, Mom. I mean, we've gone on one date. If you're worried about us moving too quickly, don't. He takes things at a snail's pace." I hope they're getting the picture without me having to draw a diagram.

Relief floods my dad's face. He looks quite happy the assumption he made when he found Sawyer at my house that morning was wrong. "I still don't like it, Jessie." He and my mom share a deep, knowing look. They're doing that thing where they talk with their eyes.

"Everything is fine, Dad. I promise. Plus, this way Sawyer can spend more time helping Colt. And that benefits everybody."

"Hey, guys. Family meeting?" Wyatt walks into the living room.

He says hello to my parents and gives me a side-hug. "Why are you here?" I ask him.

"Dad asked me to go with him to look at a horse he's thinking of buying."

"Your sister is picking up strays again." My mother's

tone is cold, and it surprises me. I thought we were past this. She was nice to Sawyer when he was here teaching everyone some basic ASL, and now she's frigid?

"That's rude, Mom. Sawyer isn't a mangy cat."

"Why is Sawyer a picked-up stray?" Wyatt asks, and I give him a dirty look for using the word.

"Because he's staying with me."

"Because of The Sierra?"

I nod.

Wyatt frowns. "That's going to take months."

My annoyance flares. "I didn't say he was staying with me till the end of time."

Wyatt lifts his hand in a show of innocence. "Okay, okay. I'm just a little surprised. I didn't know you and Sawyer were a thing."

I throw up my hands. "We've been on one date. That's hardly enough to call us a thing." My frustration with Sawyer's slow pace is beginning to seep through.

Wyatt nods, scratching the back of his head with two fingers. "Did Sawyer tell you about his wife?"

My head rears back, as though I've been slapped. It's made worse by the fact I'm learning this in front of the people who think I'm out of my mind for letting him move in. "What wife?"

"Former wife, I guess. He's a widower."

I blink hard. "You should have led with that."

Wyatt presses his lips together, then slowly peels them apart. "I don't know much about the marriage, honestly. But when I learned who Sawyer was after he bought into Wildflower, I asked him why he was back in Sierra Grande. He said he'd lost his wife, and that he returned to the last place he could remember feeling happy."

Something slices across my chest. Sadness for Sawyer. Sympathy for what he experienced. And so much understanding about why he is the way he is.

"I'm sure he would've told me eventually." I smile, but it feels weak.

Wyatt studies me. "You sure you know what you're doing, Calamity?"

"I sure as hell do not know what I'm doing, but when has that ever stopped me?"

My bravado works. It causes my dad to grunt irritably, and Wyatt laughs. My mom bites into her lower lip and looks a million miles away.

"I love you all, I really do." I back out of the room. "But at some point, you're going to have to let me live and not question everything I do just because you don't understand it." I blow a kiss to the three of them and walk out of their eyesight.

So much for waiting around to see Wes. I think I need a break from my family for today.

I love them dearly, but I can't figure out the person I'm growing into if my family is constantly reminding me who I've always been.

20

SAWYER

I'm trudging up the stairs when a throat clears. It's Jessie, perched on the front porch swing that hangs from the ceiling. She has one leg curled up on the seat, the other planted firmly on the ground. Her face is free of makeup, and she wears a low-cut tank top, shorts, and a thin cardigan. Her hair looks damp.

"How did it go with Wes?" I ask, coming closer.

She doesn't say anything. Her head tips, exposing the length of her neck, her delicate skin the color of fresh cream. There's a tugging sensation in my chest, a pull that creeps up into my throat. I try to think of Brea, but when I do, all I see is Jessie. It makes me want to run and hide in that child-size bed I'm sleeping on.

At some point, something has to give. A dam can only hold so much water until it bursts.

I stop, standing in front of her, and when she scoots over, I take the silent invitation and sit down beside her. "You worked the ranch today?"

She shakes her head.

Ah, that explains it. She's emotional because it didn't work out with Wes.

"I went to the homestead but he wasn't there, and I didn't want to wait around for him. So I left him a note at his cabin, telling him I'm prepared to beg, borrow, and steal my way back onto the ranch."

Jessie's words are delivered with less enthusiasm than usual. Something has really upset her. "I admire your persistence," I tell her.

She picks at the loose strings on the bottom of her shorts. "I didn't realize you are a widower."

I stare at her profile, trying to slow my racing heart. "How did you know?"

"Wyatt mentioned it."

I look away, biting on the inside of my cheek.

"Why didn't you tell me?" She sounds curious, but not hurt. I look down and watch her fingers move on to the hem of her cardigan.

"I don't like to say the words out loud. They sound wrong. Sometimes it feels like it was yesterday." Now I see Brea's face, clear as day in my mind. I swallow the lump in my throat at the image. I lean forward, balancing my elbows on my knees. My gaze focuses on the wooden plank floor, but I see the crashing ocean, the salty spray. "We had a little place right on the beach. Brea went out for a swim one day. And she never came back." Tears roll down my cheeks. It rips me apart to think of what she must've experienced. Even if she was able to scream for help, I don't know that she would have. She spoke very rarely, choosing ASL instead. But maybe, in a moment of panic, she tried to use her voice.

"She was recovered seventeen hours later. I was a maniac for those seventeen hours, searching the beach for miles, swimming out farther than I'd ever swam." My eyes squeeze shut as I push away the image of her being pulled from the water. The recovery team told me to walk away, but I'd refused. I regret that deeply now. The image is burned into my brain, and if I could snap my fingers and make it disappear, I would.

Jessie's palm finds my back. She brushes her hand against me in reassuring strokes. "How long were you married?"

"Five years." I rub at my eyes.

"I'm so sorry for your loss, Sawyer."

I crane my neck to look back at her. Her eyes are shiny. She looks so sad.

My gaze remains locked on her as I try to reconcile this feeling in my chest. I'm splitting in two, a crack made by an earthquake. By a calamity.

Calamity Jessie.

I came to this town, positive I'd never need to move past what happened to Brea. To my marriage. How is it that I'm not only *needing* to deal with it, I'm *wanting* to?

"In the spirit of honesty," Jessie begins, turning her full gaze on me. "Do you know about your dad and my dad?"

My eyebrows tug. What is she talking about?

"I'll take that as a no." Her lips twist. "I don't know details. I haven't asked for them, but we can if you want. All I know is that there was bad blood between our dads back in the day when you lived at the Circle B."

So that's why my dad freaked out when he heard Jessie's last name. It would've been nice if he'd just told me about it. He probably didn't want to say anything that would hinder my forward progression, and he feared that would do it.

Juliette's response to me makes a hell of a lot more sense. But Beau's response is nothing shy of confusing. He seems like a man who would hold a grudge, so why is he welcoming to me?

He's caught me with his daughter, so to speak, and not killed me with his bare hands or shot at the ground while I ran off his land like a come-to-life cartoon. It doesn't make a whole hell of a lot of sense.

"We make quite a pair, huh? You're scared to move on, and our dads used to hate each other." Jessie laughs, but it's empty.

Both of these things are true, and neither is going to keep me from her. That's what I decide in this exact moment.

I sit up straight, and wrap an arm around her shoulders, and she leans over, a half hug. It's not the right time for our first kiss. Not yet. I don't want it to come on the heels of this kind of a talk, in a somber mood. Jessie deserves better.

I look down at the top of her head, lowering my nose until it hovers just above her hair.

She smells nothing like Brea.

She is one-hundred-percent, totally and unequivocally, Jessie.

21

JESSIE

The note I left for Wes worked.

Monday through Friday, plus a Saturday turning out bulls. That's how many days Wes has asked me to help. Honestly, I thought I'd driven the final nail in the coffin when we had our argument over dandelions.

Over the course of the week I managed to slip into conversation some of the ideas I have for the HCC. *I bet we could turn a handful of unused HCC land into a pick-your-own farm. Seasonal attractions would do well out here and create a sense of community. I wonder how much people would pay to rent plots for a community garden?*

Not only did Wes absorb every word, he didn't argue with me about what I'd said.

Could it be he actually finds me helpful? Knowledgeable? Valuable?

Gasp.

My entire body hurts, but I'd never admit it out loud. Every night I soak in a bath, the water as hot as I can stand. I stretch every morning and night, wincing the first time I lift my arms above my head.

I've never felt more like I deserved a day off. Sunday, blessed Sunday. The Lord's day, my grandma Janice called it. Then she'd cuss on a Monday. God, I miss her.

Sawyer is in the backyard, sitting in a chair he bought this week. It reclines, and he geeked out on it being zero gravity. He'd asked if I wanted one, and I told him I'm perfectly fine putting my ass in chairs that don't feel like a carnival ride. He'd laughed and reached out, playfully tugging on a strand of my hair. He also added an outdoor grill to my backyard, and that's an addition I will definitely use.

The sexual tension between us has become nearly unbearable. I've always wanted him to make the first move, and now that I know he's a widower, I've double-downed on that stance. Still, it's killing me slowly. I feel it on him too, desire rolling off his skin.

Every night we watch TV together, snack on the couch, and laugh at the same punchlines. And if I weren't giving myself sweet relief when I climb under my covers after I say goodnight to him, I think I'd be in pieces on my living room floor by now. *Here lies fragments of Jessie, she died of extreme desire.*

The more I get to know Sawyer, the more I like him. Before bed he pre-measures his morning coffee, and I thought it was nerdy until I witnessed him dragging his tired feet into the kitchen one morning, eyes in sleepy slits, and sloppily reached out for the button on the coffee maker. I liked seeing this about him. He's so buttoned up all the time, so *composed*. Witnessing this part of his personality made me feel like I was in on a secret. A special Sawyer secret.

"Good morning," I say, joining him once I've poured a cup for myself and added creamer.

He glances over. The sun skirts over the top of his head, burnishing his brown hair in shades of caramel. His eyes, however, remain stormy gray. The sunlight cannot change that.

"You slept in," he remarks, setting his phone on his thigh. By now, I know he reads news from various sources every morning.

"Long week," I answer, sipping my coffee and flinching at the temperature. "But don't you dare tell Wes I said that."

"I would never," he answers, giving me a wink over his coffee cup. "What are your plans today?"

There was a time not too far from now when I might've said something along the lines of *boozy brunch with Lindsay and watching a movie*. Now, that's not even in the realm of things I want to do. I am so beyond satisfied to be where I am, I can't imagine how that used to be my Sunday norm.

"I need to get a few things for the house," I incline my head back to the cabin that is feeling more and more like mine every day. And Sawyer's. Mine and Sawyer's. How bizarre. "You?"

"I'd like to go exploring. I haven't seen very much of the HCC."

I blow across my coffee. "Screw shopping for the house. That can happen later this afternoon. How about I take you to a place I consider to be one of the most special places on the HCC?"

Sawyer nods. "It's a date." His eyes meet mine, gray seeping into blue, a storm over an ocean.

I duck my head and drink my coffee. "It's a date," I echo.

* * *

"Please don't give me one of those horses Wyatt is known for taming." Sawyer gives me a warning look.

I roll my eyes and set out for the stable. It's a bit of a walk, but I don't mind. It's beautiful out.

"I wouldn't even go near one of those horses, and I've been riding as long as I've been able to walk." I smile over at him. "Don't worry, I'll give you the mare every one of the grandkids learns to ride on."

Sawyer makes a noise with his lips. "Great. What's next, a child-size table and chairs? I'm already sleeping in a twin bed." He wraps a hand around the back of his neck and rolls it, making a few circles in both directions. Just for emphasis, I'm positive.

"Why don't you buy yourself a bigger bed?"

"I'll order one when we get back."

"While you're at it, maybe invest in a pair of real boots." I grin at him.

Sawyer looks down at his feet. "These are boots."

"Not cowboy boots. You're on a cattle ranch."

"So? These work. And I've seen Wyatt wearing a pair very similar." He gives me a pointed look. "Cowboy boots aren't my thing."

"How about cowboy hats? Are they your thing?"

"I don't know. Are they yours?"

"Cowgirl hats? Sure. I have enough of them."

"No." He shakes his head. "Cow*boy* hats. Are they your thing?"

Oh. Ohhhh. "I've been known to appreciate a cowboy hat on a man a time or two. But it's not my thing, necessarily."

"What is your thing?" He stresses the last word.

"I don't know." I brush my hand over the bumpy bark on the trunk of a pine tree as we pass it. "I tend to like nice people. Men who are strong. Tough and rugged, I like to think, although I don't know that I've ever actually seen a man I was attracted to in a situation where he was called upon to be tough and rugged. Growing up around men has had a hand in shaping what I think a man should be." And Austin was none of those things. After putting distance between me and ASU, it's hard to know what it was I saw in him in the first place. I think it's safe to say I'm so far over him. Apparently he is so far over me too, given that his phone calls ceased only a few days after I broke things off with him.

"So," Sawyer slips his hands into his pockets as we walk. "You're saying you like men who are nice, strong, tough, and rugged."

"Among other things."

"Such as?"

"Well, I'm told I'm a handful. Determined, driven, and tenacious, to name a few." I smirk at him. "So I guess my *thing* is a person who doesn't try and water me down. I need to be able to take up space in a room." I gesture out around me. "If I were forced to be small, I think it might kill me. Not literally, but it would kill my spirit."

Sawyer nudges me with his shoulder. "Is that a word of warning?"

I chuckle. "Only if you choose to take it as one." I want to ask him what his thing is, but I'm too afraid. I don't want to make him think of his wife.

I want this morning to be about us. It's not that I don't want him to remember her, I just don't want it happening at this exact moment. It's too perfect. Too enjoyable.

We get to the stable and walk inside. It smells of horses and hay, leather and wood. I introduce Sawyer to Priscilla, the gentle mare he'll be riding. She's old, dead broke, and won't give him a hard time. A leisurely ride is exactly what she'll provide, and exactly what we want.

Sawyer runs a flattened palm down her side. "I think she likes me," he says, looking proud.

I don't have the heart to tell him she's like that with everybody. Not when he's smiling at me that way. "She definitely likes you."

Next I move to Hester Prynne and get her ready to ride. I slip a saddle over her and buckle the straps, then give her a little love. She moves her face around under my touch. "I love you too, girl," I whisper.

When I was younger, she was an extension of me. I rode her less as I got older, and busier. And then, of course, going to college meant I only saw her when I came home. Wyatt rode her for me when I was gone, making sure she received love and attention. He texted me once while I was away to tell me she seemed sad and he thought she missed me.

"You ready?" I ask Sawyer.

He places his excuse for a cowboy boot in the stirrup. He swings his leg over, situates himself in the saddle, and does a cowboy nod. "After you."

* * *

"It's up here," I say back to Sawyer, risking a quick glance his way. He's a natural in the saddle, his body relaxed and rolling along with Priscilla's movements.

He doesn't look like a cowboy, but I don't think he needs to. He's just... Sawyer. Tall, strong, assured. *Cowboy* is an attitude really. Much like *cattle rancher*. It's more in how you approach life, not necessarily the occupation itself. And it looks good on Sawyer.

We arrive at the copse of bald cypress trees, and I stick out my arm, pushing away the flimsy lower branches as Hester Prynne walks through.

She comes to a stop on the other side, and Sawyer joins me. "There isn't much right now, but when there's a good rain, the little pond fills up, and the elevation forms a small waterfall. The water slips down through all those boulders"—I pause, pointing up to the oversized rocks—"and it sounds soothing as it flows through."

Sawyer looks over at me. "This is your favorite spot on the ranch?"

"Yes. I know it doesn't look like much now." The water is mostly dried up, the cracked earth the only evidence it existed at all. "But I promise, it's incredible when it rains. And there's more. Let me show you a second reason why." I dismount and lead Hester Prynne to a tree where I tie her reins. Sawyer does the same with Priscilla.

"Alright, I'm ready. Show me the ranch's secrets."

"Come on." I start out and gesture for him to follow. His long stride catches up to me immediately, then he shortens it to stay beside me.

"It's right there," I point at the other side of the small, dry pond.

"Those bushes?" he asks.

"Not just any bushes," I announce, grinning. I reach in, plucking off a ripe fruit and tossing it in my mouth.

"Blackberry bushes. The most delicious ones you've ever tasted."

"I'm allergic," he says.

My mouth opens. "What? Seriously?"

He grins, and I playfully smack his arm. "Asshole."

He laughs and pulls a berry off the bush. He pops it in his mouth and chews. "Delicious."

"Told ya," I respond, gathering two more and eating them.

He reaches across me and plucks off a few more. "This is where you can find me from now on."

Warm happiness spreads through my belly. I love that I was able to share this with him, this special place that's just another reason why I love this ranch with my whole heart.

Sawyer chews and swallows, and I can't help but laugh. There's juice on his lower lip. I reach out, using the pad of my thumb to swipe it away. The juice is gone, but the purple color remains. My gaze lifts to meet his, and the smile on my face dies.

His gray eyes are a squall, a monsoon, a churning and violent storm. He swallows so hard his Adam's apple rises and falls.

"I apologize." My hand returns to my side. "I should've asked before touching you like that. I don't know why—"

"Do it again." It's not a whisper or a command, but something in between.

My entire body awakens, the tiny hairs covering my flesh standing at attention. My legs are somehow strong enough to keep me upright, though I'm certain they're made of vapor right now.

I follow his instruction, raising my hand, my eyes

locked on his. My thumb grazes his lower lip, exerting more pressure than last time, allowing my touch to push at the fullness. His eyes close and I drag my finger across his mouth. A low groan slips from him, vibrating my thumb.

His eyes open, hunger burning through them. He reaches for me tentatively. What must it be like in his head right now? The desire propelling him forward, the guilt binding him to his past. It must be hell. He reaches for my hip, his hand curling around me. I draw in a shaky breath. He drags two knuckles up my side, traveling up my throat. He imitates my touch, dragging those two knuckles over my parted lips. "Your lips are purple, too."

My tongue darts out instinctively, as though a swipe of moisture will somehow remove the stain. Sawyer watches the motion. He takes a deep breath and leans forward. Inches separate our chests, but still I feel the racing beats of his heart.

"Sawyer," I whisper, and he pauses, his breath warm on my lips. "Are you ready for this?"

He's on the precipice. Does he shift into reverse? Or does he let off the brake and keep going?

"I'm ready for everything to change, Jessie."

I can tell he means it. His voice holds so much conviction, it would be impossible not to believe him.

He lowers his mouth to mine, and for a moment it stays there, frozen, as if he cannot believe it's happening. Then he thaws, and suddenly I'm wondering how it's possible this is our first kiss. He presses his lips against mine expertly, like we've done this a hundred times. My mouth opens and his tongue sweeps inside, and now I'm acutely aware this man set my whole world on fire the first time I saw him. There is no other explanation for this heat, this intensity.

His arms wrap around me, bringing me flush against him. My hands run up his neck and thread through his hair, my nails lightly scratching his scalp.

We eventually need to breathe, but he doesn't pull away. He drags his mouth sideways, the same way I started all this by dragging my thumb across his lip, and places a peck on the corner of my mouth. "That was... phenomenal." He pants the words, his chest expanding into mine as he breathes.

I nod, the stiff shadow on his face scraping against me. "By far, the very best kiss I've ever had."

Sawyer doesn't echo my sentiment. I don't blame him for it, but I wish he would say it anyway. A teensy lie, because I've made myself vulnerable with those words.

From somewhere in the vicinity, the sounds of pain-filled mewling fill the air. Across the desiccated pond, Hester Prynne whinnies. I look over to make sure she's good, and catch movement beyond the trees. Without a word to Sawyer, I start for my horse.

Behind me Sawyer asks what's wrong, and I motion over my shoulder with one finger. The movement hasn't stopped, and through the trees I see horses hooves.

I'm running now, untying Hester Prynne as fast as I can. It could be nothing, but it doesn't feel like it. Something about the mewling makes me nervous. I hop on and take off through the trees. From the sounds behind me, I assume Sawyer is doing the same.

By the time I make it through, there's nothing to see and no way to tell which way the horses went.

"Motherfucker," I hiss, and Sawyer looks at me with questioning eyes.

I move the reins left and make a sound with my mouth, urging Hester Prynne into action. "We need to find what that sound was," I tell Sawyer.

He rides beside me, and even though I'm distracted by our searching, somewhere in the back of my mind, I'm impressed by his riding skills. We're going faster than we were on the way out here.

Twenty yards out, I spot the reason for the crying sounds. Two mountain lion cubs circle their mother, pushing at her with their noses. She lies on her side, unmoving.

I slow down, approaching slowly. Not because I'm being cautious, but because I already know what I'm going to see.

"We should probably stay back," Sawyer says, but I shake my head.

"She's dead. There's no way she'd let us get this close if she weren't."

We stay back ten feet, in an effort not to scare the horses or the cubs, and even from here I see the open wound, the bloodied flesh. I shake my head, rage filling me, and crane my neck. It's useless, though. Whoever shot her and left her to die is long gone. Maybe they were going to take her, and then realized Sawyer and I were nearby.

"Who the fuck would do that?" Sawyer asks, disgusted. "And why? It's not even mountain lion season."

Tears prick my eyes. "And she's a mother. These cubs won't survive without her. They depend on her for food for two years, and I don't think they're even half that old."

"What are you going to do?"

"We need to go home and call the game and fish department and tell them about the cubs. They'll come and get them. Even if they somehow manage to survive and grow up, they can't be here. They'll eventually hunt the cattle."

"Do you think the mom was here to hunt the herd?"

I look down at the big cat's blank, glassy-eyed stare, her thick tongue lolling out of her mouth. "She may have been."

"So maybe whoever did this, did you a favor?"

I shake my head. "No. If she'd been seen alive, we would've called Game and Fish and reported her. They'd send out a hunter to run her off the land. It wouldn't be about eliminating her, but putting her in a place where she and her cubs could live." My jaw clenches until it's painful. "Someone took that choice away. And they broke the law while doing it." I turn my horse around, stopping and looking into Sawyer's eyes. The heat of our kiss still burns, even if it's hard to think about at the moment. "Let's head back so I can call about the cubs."

We return the horses to the stable and put them up. Sawyer doesn't kiss me again, but he does take my hand as we walk back to my cabin.

I call the game and fish department, but it's a Sunday. The best I can do is leave a message.

My mood for the rest of the day is ruined. Someone is hunting on my land. Not just hunting, either. They're killing in an injudicious, cruel manner.

And I won't have it.

22

SAWYER

I'VE BEEN TRYING TO GO TO SLEEP FOR A LONG TIME. AN impossible task.

Jessie was torn up about the mountain lion. I wanted to bring her back here and do all the things to her I've been holding back. The dam has opened. But her heart was hurting, and it worried her to know there are hunters on the HCC.

When I make love to her, I need her to be all in. And after a kiss like the one we had earlier today? What we do with our bodies is going to be nothing less than extraordinary. I can already tell.

I reach down, adjust what's going on in the front of my pants, and deny myself the release I'm dying for. Every night this past week I have not denied myself.

Sighing, I roll over and wince as the bone on the outside of my wrist meets the corner of the nightstand. The startling pain makes me even happier I ordered a new bed earlier this evening. I have no idea how long I'll be staying with Jessie, but I can't keep sleeping in a bed that's too small for me. Soon I'll be back in a bed meant for a man my size. I push back the comforter and stand up. I pause, hovering beside the bed and contemplating my next move.

I want to go to Jessie. I like her soft hair and that sweet interior she hides behind her tough exterior.

Maybe I can just lie down with her. Hold her in my arms.

I leave my room and walk down the hall. I stop outside her closed door, take a deep breath, and push it open. It takes a moment for my eyes to adjust, and when they do, I frown. Her bed is still perfectly made, even though we said good night an hour ago.

I back out of her room and look for her in the rest of the cabin. I even flip on the outside lights and walk the perimeter. Her car is gone.

A ball of anxiety gnaws on my stomach. Jessie could have a hundred reasons why she left. She doesn't have to report to me.

Brea had a hundred reasons to be missing that day too. Nor did she have to report to me. But I've never been able to shake the feeling that if I'd reacted sooner to her absence, things would've turned out differently.

I turn off the lights, go back inside, and call Jessie. It goes to voice mail.

I could go to the homestead and tell them Jessie is missing, except she's not really missing. Her car is gone, which means she *went* somewhere. Late at night.

So I sit down on the front porch swing, bathed in utter darkness, and wait.

23

JESSIE

"Hurry the fuck up," I whisper, giving him my sternest look.

He pulls his head through his shirt and stands up straight, his mouth a hard line. "You showed up at my house late at night to help you hunt down people you never even saw. Chill the fuck out and let me get dressed."

"I didn't need to see them. She was fresh, Wes. I bet every blade of dried out grass on this land that whoever did it is still out there, hunting on private property. HCC land. I'd hate what they did no matter where it was done, but I hate it even more because it happened on our property." Yeah, I said *our*. My last name is Hayden, too.

I turn to look at Dakota and she shrugs apologetically. "I'm with Wes on this one," she says. "You scared the shit out of me when you knocked on the door."

Wes grumbles something unintelligible, shoving his feet into his boots. He leans over Dakota and kisses her. "I'll be back soon." She starts to hug him, but he shakes his head quickly and gently unwinds her arms.

What the fuck was that?

Dakota doesn't seem upset by his brush-off, so I don't make a thing of it either. I say goodbye to her and we set out on horseback. In hindsight, it was probably the fact that I showed up with Wes's horse, Ranger, that made him take me seriously.

"Tell me one more time what happened," Wes commands, Ranger's nose just a hairbreadth in front of Hester Prynne's. Of course my brother's horse would insist on being the leader.

"Sawyer and I were out for a ride," I begin, my cheeks heating as I remember Sawyer's lips on mine, his tongue exploring my mouth, the way I lost my mind when he ran his hand up my neck. Luckily my blush is hidden by the night. Wes is a lot of things, including observant. If the sun were shining, he'd pick up on my thoughts in an instant.

"Didn't know the guy could ride a horse," Wes remarks.

I roll my eyes. Another thing he can't see. I know Wes likes Sawyer, especially considering the time Sawyer is spending with Colt, but he gives him shit just like Wyatt. I'm starting to think my brothers are feeling protective of me.

"He used to live on a ranch," I remind Wes.

"I don't need the reminder," Wes counters.

For Wes, tales of the Circle B where Sawyer lived isn't Sierra Grande lore, but real memories. I tend to forget that.

"Anyway," I say pointedly. "We heard this keening sound. And then I noticed horses moving behind some trees. We were out at the pond on the northwest edge of our property."

"The one with the blackberries?"

"Exactly."

"I tried to go after them on the horses, but they were gone by the time I got through the trees."

"So you weren't on horseback when this all happened?"

"No." I make a face. Why does that matter?

"What were you doing? I thought you were riding?"

Shit. He's going to make a great dad to a teenager.

"We'd stopped off to pick blackberries." This is true. Just not a blow by blow of everything that happened.

"So you get on HP and start for the trees?"

"Pretty much," I answer, pushing away my irritation at his shortening of Hester Prynne's name. She's not a computer. "Whoever was there was long gone, but Sawyer and I looked for the source of the original sound and found the cubs. And the mama." Sadness settles over me. "It had to have been whoever was riding those horses."

"Why didn't you hear the shot?"

I shrug. "Silencer?"

"You think a couple hunters came out here with a silencer?"

"How should I know? Maybe they're some rich pricks who spent money on guns and now they're itching to use them. Shit like that happens."

"I'm aware," Wes says roughly, and it reminds me to cool it. Wes struggles with PTSD from his time in the army. I'm not trying to trigger him. "So what's your plan?" he asks.

"My plan was to go back out to the place where I

saw the mountain lion and go from there. But..." I slow my horse and point up at the sky. "I may not have to."

Wes stops too, and looks up. The moon is waning, so we don't have much to go by in terms of light, but there's an unmistakable finger of smoke curling up above the trees about a mile away.

Wes nods at me, and we continue on. "So you were showing Sawyer your favorite part of the ranch?"

I balk. "How do you know that's my favorite spot?"

His soft chuckle floats my way. "You asked to go there a lot when you were little."

"I don't remember that."

"Of course not. You were too young. But I remember it. I took you out there before I shipped out."

I'm not sure what to say. Hearing he took me out to my favorite place makes me feel odd. Sad that I don't remember it, and wishful that I did.

"Yeah, I showed Sawyer." I'm not sure what else to say. Everything about this conversation is uncomfortable, for different reasons.

"I hear you're roommates now."

I frown. "Mom and Dad have big mouths."

"Wyatt told me."

"Of course he did." I blow out an annoyed breath. "How about you?" Let's see if he likes the tables being turned on him. "What was with that awkward hug back at your place? Dakota tried to hug you and you pushed her away."

"I'm strapped, Jessie," Wes explains. "Dakota understood right away."

"Oh." Then I remember the tense conversation I walked in on at the homestead a couple weeks ago. I ask him about that and it takes him almost a full minute to respond.

"First off, I should apologize to you. I asked you to come see me, and when you arrived, I snapped at you. Life has been stressful lately. More than I bargained for." The strain in his voice stretches across the space separating us. I have the uncharacteristic desire to hug him. "Dakota wants me to pull back from the ranch while we work with Colt. She's overwhelmed by his disability, which I understand. But I have to work. If I don't work, everything falls apart. Those cochlear implants cost money, and—" he pauses, weighing his words. "Everyone is depending on me. And I'm shorthanded—"

"You don't have to be."

"You know the deal. The ranch has always been run by Haydens. Warner gave it up, and Wyatt's not interested."

"Last I checked, I'm a Hayden."

"Jessie, you know—"

"Shh," I say quickly, as a light at eye level shines nearby. I turn my horse, and we take a circuitous route toward the smoke.

The closer we get to the source, the more I can see Wes. He looks at me, indicating through the trees with his chin. A man lounges on a chair, his feet stretched out toward the blazing fire.

A fire on this dry ass land? Strike number two.

We creep forward until we get to the edge of the clearing where they've set up camp. The man's eyes are closed. Soft snores slip between parted lips.

I gasp, my hand flying to my mouth. It's one of the assholes from a few weeks ago, the hunters I came across on my way to meet Marlowe. My blood boils as I remember them, their fancy truck and dirty name-calling, the way they spun dirt around my car, laughing. So contemptuous. More than that, though, it was the way they thought they deserved to behave however they wanted.

From my saddle bag, I produce a length of rope.

"Jessie," Wes whispers a warning, but I hold up a hand.

"Trust me," I whisper back.

He falls silent.

I climb silently off my horse and inch forward, coming up behind the sleeping guy. Carefully, I slip the rope over the sleeping guy's head. Judging by the half-empty bottle of expensive bourbon at his feet, I'd say the weight of the rope isn't likely to wake him.

Two minutes later, the second man, the one carrying the light we saw, stumbles into camp. It takes him a few seconds to register the additional two bodies, but when he does, he stutters to a stop. He reaches into his pocket, but Wes is faster, producing his pistol first.

The guy pats all his pockets, his eyes flying toward his tent.

I cock my head. "Bet you wish you had that gun with the silencer now." It's a leap to assume that's what he has, but apparently not too far of one. He doesn't deny it.

His eyes are wild, his alarm causing him to twitch.

"I'm not a defenseless mother with cubs though. Might be a little more difficult to shoot me."

His eyes are on me, the campfire reflected in his irises. "I've seen you before." His voice quakes, but his tone holds righteous indignation.

"Right. The first time we met, you called me a cunt and tried to hit me. I told you you weren't welcome to hunt on my land. And yet," I spread my arms. "Here you are."

"Are you fucking kidding me, you crazy bitch?" he yells.

The volume causes his friend to stir. He sits up and looks around, blinking as he takes in the scene. He looks down at the rope, and when it registers, he begins to panic. "Careful there," I reach out a hand in warning. "She's prepared to take you for a ride."

Everyone's eyes widen. Including Wes's. His arms remain still, his gun trained on the untied man at the edge of camp.

I look at the man whose neck bears my rope. The very same rope I looped around Hester Prynne's neck. "I wouldn't move, if I were you," I advise him. "Or yell. The most you can do is breathe. Maybe piss your pants, if you want."

"Why are you doing this?" the other guy asks.

"There's a lot I can tolerate. But something I can't stand? The defenseless being preyed upon. You did that today. Even after you were told *by me*"—I point back at myself—"to stay off this land. You returned. You must've thought I was kidding."

He twists his hand in front of himself, palms facing out. "Look, look, we don't want any trouble."

"Oh, really? Is that why you shot the female mountain lion with the cubs today? With a silencer? When it's not even open season? On private property? Sounds to me like trouble is exactly what you wanted." I smile at him. "Can we make an agreement here, tonight, under the moon and the stars and God himself?"

"Yes, yes," the man with the rope around his neck rasps.

"You get the fuck off my land. And you stay the fuck off my land. Forever."

Both men nod. Wes backs up, keeping the gun trained on the man at the edge of camp. He mounts first, and I pause with my foot in the stirrup.

"Cut him loose," the man cries, pointing at the rope. "Cut him loose. We agreed."

"Hmm." I mount Hester Prynne. "I'm not certain I believe you."

"I promise," the man with the rope moans. "Please. Please. I have children."

"So did that mountain lion. You killed her in front of her children."

"I'm sorry. So sorry." He's crying.

I lift my leg, prepared to kick Hester Prynne. And I do. But, a moment before, I use the knife Warner gave me five years ago to slice through the rope.

Wes and I are off, galloping across our land, the night air smacking our cheeks. We don't stop for a long while, and when we do, he is smiling from ear to ear. Happiness spreads through me at the sight of my oldest brother feeling unadulterated joy.

"You are fucking unbelievable, Calamity."

It's the first time in a very long time that my nickname hasn't sounded like a bad thing.

24

WES

Jessie leaves me at the stable after I decline her offer to walk me back to my cabin. I need some time to figure shit out.

I'm not sure what to think of her. Everything I thought about my sister seems to have been more than a little wrong. I don't like thinking of how I've been short-changing her. Besides, there isn't much I can do about that now.

But there is something different I can do moving forward. Dakota was right when she said I needed to pull back from the ranch while we get Colt's hearing challenges sorted out. I knew she was right, of course. My wife is an intelligent woman. A warrior, of sorts. But she needs me now, and so does my son.

I'm passing through the front yard, my boots bending the blades of grass with every step, when a deep voice sails through the dark.

"What are you doing, Wes?" It's my father, sounding confused and tired.

I change my route and head for the stairs, taking

them two at a time. He's sitting in a chair, an ankle crossed over the opposite knee. His pajama pants and messy hair tell me he'd been having an unsuccessful night of sleep.

I don't feel much like sitting, not after the night I've just had, so I lean my ass back against the porch railing and cross my arms. "Jessie came and got me. Told me she'd found a dead mountain lion out on the northwest edge."

"Natural causes?"

I shake my head slowly, still reconciling what I saw tonight with everything I thought of my baby sister. "Bullet. Recent, too, according to Jessie."

I wait while my dad has the expected reaction. When he's finished swearing, he asks, "What now?"

I shake my head. "Nothing. Jessie took care of it."

He uncrosses his legs and leans forward, resting his elbows on his knees. "Took care of it, how?"

I recount the entire story from beginning to end, and my dad interrupts a few times to ask questions. The wonderment and conflict I feel? It's plain as day on his face too. "She was like you, Dad. That's the best way I can describe it. She did what you would've done. I provided her with security, but she commanded the situation."

My dad's hands steeple and he presses the sides of his fingers against his lips as he thinks. "Jessie did all that? No direction from you?"

"None of it was my idea. She walked into that situation with absolute confidence. She laid down the law, and when they challenged her, she showed them what the consequence would be for noncompliance." I take a deep breath, one I've been holding ever since Warner left his position at the HCC. "I'm going to ask her to run the ranch with me. Be my second-in-command. She has ideas, Dad. Good ones. She's everything this ranch needs."

He nods slowly, the tiny muscles around his eyes tightening as he mulls over my words. "Okay, Son. I trust your judgment."

I nod. "It's settled then. I'll talk to her tomorrow. I don't think there's a chance she'll say no."

"I doubt it. I've only seen her love for this ranch in one other person." He eyes me meaningfully. "You and Jessie are a lot more alike than I ever realized."

I look down at my boots, but the corners of my mouth turn up. "Get some sleep, old man." I push off the railing.

"Same to you," he counters.

I head back to my cabin, to my pregnant wife and my son, my steps lighter than they've been in a long time.

25

JESSIE

A TALL, FILLED-OUT SILHOUETTE GREETS ME WHEN I PULL up to my place. *Sawyer*. He's on the darkened porch, leaning against a column. I climb from my car and walk over. The closer I get, the more I see the worry in his eyes.

"Everything okay?" he asks. I think it's his way of asking where I've been without directly asking the question.

"I'm good," I answer, coming up the stairs. There are only three of them, and now I'm on the landing. "Wes and I went out and found those hunters. I don't think they'll be back."

It was by far the boldest thing I've ever done. My hands shook the entire ride back to the stable after, and I think Hester Prynne sensed it. She was jumpy, too.

I never would've ridden off with that man tied behind me. The hubris was for show. A message. I think he got it.

Fear and concern crinkle his eyes. "What did you do?"

"We gave them a warning."

"What kind of warning?"

I break down and tell him. Sawyer remains stock-still, his face a mask of disbelief when I tell him about the rope and the horse.

"I wouldn't have done it," I assure him. "My purpose was to incite enough fear that they won't come back. And, hopefully, some respect." They didn't show me any respect the first time I encountered them, and I was nice. So this time, I went a new route. For some people, you have to travel a different road to arrive at the same destination.

We go into the house, and I turn on the overhead light in the kitchen, blinking at its brightness after spending the past couple hours in the dark. All I want is a drink of water.

"You're a mess," Sawyer says, coming up behind me. I look down. A layer of dirt covers my jeans.

"Wes and I had a little race near the end of the ride. I won," I smirk proudly. "We must've been kicking up a lot of dust."

"Your hands," Sawyer says, his eyes on my palms. "Are they burned?"

"A little," I admit, looking down at the red marks. "Rope burn. I was a little careless when I was preparing it."

"Do you have anything for that?"

"There's some balm in the medicine cabinet in the bathroom."

He strides away, returning with the tube. "Sit down," he says, motioning to the chair.

I sink down, letting my body relax into the hardwood. It's not comfortable, but in this moment it's all I need.

Sawyer gets down on one knee, propping a forearm on his thigh and leaning forward. "Let me see," he says, unscrewing the cap and extending a hand. I place my hand face up in his. Gently, as if he's touching thin glass, he smoothes the balm over the abrasions.

I moan quietly. I don't mean to.

He stops, worried eyes on me. "Did I hurt you?"

I shake my head quickly. "No."

His fingers move from my injury, but stay on my skin. "Did I do the opposite of hurt you?" His eyes seek mine, softening at the corners, and his lower lip peels away in anticipation of my answer.

My heart races across my chest, beating throughout my body. "I like when you touch me."

He drops my hand and cups my cheeks in both of his. "I want to disappear into you," he says, his low voice rumbling deep down into me, slipping into hidden crevices.

I close my eyes against his words, his steadfast gaze, the emotions I feel pouring off him. "Are you sure you're ready for this?"

"I've never been ready for anything as much as I'm ready for you."

That's all it takes. Our lips meet, and even though our mouths no longer taste of blackberries, the incredible fire is there, the utter disbelief that this is new to us.

We are exploring tongues, roving limbs, hands that roam. Sawyer, still on one knee, pulls my shirt over my head, followed by his own. He pulls back to look at me, and I remove my bra. He grips my hips, dragging me forward on the chair. "Wrap your legs around me," he instructs, then brings us both to standing. His tongue slips over my neck and my hands wind into his hair as he walks us into my room.

He lays me on the bed, and it takes two of us to work these tight jeans over my hips. He smiles down at me, a grin incongruous to those stormy eyes.

"Finally," he says, tossing the jeans on the floor. He steps from his pajama bottoms at the same time I slide my underwear down my legs. He stands beside the bed and looks down at me. I can't decipher his expression except to say he looks astonished. His eyes rake up my body, then he leans down over me.

He trails his fingertips over my skin until every square inch of me is at attention.

"Sawyer," I beg, squirming.

Climbing onto the bed, he covers me like a blanket, and parts my lips with a slide of his tongue. We kiss for so long I become impatient, and when I buck my hips into him, I feel him smile against me. He sits back, settling between my open thighs, and smiles down at me.

"Where is your patience?" he asks, dragging himself along me.

My core clenches in anticipation. "Long gone."

"Fucking hell," he says suddenly, pulling away.

"What's wrong," I ask, sitting up on my forearms and blinking at the sudden change. Is he remembering the woman who came before me?

"I don't have a condom."

Five glorious words. I sigh in relief.

"I do." Pointing, I say, "Nightstand." He reaches in and finds it easily. I haven't lived here long enough to create a disorganized bedside drawer.

Once it's in place, he grabs my hips and hauls me to the edge of the bed. He leans over me, and without hesitation, thrusts inside. I gasp against his cheek at the delicious feeling of fullness, and he turns his face, pressing his lips against mine. I don't know how he manages to be both gentle and merciless within the same action, but he does.

He fucks me without reservation, and I match him. We are sweaty, and fierce, his mouth searching my chest, needy for me. I've never felt so cherished. So wanted.

He rolls us over, and now I'm on top of him. It's a position I've never been in, and I tense. Sawyer takes over, cupping my backside, lifting me. He does the work at first until I find a rhythm and take over. The heat builds, and even as my body lifts and lowers, inside me there is only rising. Higher and higher, until my legs quake against him and my fingers grab at his chest. My head tips back, and it's the first time I've felt something so intense and exquisite.

I scream his name, and I don't think I meant to, but it spurs him on, and just as I'm coming down from my high, he pulls me flush with him. He kisses me with so much emotion, holding me tight as he tenses and jerks, then stills.

I've gone limp, a deadweight on his expansive chest. His hand runs over my back.

"I've..." I try to say. "It's never..." I sigh quietly. "Those feelings. I've never felt anything like that."

Sawyer doesn't say anything, and after a few seconds, I tip to the side and roll onto the bed. He pulls off the condom, ties a knot in the end, and tosses it on the ground.

"Come here," he says, arms out. I back into him, and he folds over me. His lips brush my hair. "I said you scare me, but it's more than that. You *terrify* me."

"Enough to make you want to stop?"

Sawyer drags in a breath, and although I know he's getting oxygen, I get the feeling he's breathing in *me*.

"Enough to make me never want to stop."

I don't know how to respond, and I don't know if a response is even needed. The events of the night settle into me, and suddenly I'm exhausted.

I'm almost asleep when I register his lips against my neck, his softly spoken words drifting over me. "I've never felt anything like that either."

* * *

Wes is knocking on my door. I know it's him because he texted a few minutes ago, telling me he was on his way over. My guess is that he remembered I'm not currently living alone, and thought he might want to announce himself.

Good idea on his part, considering what just happened in the living room. Sawyer and I woke up together, fixed coffee, and when it began to brew, he turned hungry eyes on me. I pretended to run, but he caught me easily, and started by bending me over the couch.

I glance at the living room window, double-checking the curtains are completely drawn, and finish tying my robe.

"Hi," I greet Wes, pulling open the door halfway.

He stands on the welcome mat I added last week,

dirt raining off his boots as he wipes them. He says hello and asks to come inside.

I look over at the living room. It's still in a state of disarray, but am I supposed to say no?

"Sure," I open the door and gesture inside. Wes walks in, takes one look at the cushions on the ground and the papers that were so obviously pushed off the coffee table, and blushes. Which makes me blush.

"So," he starts, turning his back on the mess. "It looks like you and Sawyer are getting along."

"Don't lecture me. You have two kids. They are like living sex trophies."

Surprisingly, Wes bursts out laughing. "I had a sergeant who called his kids 'fuck trophies'. But not in front of his wife."

I laugh, too, and at the same time try not to marvel at how this conversation is making me feel more like an equal than I ever have. "I don't think you came here to tell me that. What's going on?"

"I talked with Dad, and I'd like to ask you to join me in running the HCC."

My breath steals away, locking up somewhere else inside me. I palm my chest. "Wes, is this a joke? Because this is... everything. This means everything to me."

"You deserve it, Jessie. I know we all call you Calamity, but sometimes I think that nickname is earned, and other times I wonder if the nickname has given you license to behave certain ways."

"Maybe a little of both," I admit. He has a point.

"After what happened last night, the way you defended our property and our name, it made me realize we've been selling you short. Maybe what this ranch needs is some young blood. Someone to usher the HCC into a new age."

I want to hug Wes, but I'm naked under my robe, so I settle for a handshake. I think he understands, because he blushes again, which isn't something I can recall Wes ever doing. It's both odd and comforting, these new things I'm learning about him. I'm getting to know my big brother in a way I was deprived of due to our age gap.

"Oh," I say, remembering the voicemail I listened to after I saw Wes's text. "Game and Fish called me back. They're sending out a hunter to find the cubs. Someone named John Reynolds. He's going to stop at the homestead to introduce himself before he starts."

"Got it," Wes says, nodding. He leaves, and I cover my face with my hands. I want to yell, squeal, jump and dance. I am too overwhelmed to do any of that, so instead I stand here, my excited screams reverberating throughout me.

The HCC. It's everything I've ever wanted.

Sawyer walks into the room. Moisture darkens his hair. He is freshly showered.

I'm trying to wrap my head around how my life is coming together so perfectly, but it's difficult.

So I try not to think about it. I wrap my arms around Sawyer's neck, and I tell him my good news. His grin reaches his ears. Later that night, he takes me out to dinner, stops at the wine store on our way home, and buys the most expensive bottle of champagne.

We get tipsy, and Sawyer does gloriously unspeakable things to my body.

My cheeks ache from smiling.

26

SAWYER

"Where's your head, Sawyer?" Leon backs up, dropping his hands. "That's the fifth time you've made a mistake."

"I'm fine," I grunt, wiping my brow on the inside of my upper arm.

"Sell your lies to someone dumb enough to buy them."

My entire body is too exhausted from physical exertion to laugh, but I manage to nod my head. "Again."

Leon readies himself, lifting his pad-covered hands. "So what is it?" he asks the first time I hit him.

"I told you I'm fine."

He makes a face. "You're not yourself today."

"I'm struggling," I admit. *Jab, jab.*

"What's going on?"

I'm confused as hell, not that I'm going to tell Leon. At this point I'm certain I'm falling in love with Jessie. She rules my thoughts. My choices. I fall asleep every night with her in my arms. The two of us together feels like the most obvious pairing in the world. My attraction to her is a wildfire, unconfined and uncontrolled.

It's not a bad thing, not at all. But it's forcing me into an uncomfortable place. I have to examine what I'm doing with my life, and where it's going to go from here. I froze over when Brea died, and now I'm thawing, and it's making a huge mess.

"There's just a lot of shit for me to wade through, Leon."

"Then you've come to the right place, my friend." He pulls off his pads, tossing them onto a nearby bench. "I'll be right back," he says, and when he returns, he's wearing his boxing gloves. "Let's spar."

I clear my throat and shake my shoulders, trying to keep them loose. I've never sparred before, and he knows it. I don't ask him to take it easy though. This is probably the best thing for me right now.

Leon calls out pointers as we go.

Widen your stance.

Keep your weight on your front foot.

Follow through.

Then he gets me right on the cheek. I swallow the pain and keep going.

A minute later, we call it. Leon pats me on the back with his gloved hand. "You did good for your first time. Sorry about your cheek," he says. "Bleeding just a little."

"All good."

Two guys walk in, dressed to exercise and carrying gym bags. I recognize one from some work he's done on Wildflower. He must recognize me too, because his eyes light up. "Wildflower Ranch, right?" he asks, approaching with an extended hand. "Connor Vale. I did a bunch of work out there before your opening."

I nod. "I thought that's where I knew you from. I'm Sawyer Bennett."

He snaps his fingers. "Sawyer, that's right." He thumbs toward his friend. "This is Finn Jeffries."

Leon comes up behind them and puts his hands on their shoulders. "Maybe you two can get him to tell you what his problem is. He wouldn't tell me a thing, but I'm pretty sure it has to do with a woman."

"Thanks, Leon," I deadpan.

Connor and Finn laugh. "Been there," Finn says knowingly.

"Uh, yeah," Connor agrees. "Anything worth having is worth working hard for, and that includes a woman. That's what my dad always said." A flicker of pain crosses his face, and I get the feeling talking about his dad in past tense is a recent development.

"Thanks, guys." I nod at Finn. "It was nice to meet you. I'll let you get to your workout."

After I've showered and stopped in Sugar Creek for those to-die-for blueberry muffins, I'm on my way back to Sierra Grande. I don't feel all that much better after boxing, but I feel lighter. Light enough to turn on The Rolling Stones and tap my thumb to the beat on the steering wheel.

Out of nowhere, there's a thump. A bump. A grinding cough from my car.

"Fuck," I groan, taking my foot off the accelerator and braking carefully. My car hobbles off the road and comes to a stop.

There's nothing around for miles. I'm between Brighton and Sierra Grande, in a sort of no-man's-land. Mountains tower on either side of me, and I'm down at the bottom of them. No cell service.

I pop the hood and get out, walking to the front of my car. I lift the hood, scratch the back of my head, and stare at the complicated machine in front of me.

I don't know shit about engines.

I reach for my phone to search the internet for a reason a car would stop mid-drive, then remember I don't have service. My hands run through my hair, fisting in my frustration.

How many miles is it to Sierra Grande? Eleven or so? Same to Brighton. I'm equidistant, stuck between two towns. It's disarming how ill-equipped I am to deal with this situation.

I'd bet a hundred bucks Jessie knows her way around a car engine.

Jessie, with her honey hair and beautiful face. Her high cheekbones and her perpetual readiness, like any challenge that comes her way will be met with force. There's something about that I find undeniably attractive.

I can't spend any more time thinking about Jessie. I have to get myself out of this situation. Which means I'll be walking back to Sierra Grande. I'm not going to even calculate how long that's going to take. Knowing isn't going to change anything.

I get back in my car, grab my water bottle and double-check I have my wallet and currently useless phone. Time to walk.

I'm two miles in, my mind one-hundred-percent on Jessie now that I have nothing but time on my hands, when a late model truck comes sputtering down the road. There isn't much about the driver I can see from here, except the hair. I'd recognize that bottle-dyed red color anywhere.

"Sawyer," Greta calls, rolling to a stop. She presses a forearm to the base of the open window and leans out. "What are you doing out here?"

"Going for a stroll," I answer, and Greta laughs her thick, hearty guffaw.

"More like that fancy car of yours couldn't handle the back road."

I smile at her. Despite having unforeseen car trouble, Greta is a person who always makes me grin. She's one of the first people I met when I showed up in town, and I see her at least once a week for the delivery of her blueberry muffins.

I nod. "You might be right about that, Greta."

"Tell you what," she says, glancing east, "I'm on my way to Lady J bakery right now. Her delivery truck broke down yesterday and it's still in the shop. Help me load up all those muffins and I'll give you a ride back to Sierra Grande."

"Done," I answer, walking around and climbing in.

We make small talk as we go, and Greta smirks at my *fancy car* on the side of the road when we pass it.

"It doesn't shock me you like fine things." She winks at me. "Your mom was always dressed up and elegant. Pretty nails, hair curled." She motions to the ends of her hair with a flattened palm when she says this.

It's hard to focus on what she's saying now, though, because all I can think about is my mom. And the pink nail polish she always wore, and the curling iron lying unplugged on her bathroom counter.

I had no idea these memories existed in my brain, and now they're here and they feel real enough to touch. Like I could walk into what is now Jo and Wyatt's bedroom at Wildflower and see my mom's makeup bag on the counter, her floral-printed robe hanging on the wall hook.

"You knew my mom?" I ask Greta, doing everything in my power to conceal my shattered heart.

She shrugs. "As much as a person can know an acquaintance. I had only opened up shop a couple years before you and your family arrived. Your mother had a thing for my lemon scones. But she was the only person who bought them, and I stopped making them after—" Greta's apologetic gaze locks on me. "Listen to me, going on and on. You'd probably appreciate some peace and quiet."

"It's okay, Greta. You don't have to avoid talking about her." I say it offhandedly, like it's not a big deal, but my hands are shaking. The micro movements aren't from pain, though. It's *exciting* to talk about her. To hear about her. For so long she has been a figment, and these anecdotes make her real.

But Greta must think I'm only placating her, because she changes the subject and tells me about emigrating to the United States when she was fourteen. She says she missed the Ukraine at first, but then met a man when she was just seventeen, and married him two years later. "I didn't love him at first," she admits. "But over time, love grew. There are rarely right answers." Her shrug tells me how much she believes these words. "Sometimes, there are just best fit answers. And they will have to do."

I smile at her. She says, "Do you like lemon flavor, Sawyer?"

I nod.

She pats my thigh motherly. "Good. Because I was

thinking maybe I should put lemon scones back on my menu."

It's in this precise moment I realize how much the town of Sierra Grande is beginning to feel like home again.

* * *

GRETA DROPPED ME OFF AT THE BODY SHOP, AND I HAVE A forty-five minute wait until the tow truck arrives with my car. To pass the time, I return my friend Sebastian's phone call.

I use the term 'friend' loosely. Sebastian is a bit of a dick, and he was never my choice of friend in the first place. He was a friend of Brea's family, and he was always showing up at functions, though he never really fit in. When I questioned Brea, she explained he was the son of her dad's client. His presence made more sense after that.

After Brea died, Sebastian decided it was his job to help me through my grief. I didn't have the heart to tell him to pound sand. That was a huge mistake on my part, because he showed up in Sierra Grande for a surprise visit. I don't think he'll be back, not after his run-in with Beau Hayden.

"Bennett," Sebastian booms into the phone, sounding more dudebro than any adult male should. "What's good, brother?"

"Not much," I lean against the wall out front of the body shop. The smell of body odor and lunch meat was getting to me, so I came out here for a breather.

"You getting sick of small-town life yet?"

I think about the Hayden ranch and Jessie's cabin.

When I sit on the back porch and look up at the sky, it feels like the first time in a long time I've been able to take a real breath.

"Not quite," I answer.

"Have you managed to meet Tenley Roberts? I'm dating this new girl and she was talking about how the actress traded LA for Sierra Grande, and I realized you've kinda done the same thing."

"Uh, yes, I've met her. She's nice." No way in hell I'm telling him Tenley is the sister-in-law of the woman I'm dating.

"You should make friends with her and get some dirt. Bet you could make a mint selling her info."

My eyes close and I shake my head. The expensive suits Sebastian wears can't clean up his dirty moral code. "I'll pass."

"Then at least share that shit with me. I'll cut you in on the profits, sixty-forty. I could use the cash. You owe me, anyway."

I frown. "How's that?"

"You didn't do anything but laugh after that cowboy motherfucker ran over my car at the gas station."

"I wouldn't say he *ran* over your car. Pushed it, yes. And that was your own fault. You were being a prick."

"I thought I'd get a middle finger, not have my car nudged out of the way by that giant truck."

I laugh silently at the memory of Beau in the driver's seat, his face stoic. Sebastian had most definitely underestimated how Beau levels his own personal brand of justice.

"I seem to remember someone inside that truck flipping you off." *Wyatt.* He'd given Sebastian a stiff middle finger as they drove past. The tow truck rounds the corner. He's early, and I'm grateful. "I have to go," I say. If I never talk to Sebastian again, it will be too soon. Next time he calls, I won't call him back.

I hang up and stand by, watching the tow truck driver work the platform and chain. My car rolls off the truck, and I pay the guy. He's missing a chunk of his nose, as if a dog bit it off, and I do my best not to stare.

The mechanics get the car into the bay, and after a few minutes of looking at the engine, come back into the waiting area and tell me it's my timing belt. They don't have one in stock for this type of car, he says. Behind his words is an amusement that I'd even expect them to have one. He tells me he can get one by tomorrow, and have it ready for me the day after.

I know better than to ask him if he knows how I can get a rental car. I thank him and head outside. The grocery store is a couple streets over, so I go there and grab a ready-made turkey wrap and bottle of water, then settle in the park that's in the middle of town. I'll give it a little time, knowing how busy Jessie is on the ranch, then give her a call and—

"Hello, Sawyer."

I startle and turn. I hadn't heard anybody approaching, but there Beau stands, just a few feet away.

His Wranglers aren't nearly as tight as his sons', but he still manages to look like a person they'd use in an ad campaign. Lined face, shrewd eyes, and a grizzled air about him. The consummate cowboy.

And Jessie's father.

I sit up straight on the bench, then decide to stand. Shake Beau's hand. Start to say something but realize it's stupid to comment on the weather.

I've been reduced to a bumbling teenager.

Beau takes a seat at the end of the bench. I sit back down and move my empty food container to the other side of me, so it's not between us.

He crosses an ankle over the opposite knee and looks out at High Street. "I remember when all this was different. The buildings are getting taller now. Fancier. Clothes are more expensive than I remember them being." He laughs once. "Listen to me. I'm starting to sound like an old man." He glances at me. "Feel free to roll your eyes. That's what I used to do when my dad told me how he paid a dime for a hamburger."

I chuckle. There's zero chance I'll be rolling my eyes. Not only is he Jessie's dad, he's fucking Beau Hayden. "When I complained about something when I was young, my dad would tell me he walked to school in the snow and it was uphill both ways."

Beau cracks a smile. Suddenly I remember what Jessie said about Beau and my dad. I don't know anything more than what she told me, because my dad hasn't answered either time I've tried to call him.

"How is your dad?" Beau asks, scratching at his nose. His nonchalance feels forced.

"Alright, I suppose. Jessie tells me you knew each other back in the day?"

Beau nods slowly. "We did. Didn't like each other much, either."

"Why not?"

Beau's mouth opens like he's going to answer, but he pauses, and I sense his shift from whatever he was going to say, to the answer he decides to give. "I think your dad should be the one to answer that. If it were one of my boys asking him the question, I'd hope he'd do me the same courtesy."

"Sure thing," I answer quickly. Beau's non-answer brings relief. If the blood between him and my dad had been that bad, he probably wouldn't hesitate to tell me. Allowing my dad the chance to speak his side first implies a level of respect. And that, in turn, tells me the bad blood between our dads is a non-issue for me and Jessie.

I change the subject and tell Beau about my car troubles. He smirks at my story, and I see Wyatt in his features. "That's what happens when you don't drive a truck," he quips, giving me shit. "You need a ride back to the ranch?"

"Yessir," I nod my head at him. "I'd appreciate it. It'll keep me from calling Jessie. She's busy." She's knee-deep in running the ranch with Wes, and I'm damn proud of her for fighting to reach her goal.

"That she is," Beau answers, getting to his feet. "You ready to go?"

I toss my trash in a nearby bin and walk with him to his truck. He's quiet for a good portion of the drive out of town, but when he takes the turnoff for the ranch, he looks my way.

"Wyatt tells me you used to be married."

"I was," I nod. Nerves shoot around through my stomach. "I'm widowed now."

"I'm awfully sorry to hear that."

"Thank you."

"Have you dated much since your wife's passing?"

I bite back a smile. Beau's fishing, trying to figure out what I'm doing with his daughter. "Jessie is the first."

He nods. "She's a handful, that girl. But she deserves the best. And she'll give you her best, too." He takes his gaze off the road long enough to fix me with a meaningful stare. "Make sure you're worthy of it."

A feeling rips across my chest, like a profound honor has been bestowed upon me. The chance to be Jessie's man. To care for her, to step in and fill her father's shoes.

Jessie would say she can fill her own shoes, and she's not wrong. But she's not completely right either. She can manage on her own, but how much better can we both be if we're together?

A euphoric thought hits me, quite suddenly and violently. *Some of the best days of my life haven't happened yet.*

With this one simple understanding, a weight floats from my chest.

I don't *have* to stay stuck in place, putting all my energy into grieving my mom and Brea. My heart has known this since the moment I met Jessie. The tilt of her head, the lift of her chin, the spark in her eyes, they've all beckoned me from my hiding spot safely behind my pain. It was my brain that remained stubborn. Funny how the heart and the brain can go to war with one another.

The white flag has been raised. My heart has won.

"I won't hurt your daughter, Beau. You have my word."

He doesn't say anything else until we arrive at Jessie's cabin, and even then, all he says is goodbye. But he's pleased with my response.

I go inside, work for a few more hours, then get dinner ready.

My steps are light. My limbs loose. The physical

body holds on to emotion, and when you make a choice to release the pains of yesterday, the body knows it.

I'm not saying I'll never think of Brea again and feel a flash tear across my chest. I fully expect to. But will it debilitate me like it used to? No.

There are still loose ends to tie up in California. But for now?

Sierra Grande is looking more and more like my forever home.

27

JESSIE

Sawyer plays with Colt for an hour almost every morning. He told Dakota the best way for Colt to learn ASL is through repetition.

Sawyer is a natural. Not just with teaching, but with Colt. I think he's surprised himself with how easy he takes to it. When Colt picks up a new sign, an elated grin lights up Sawyer's face, and it does something to my heart. Sawyer isn't just being kind to Colt for my sake. He has a genuinely kind soul, and a desire to help Colt understand the world.

We each bring into our relationship our past selves, and ASL is what Sawyer has carried with him into this next step of his life. And I honestly love this about him. He has a little superpower to go alongside all his other wonderful qualities.

To say things are going well between us would be an understatement. I had a hard time tearing myself from his arms early this morning and putting myself through the motions of getting ready for my day. I managed it, of course, but only just barely.

The Calamity

Just as I walked out the door, Dakota arrived with Colt and two bags of toys. She's learning ASL too, but it's more difficult for adults. Old dog, new tricks.

I'd kissed the top of Colt's head, hugged Dakota, and watched as Sawyer reached for Colt's hand. Colt's small fingers wrapped around two of Sawyer's, and my heart did a stutter step. There is something special between Sawyer and Colt, and I know I'm not the only one who sees it and feels it. When Sawyer first began playing with Colt, I'd worried Wes would be irritated, upset, or jealous. I think if I were in his shoes, deep down I'd want to be the hero who could help my son.

But Wes has surprised me by being completely the opposite. He's grateful for Sawyer, and what he can teach Colt. For me, it's the ultimate example of selfless love. Colt's learning and increase in quality of life far exceeds Wes's pride and ego.

As much as I'd have liked to stay and watch Sawyer play with Colt, and join in myself, duty called, so I kept on my way.

Wes and I spend the day cutting, baling, and stacking hay. We divide the cowboys into two groups. Half stay and help us, the other half ride out to check on the grazing cows. In the late afternoon, Wes informs me he'll be taking a few days off next week to go to Phoenix for Colt's surgery.

"You'll be on your own," he says, his tone almost a warning.

"I'm aware," I answer, looking around to make sure we're the only ones in the barn before taking off my long-sleeve button-up. I'm wearing a white tank underneath, but I don't want to be in such a small piece of clothing in front of the cowboys. Tiny pieces of hay rain down onto the ground as I shake out my shirt. "I'll be fine," I assure him.

"I know you will," he responds. I'm not sure if he means it, or if he thinks if he says it enough he'll convince himself it's true.

We end the day before sunset. I'm exhausted and filthy, and the shower calls my name. But first, I want to stop in and see Hester Prynne. I wasn't able to ride her today, so the least I can do is give her a treat. I make my way to the stable after a quick stop to grab an apple from the kitchen at the homestead.

The horses are all put up for the day. They greet me as I pull aside the door and walk in. Hester Prynne is near the back, so I walk that way, glancing over the horses I pass to make sure everything looks as it should. She nickers when she sees me, and I run a knuckle up her muzzle to say hello.

"This weekend, okay? We'll go for a long ride." She noses the apple in my pocket and I feed it to her. I stay with her a little while longer, then start for my cabin.

A shiver of excitement ripples down my spine, knowing Sawyer is there waiting for me.

28

JESSIE

Sawyer makes love to me in the morning. It's the slow, unhurried kind. Saturday morning love, with lingering touches and tips of noses pressed together. I'm on birth control now, so there's no longer a barrier between us. It's a closeness I relish. Love, even.

By now, I know I'm in love with him. Telling him how I feel is tricky. He has far more baggage than me. I come to the table with what now feels like a silly fling with a professor. Sawyer brings a past life, and a very real heartbreak.

He never talks about it, but I can only imagine how difficult it is to let himself move forward with me. For now, I'll keep the way I feel to myself, and take what he can give. Currently, that means his body. It's enough for me. This form of communication is very effective.

"Come with me," he murmurs, lips grazing over mine with every thrust.

"So close," I whisper. Sawyer reaches between my legs, working as my thigh muscles coil and I shatter beneath him.

His body tenses. He kisses me, and we moan into each other's mouths, swallowing the pleasured cries.

Sawyer collapses on top of me, his weight almost too much but not so much that I can't bear it. I drag my fingernails across his back, lightly tickling him. "That was magnificent," I comment, looking up at the ceiling. His shoulders quake with his chuckle. "Can you believe we have to go on living normal life after that?"

He turns his head to the side so he can speak. "Travesty."

We lie quiet and spent for a few more minutes when I remind him I promised Hester Prynne a ride today. "Do you want to join?"

"Not if I have to ride Priscilla again."

"Wes will have a conniption if you ride Ranger. But Warner won't care if you ride Titan. He's not as attached to his horse as Wes."

"Or you," Sawyer says, lifting himself to hover over me. He drops a kiss on my forehead and climbs off me. "Let's eat first."

* * *

"I don't know. I'm not sure he likes you." Titan makes an irritated noise and flicks his head. His black coat shines in the sunlight.

"He's fine," Sawyer insists, even as Titan takes a few steps to show his displeasure. "He's just mad because he wants the rider to be Warner. He'll get used to me."

We ride out past the homestead, and I wave at Gramps. He's sitting on the porch, hands folded in his lap. Farther and farther we go, past the cows who're still grazing, and the bulls who're doing what they can to inseminate them.

I steer clear of the pine and the cottonwoods and go lower in elevation, where the land flattens out and looks like a sea of yellow. We're still too high up for the saguaros to make an appearance, but they are out there, in the far-off distance.

We pause for a moment, and I sit up in the saddle, gazing out at it all. It almost takes my breath away, this love I feel. For my land, my heritage, what the men before me built. I look over at Sawyer sitting on Titan beside me. *For Sawyer.* He robs me of breath, too. And my heart. He's stolen that, also.

He's wearing the cowboy hat I gave him, and he takes it off, pressing it to his chest and leaning over to kiss me.

I smile at Sawyer and start across the plain. Thoughts drift through my mind, mostly about how perfect this moment is. This day. How excited I am for whatever is going to happen next in my life.

It's one of those thoughts that should come with a warning on its heels.

What happens next is anything but perfect.

Three-quarters of a mile later, Hester Prynne takes her last step. It happens so suddenly, this faulty movement. A deep step, an unnatural lowering on one side, a horse's equivalent of a scream. She goes down, all of her limbs bending, but only one is broken. My knees pull up and I sink down with her, rolling to one side. Sawyer yells my name but I can hardly hear him. My own screaming and sobbing is too loud in my ears.

"No no no," I cry, trying to get close to my horse, my very first love, but Sawyer holds me back. Hester Prynne tries unsuccessfully to get up, and he's keeping me from getting in the way of her frantic attempts.

I look out, staring down at the land, and see what I missed before. Gopher holes. "Fuck," I scream, covering my eyes.

Sawyer pulls his phone from his back pocket and dials Dakota. "Can you please tell Wes we need a vet? Jessie's horse is hurt." He pauses. "Where are we, Jessie?"

"Southeast. A couple miles from where the Rioja River meets the Verde."

Sawyer repeats me. "Get out here as fast as you can. I—" He halts, looking at me. "I don't think it's good."

I shake my head. Not because he's wrong, but because he's right and I can't believe it.

"Jessie, even if they hurry, it'll still take a while. There's some shade a ways back where you can wait for them."

"Absolutely not," I say, my voice hard. I sink down in front of Hester Prynne. She has quieted now. I stroke her muzzle and gaze into her large eyes. There's so much soul in them. "I will not leave her."

Sawyer settles beside me. The sun beats down as the minutes tick by. Sawyer removes his shirt and tents it over me.

"Thank you," I whisper. My heart feels like it's been hollowed out with a dull knife.

"Tell me about her," Sawyer says. I feel his kiss on the side of my head. "Tell me about the first time you saw her."

"She was a foal. I watched her mother give birth. For a long time after, I thought we were all born in sacs." Tears sting my eyes. "I didn't ride her for a couple years, not until she was fully mature. While I waited for her to be strong enough to carry my weight, I played with her. Fed her. Walked around with her. She was like all children. Very playful." My face is coated with moisture as I begin to sob. I can't speak after that.

Wes drives up with the vet, Dr. Zahn, trailing behind him. He checks her out and tells me what I already know. Her leg is broken. He starts telling me the prognosis, but I stop him. I don't need to hear it. I've seen this before. I've just never felt it. Not like this.

"I know what you have to do. Just do it."

Wes speaks up. "Jessie, I think you should leave first. Nobody should have to see their horse euthanized."

I surprise myself by agreeing.

Wes gives his truck keys to Sawyer. "Take her home. I'll help Dr. Zahn make arrangements and ride Titan back."

Make arrangements. For the removal of Hester Prynne's body. A fresh round of tears spills from me. I hug my brother and see him trying to hold back his own tears. Sawyer holds my hand and opens the passenger door for me. I climb inside and keep my eyes on my beloved horse in the side mirror.

And I cry. I cry and I cry until my head throbs. We arrive at our cabin, and Sawyer carries me inside. He lays me in the bed I've come to think of as ours, and brings me headache medicine and a glass of water.

"It was just supposed to be a fun ride," I whisper, lying on my side and looking out the bedroom window, my gaze on the land I work hard for every day.

I've never felt so betrayed by it.

29

SAWYER

I'VE SEEN THIS HEARTBREAK. I *KNOW* THIS HEARTBREAK.

There's nothing I can do for Jessie now, except be there for her. I make her dinner that night. She picks at it.

I make her breakfast, lunch, and dinner the next day. She moves it around with her utensil.

Jessie told me she blames the land. I understand the need for blame. How else does a person make sense of the senseless? Grief is an antagonist all its own. A thief of reality, a shape-shifter.

She emerges from our room on Monday morning. She's dressed, her hair pulled into a ponytail, and she manages a small smile. "Do I look like the boss?"

Wes leaves today for Colt's surgery in Phoenix. Jessie will assume his role while he's gone. "You looked like the boss to me long before you were actually the boss."

She steps into my open arms and hugs me. "Thank you for everything this weekend. You took care of me."

I curl a finger under her chin and urge her eyes to meet mine. "I like taking care of you." The words feel as natural as our first kiss, as familiar as the first time I touched her. Like it was all an eventuality and we needn't have worried ourselves about any of it.

Jessie rises on tiptoe and kisses me before she leaves for the meeting she's called with the cowboys.

I watch her go, feeling grateful she's managed to get herself up and out the door this morning. It's not the first time I've been astounded by her strength. I doubt it'll be the last.

Jessie runs the ranch for the next three days, until Wes arrives home from Colt's surgery, and then two more after that, because Wes wants to stay at home with his little boy. It's a blessing, because it allows her to keep her mind off the loss of Hester Prynne.

We spend the weekend in domestic bliss. We nap in the hammock, I help Jessie plan a backyard garden, and in the evening we drink too much wine and I make love to her on the kitchen table. Jessie calls it fucking, which gives me the greatest opportunity of all time.

"That wasn't my definition of fucking," I tell her, lifting my head in challenge. She dares me to show her what I consider the word to mean, just like I knew she would.

"You've walked right into my trap," I tell her, wiggling my eyebrows.

She grins and taps the tip of my nose. "I know."

Two hours later, after a shared bowl of mint chip ice cream, I instruct her to get on all fours. Then I grab a fistful of that honey-blonde hair and show her exactly what I mean.

We fall asleep wrapped around each other.

It is absolutely, utterly perfect.

* * *

Jo called me earlier and asked me to come by. She said she thinks she's found something that belonged to my family.

The prospect makes me nervous. And a little sick.

I've learned there was a lot of stuff left behind in this house when we left town, items my ten-year-old brain didn't notice. Jo once told me there was a fully stocked kitchen when she took over the ranch. Like someone could walk in and begin cooking dinner. She'd offered me the kitchenware since it was technically property of the Bennett family. I'd declined. If anything, I would have donated it. I certainly couldn't send it to my dad.

I walk into the front door of Wildflower. There used to be a wall separating the living room and the dining room, but Jo had it knocked down. Very little about the interior of the house is similar to when I lived there, but it's still familiar to me. My mom walked these floors. She comforted me in my bed after a nightmare. She served peanut butter and banana sandwiches to me at the breakfast nook and read books on fishing with me.

Jo pops up from behind a cabinet in the kitchen. "Sawyer, in here," she calls, waving me over.

I walk in. The kitchen is a disaster. Jo grins happily, brushing hair from her eyes. "Have you ever made lunch for a bunch of boys? Quite the task."

She doesn't want an answer, because she probably already knows it.

"Here." She spins, hefting a box off the counter. I take it from her and peer down at the lid. It doesn't look like anything special, but there's a sinking feeling in my core.

"I found this at the very back of my closet, on the tallest shelf." Jo swipes a finger over the top. "I dusted off the lid. Can't vouch for the inside though. I didn't open it, so I have no clue what you'll find in there."

I hold the box out in front of me, turning it this way and that. No markings, no names. "How did you determine this belongs to me?"

Jo shrugs. She turns back to the lunches. "Who else would it belong to?"

She has a point. I thank her and leave. I set the box in my passenger seat, then climb in the driver's seat and look over. I don't think I want that box staring at me while I drive. An ominous feeling drifts through me. I'm not a superstitious person, but I'm acting like one right now. I get out, remove the box, and place it in the trunk.

* * *

JESSIE IS BUSY WORKING. I AM TOTALLY ALONE OUT HERE in the cabin.

I make a pot of coffee and stare at the box I've set on the kitchen table while the strong brew percolates. A part of me wants to tear off the lid and discover what's inside. There's another part of me, equal in size, that never wants to know what the box contains.

I pour myself a cup of coffee and open the box.

Clothes? I sift through the sweaters. They are covered in dust. I find two dead spiders, one bigger than the other even with its legs folded, and I shudder when my hand brushes against its petrified body. And then, nestled down in the folds of a corduroy jacket, almost as if someone had placed it there on purpose, is a leather-bound book. My thumbnail leaves a discolored mark as it scrapes across the cover. It is tied with a string made of the same material.

It's the string that tells me what this is. A journal.

I swallow the lump in my throat. I open the journal. Tears spring instantly to my eyes. My mother's handwriting.

April 2, 1999

A cattle ranch! I can't believe it. We did it. We really did it. We have no idea what we're doing, but so what?! We'll learn on our feet. Time to buy some boots and a new hat!

April 30, 1999

Sawyer is settled into the elementary school and he's happy. He's made some friends, and they seem nice. I made a friend too, on my morning ride.

August 13, 1999

What happened today... well, it wasn't supposed to happen. I love my husband. We are happy. It's just that sometimes, I feel sad. And he caught me in a blue moment.

September 4, 1999

Who is the man I married? Where is the man I married? This was supposed to be fun. Cattle ranching has turned him into a person I don't recognize. He talks constantly about the beef industry, and bringing cows to market. And the Haydens. He is obsessed with the Haydens. He is not the only one.

. . .

<u>October 28, 1999</u>

Why should I stay and suffer if I'm not happy? This is the question I've been asking myself. What does it teach Sawyer? Is it better that he sees his mother care about her well-being and happiness? Or will I hurt him no matter what I do?

<u>December 31, 1999</u>

A few more hours, and it will be a new year. The turn of a century. This Y2K business is nonsense. This is the year I'm finally going to be happy.

<u>January 4, 2000</u>

We did it. I did it. It didn't feel illicit or wrong. It felt like the best decision I've ever made.

<u>February 14, 2000</u>

I love him.

<u>March 16, 2000</u>

I'm going to start a new life with the man I'm meant to be with. I've never been happier than I am right now.

Tears drip down my face. I'm a grown man, but I'm crying like a ten-year-old again. Not for the mother I lost, but the one I never knew.

She was cheating on my father when she died. He must've known. That has to be the reason why he never talks about her. Why we left town in a hurry, why he left so many of our belongings behind. He was furious with her, he didn't want her things. He didn't want to be reminded of her.

I call him, but it rings and rings. I drink coffee that is now cold. It's bitter, but not any more bitter than the truth.

He calls me back twenty minutes later, and I haven't moved.

I hit the speaker button. "Hello?"

"Sorry I missed your call. How's it going?"

"Did you know, Dad?"

He doesn't say anything. Do I need to explain my question? Does he understand just from the tortured sound of my voice?

"Know what, Sawyer?"

Why is he making me say it? Isn't it obvious? "Mom was cheating on you when she died."

He draws in a noisy breath and releases it. "Yes, I knew."

My world spins, tilts, flies off its axis. I can't tell how I feel right now. Anger, sadness, confusion, disgust. I feel tricked, but I don't know why. She cheated on my dad, but in a way, it feels like she cheated on me. On our family. How could she?

"Who was it? Who did she cheat with?"

"Sawyer, I don't think it will benefit you to know."

"Tell me before I start asking around." It's a threat, and it's not empty. "I want the name of the motherfucker." I squeeze my eyes shut after I say it, realizing how sickeningly accurate that word is to this situation.

"I'm warning you, you're not going to want to know."

"Tell me," I say, my teeth pressing together so hard it hurts.

"Beau Hayden."

The phone drops to the table. My ears pound. My vision clouds, black on all sides and tunneling down the middle. I see Beau's land, his cattle, his extended hand clinking against my glass filled with expensive whiskey as he thanks me. He knew who I was. He knew, at that exact fucking second, who I was. He brought me into his home, allowed me to help his family, all while knowing what he did to mine.

My mother died out here. She must have been coming from seeing him when it happened.

Fucking Christ. I grip my head, rocking back and forth in the chair.

"Son?" The worry in my dad's voice floats up into the air.

I pick the phone back up. "I'm here."

"Your mother and I were having problems. You can't place all the blame on her, okay?"

"Why didn't you tell me?"

"It wouldn't have helped you to know. And, flat out, it wasn't your business."

"Was she coming from seeing him when she died? Is that why she was on that road?"

"I... I can't say for sure. Given the direction she was driving, my guess is that she'd been with him."

Suddenly I understand why my dad chose Renee. I've always found it odd he would marry someone my mother's opposite, but now I get it.

"I need to go, Dad. I need some time alone."

"Sawyer, don't do anything rash. You might know the facts, but you don't know any details."

"Love you, Dad." I hang up. I pity him as much as I'm angry with him. I don't know that he deserves my anger, but I feel it in all directions right now.

The hottest, reddest, most concentrated anger, well, that's reserved for Beau Hayden.

30

JESSIE

I find Sawyer sitting in the dark. The last of the day's light filters in through the living room window, allowing me to see that he's on the couch, elbows propped on his knees, his chin resting on his hand.

"Hi," I say tentatively, flipping on a light. He blinks at the brightness.

I work my boots off my feet and look up when he doesn't respond. I don't understand the expression on his face. It's determined but also heartbroken. Something must have happened concerning his wife. Did he get a call about her? Some telemarketer looking for her? Is he spiraling because of that?

I go to him, standing in the space between his knees. "Are you okay?"

He looks up at me, blinking, like he's just realized I'm there. "I'm fine."

"You don't sound fine."

He doesn't say anything. I have no idea what I'm supposed to do now. I walk to the kitchen and open the fridge, searching for something to make for dinner.

Sawyer usually cooks, but the kitchen is free from any hints of a meal being prepared. I take out the bread and butter, the sliced cheese.

"I hope you're okay with grilled cheese," I call, then realize he's behind me, standing beside the table. I go to him, wrapping my arms around his waist. "Sawyer, did something happen?"

He looks down at me. His gray eyes flash, the storm in them raging. "Kiss me," he whispers.

"What?" It's not his request that confuses me, but his tone.

"Please," he adds, and his plea hurts my heart.

I rise on my toes, bringing my mouth to his. He kisses me softly, lips gently yielding, his eyes closed. I keep mine open.

His arms encircle my waist and he lifts me, spinning us as one, until my back meets the wall. I grunt into his mouth at the contact, and his eyes open. He pulls back an inch to look at me. His expression is indecipherable, and I know something has upset him. Hurt him. He looks wounded.

His lips lower to my neck, and he kisses me roughly from my ear to my collarbone. Whatever happened, maybe it wasn't too terrible, not if it caused him to want me like this. I'm not minding this side of Sawyer at all.

He reaches for the bottom hem of my shirt and lifts it over my head. I help unclasp my bra, and his hands rake over my skin, cupping me. His head dips down, taking me into his mouth. I groan. He bites down, not hard but not exactly gentle, and I gasp at the pleasure mixed with pain. He maintains eye contact with me, his mouth sliding down my stomach. He eases my jeans down over my hips, leaving my underwear in place. His hot breath streams through the thin fabric. He presses his forehead to my stomach, as if he's attempting to gather himself. I open my mouth to say something, but I have no words.

And then I'm unable to speak. Sawyer is on his knees, his mouth is there, and though he's been in this position before, he's never been quite so... so... unrestrained. It isn't long before my legs are shaking and I'm pressing into the wall to stay upright.

Sawyer stands, but he doesn't look at me. He pulls me off the wall, spins me again, placing his hand on my back and bending me over the table. And once again, I don't mind.

He enters me harder than normal, but given everything that's led to this point, I'm expecting it. I even like it. Everything is good, until it's suddenly not. Until it hurts. I don't know if it's the angle, or the force of his thrusts, but I cry out in pain.

Sawyer freezes. He's still inside me. "Did I hurt you?"

I lift up on my forearms and nod. His body leaves mine, and he hauls me upright, pressing my back to his front.

"I'm sorry," he mutters thickly. "So sorry."

"Sawyer, it's okay. It was an accident." A tiny drop of moisture wets my shoulder. I watch the tear roll down my arm. "What happened?"

"I can't tell you."

I turn around to face him. "You can't tell me?"

He shakes his head, not meeting my eyes. "Come on." He takes my hand, leading me into the bathroom, where he starts the shower. "I'll make you a grilled cheese while you shower."

Then he walks out. He's as naked as I am.

Dumbfounded, I step under the spray, letting it beat down on me. The warmth presses into my skin, but on the inside I feel cold. Worry gnaws at my stomach. I turn off the water, towel-dry my hair, and dress. When I come out, Sawyer is clothed again. Two grilled cheese sandwiches sit on plates at the table.

Sawyer waits for me. He doesn't pick up his sandwich until I've sat and picked up mine. I take a bite. "You're just not going to tell me what made you upset enough to fuck me like that?"

His eyes cloud over with shame. "I would never hurt you on purpose."

"I know. But there was a different emotion to that than I've ever seen from you. Something has upset you, and it worries me that you're refusing to tell me what happened."

"I just..." His shoulders slump. "I can't tell you, Jessie."

"Because it would hurt me?"

He nods slowly.

I stand, the sandwich in my hand. "You already have." I pick up my plate, and before I've thought it through, it sails out of my hand at the wall. Right where my back landed earlier.

I go to my room and lock the door behind me.

31

SAWYER

Jessie was gone when I woke up this morning.

I feel terrible about last night. I didn't mean to hurt her. The second I heard the pain in her voice, I snapped out of the role I'd allowed myself to occupy.

I'd sunk down deep in my grief all afternoon until Jessie came home. And then I saw her, and even though I love her, I was overwhelmed by emotion.

And I can't tell her a damn word of it. Because I love her. I cannot shatter her world like mine has been. She can't know what her dad did. Even as frustrated as she gets with him, he is her hero. I won't be the one to take that away from her.

I have to come up with something. Some reason for the way I behaved last night. I'm going to have to find a way to continue on like I was before, without letting on how much I'm hurting. How angry I am.

But how? How can I stay with Jessie, given what I know of her father?

How can I leave? What could I ever say that will make sense to her?

The longer I think about it, the longer I'm certain this cannot end well. Not when all I want to do is pound on the front door of the homestead and confront Beau. I haven't yet, for many reasons, one of which being I don't trust myself to see him right now. I don't have much of a temper, but given the right set of conditions, just about anybody can snap.

My dad has called three times this morning. He finally left a voice mail, asking me how I'm doing and pleading with me to stay calm and remember this all happened a long time ago. He has a twenty-plus year head start on moving past all this.

Is there a statute of limitations on lies and deceit? It's something I've been going over and over in my head, and I don't have an answer.

There are other answers I'm looking for, too. Ones that aren't subject to opinion. Something about the fact my mom was having an affair with Beau when she died is really rubbing me the wrong way, and not just for the obvious reason. Is there more to the story? It seems unlikely, but... what if?

It sounds insane, but what is insanity at this point anyway? I'm already out of my mind with shock. At this point, anything is possible.

Since waking up this morning, my thoughts have gone from red hot anger to something darker. Maybe it's just grief cycling it's way through me, but I'm the kind of person who needs to see something through once I have an idea.

Which is why I'm here. I open the front door of the police station and walk inside. The person at the front desk asks how they can help me.

"Sheriff Monroe, please?"

The guy picks up the phone, speaks in a hushed tone, then hangs up. "He'll be ready to see you in a few minutes."

A few minutes turns out to be twenty.

"You can go on back," the guy informs me, pointing to the office at the back of the station.

Sheriff Monroe stands when I walk in. This is no easy feat. He's older, and there's a lot of him to haul upright.

He shakes my offered hand. "What can I do for you, Mr. Bennett?"

I don't know exactly how he knows my name, but it must have something to do with this being a small town. "How long have you been the sheriff?"

He makes a noise with his mouth, like thinking back that far isn't possible. "Longer than you've been alive, probably."

"That's what I was hoping you'd say." I lean forward. "I'm not sure how much you know about my family, but my mother died here when I was ten."

He nods gravely. "I remember. Such a tragedy. Hit a tree."

"That's correct. Out on the HCC."

"Not quite. It was on the road that runs parallel to the ranch." He scratches at his chest. "Ten feet to the left and it would've been on the HCC."

"You really do remember it."

"I responded to the call."

I swallow hard. "You saw my mother?"

He eyes me sorrowfully. "I did."

"Did she die instantly? From the impact?" I've always wondered if she was allowed that small kindness. Alive, alive, alive, dead. A blip in time.

"Yes. She did not suffer."

"Was there an autopsy?"

His eyes squint. "Is there a reason you aren't asking your father these questions? Assuming he's of sound mind and body, he should be in possession of this information."

"My dad doesn't like to talk about her. It still hurts too much." That's another lie I've been believing my entire life. He didn't want to talk about her because he didn't want me knowing about her affair. Not talking about her was easier than lying.

"There wasn't need for an autopsy. The postmortem examination confirmed what we already knew. Blunt force trauma due to her collision with the tree."

My lips twist. There is more I want to say. I want to ask him if he questioned Beau, or if he saw a reason to. I don't know how to ask that without drawing too much unwanted attention to my questions. "Can I see a copy of the police report?"

"You bet," Sheriff Monroe answers. "We weren't using our electronic system back then, so it's buried down in archives. Talk to Bradley at the front desk and fill out a request form."

I thank him for his time and stand. Before I leave, he says, "I know it's hard to take, but listen to me. I've been in this job for a long time, and the one thing I can tell you with absolute certainty is that accidents happen. They are as awful as they are unstoppable. Searching for a rhyme or reason won't do you any good."

My head bobs, accepting his words. "I appreciate that, Sheriff."

I stop at the front desk on the way out. Bradley

hands me a form and takes it after I've filled it out. "When can I expect the report?" I ask.

"We have a four-to-six-week turnaround."

"Four to...?" If I did business that way, I'd be out of a job. "You look like you have room in your schedule right now." He doesn't appear to be doing much more than playing a game on his phone.

He shakes his head. "Rules are rules."

I don't say another word. I stride out of the station, glancing back one last time on my way out, and catch a glimpse of the sheriff at his desk. He's gazing out the window, his bottom lip pinched between two fingers. He looks a million miles away. Or two decades.

I need to get back to Jessie's cabin to accept delivery of my bed. I don't know that I'll be needing it anymore, but when I called the furniture company on my way into town, they'd told me it was too late to cancel. The bed was already on the truck.

My relationship with Jessie is seven shades of fucked up, and the bed may end up being a large, unused memento of our time together. The thought takes my fragile heart and gives it a malicious squeeze.

I either move forward and lie to her every day for the rest of our lives, or I tell her the truth and watch it break her heart.

The game is zero sum. And we'd never have had to play it if Beau and my mother didn't have an affair.

I'm nearly to the edge of town when an idea comes to me and I turn my car around. The sheriff said the files were likely never transferred to a computer, but I can't leave it at that. I have to exhaust the possibility.

Parts of Brea's death will likely always be a mystery to me. I can't experience that twice. I can't let this go until I know, one-hundred-percent, that my mom hitting that tree was an accident. And I don't want to wait for the police department to take their sweet-ass time.

* * *

Farley lets me into his apartment. He is far younger than I expected. Possibly even still in high school.

I go to shake his hand, but he says, "Sup," and turns away.

Hmm. Okay.

I follow him down the short hallway to his bedroom. It's cramped, and it smells like teenage boy. It's a scent I don't want to think too much about.

Farley sits down at his desk, where there's a large computer, and looks at me, waiting.

"I need you to find out if there was an autopsy done on a woman twenty-two years ago."

"That's going to cost you. I'll find out all kinds of shit, but government systems are a bitch. Not to mention a federal crime."

"I'll pay you whatever you want."

He watches me. "You do know it's entirely possible the results aren't in a computer, right?"

"So I've been told. I want you to look anyway."

He grunts. "Twenty-two years ago, there were like, horse-drawn buggies and shit."

I give him a withering look. "Not quite."

He glances over at his dark screen. "Five hundred dollars. Right now."

I open my phone and transfer him the money. "Get to work."

32

JESSIE

"Jessie, there's a delivery here for you." One of the cowboys peeks his head into the barn.

I sigh and walk outside, blinking against the bright sun. A white delivery truck with the name of a furniture store on the side sits idling. This must be Sawyer's bed.

I have no idea if he'll ever sleep in it. The thought takes my already twisted heart and gives it an extra squeeze.

"Follow me," I yell to the driver, motioning to the ranch truck I was given yesterday. I lead him to my cabin and point out which bedroom.

He and the other person with him carry the bed inside in pieces. He stops in the doorway to Sawyer's room. "There's already a bed in there."

"Okay?" I try to keep my irritation in check. I need to get back to what I was doing.

"We were paid to deliver and set up, not disassemble and haul away."

I tell them to hang on, then go to my room and grab some cash. "Here." I return, holding out a one-hundred-dollar bill. "Will this be enough to cover taking care of it all?"

The driver swipes it from my hand. "Yep."

I wait in the kitchen while they get to work. Since I'm here, I make lunch for myself. I'm halfway through the process when the guy comes into the kitchen. "All done. I need you to sign this saying you received the bed. And," he places a leather-bound book of some kind on the table. "We found this between the mattress and the box springs of the old bed."

"Thanks," I say, eyeing the book.

I sign the receipt he's holding out, then lock the door behind them when they're gone.

I walk back into the kitchen and stare down at the book. It could be Peyton's, but I don't think it is. A young girl wouldn't be careless with her journal. I've been there. When I was Peyton's age, I'd have grabbed my journal in a house fire before running from my room.

Which means it's Sawyer's.

I tap my pursed lips with two fingers. Does wanting to read it make me an awful person?

His behavior was bizarre last night, and he admitted something happened. He also told me I can't know, because it will hurt me. I've been envisioning the worst scenarios all day long. For hours, I've been convinced he cheated on me, even though it doesn't seem like something Sawyer is capable of. But what the hell else could it be?

I'm staring at the book when a key slides into the front door lock. I train my gaze at the door, watching as it opens and Sawyer steps in. First, he looks at me, then down to the table. His eyes bulge.

He comes toward me, arms open. "Jessie." He says my name cautiously.

I put out a hand to stop him. "I didn't read it. It's your journal. I believe in privacy."

Sawyer pulls out a chair and sits down. His forearms lean on the table, and he looks at me earnestly. I remain standing, and the journal lies between us. "It's not mine," he says, running a hand through his hair.

"Whose is it?"

A long time passes before he answers, maybe ten seconds. They feel like forever. "Jo found it at Wildflower. It was my mother's."

I lift my chin, then lower it inch by inch as I process this information. "This is what upset you so much last night?"

He nods.

I poke at the front cover. "And there is something in here you can't tell me about? Because it will hurt me?"

"Exactly," he answers, somber.

I reach for the journal. It was never a choice. I'd rather know the truth and handle the pain than be lied to. I can't imagine how Sawyer's mother, who died before I was born, could possibly hurt me now.

I open the journal. I read every entry until it ends.

"Who is she referring to?" I ask, but I already know. I don't know how, but the answer is there, a heavy stone in my stomach.

Sawyer grimaces like he is about to be sick. "Your dad. I called my father, and he told me."

I choke on a sob. "Your mother... slept with my father?" The meaning of the words dusts the surface, sinking in. "She disrespected my mother."

Sawyer's jaw twitches. "Like your dad disrespected

my dad? He slept with another man's wife." He sounds horrified.

I can't hear that right now. I can't see that right now. Not my dad. My dad with the ironclad loyalty to his family. A man who, without a doubt, would place himself between a bullet and any of his loved ones.

"Oh. *Oh*. No no no." I shut my eyes against the truth, but it doesn't work. I see only a younger version of my father, with a woman in his arms. A woman who is not my mother.

Sawyer pulls me to his chest, his big hands holding my head to his galloping heart. I cling to him, refusing to accept this new information as reality.

Impossible. This cannot be unlearned.

My chest splits open. The pain is atrocious and exquisite.

"I went to see the sheriff today." Emotion fractures his sentence.

"Why?" I ask, my face still pressed to him. I don't want to move from this spot. He smells clean and fresh, and whatever else it is that makes him *Sawyer*. The man who holds my heart.

"My mom died on that road out there." His arm shifts, and even though I can't see it from my position, I know he's pointing beyond the HCC, to the road leading to town. "And now I find out she and your dad were having an affair?"

My mind makes the connection immediately. "Sawyer, no." I pull away from the smell that soothed me a second ago, and look up at him. "What happened to your mom was an accident."

He shrugs in a *maybe but maybe not* way. I take a step back, relinquishing the comfort I found in his chest.

"What are you implying?"

His lips press together. He doesn't want to say it, but he'll hint at it? I don't think so.

"Say the words, Sawyer."

"It's too convenient, Jessie." A pleading edge strains his tone. His hands run over his face. "Our parents were sleeping together when my mom died."

I turn my chin away from his ludicrous words. My dad would never—

Except he might. Maybe. I don't *know*. I thought I knew him, but what do I know anymore?

Sawyer continues. "The sheriff said he was there the day of the accident. That her cause of death was clear."

My shoulders sag with relief, but his next words rip away the feeling. "I couldn't leave it at that. I'm looking into it further."

"You suspect your mom's accident wasn't an accident?" My tone is incredulous. "Let's pretend that's true. Then who killed her? My dad?" My fingers rake through my hair, scratching my scalp.

"I don't want it to be true, Jessie. But what would you do if you were me?" He catches my hands, gathering them in his own. The storm in his eyes has transferred into me. I feel like a ship tossed in a hurricane. "If you'd lost a parent when you were young, and then you learned something like this about them? I know you, Jessie. You'd exhaust all possibilities."

He's right. I'd turn over every stone.

And I know what all this means. If we strip away the shocking revelations, there is only one ending for us.

"We can't be together," I weep, overwhelmed with all the emotions coursing through me.

"I know," Sawyer whispers, his voice breaking. "I know."

He drops my hands, but only to capture my face and stare into my eyes. A fresh round of tears releases. I was wrong. I do not want to know the truth and handle the pain. I want to be lied to.

Sawyer holds me for a long time, then lets me go. "I'm going back to California. I can't stay here. I can't be on the HCC, or even in Sierra Grande." He shakes his head. "I have to put space between me and this place. For my well-being, and yours too. I hate your dad right now. I hate my mom a little bit too." He chokes on the admittance, tears filling his eyes.

"I understand," I whimper, my voice shaking. Right now, I hate my dad also.

I don't say a word as Sawyer leaves the room. I cry silently. He returns with his packed bags.

"I left one of my shirts on your bed. If you want to wear it to sleep in every once in a while..." he trails off. "I'd like knowing you're in the next state, wearing my shirt."

I watch him while he speaks, hearing what he has to say but not absorbing it. I'm too busy memorizing the way he talks more from the right side of his mouth, how he gestures, the arch of his eyebrows.

This can't really be it for us. Right? It was good, *we* were good, and then out of nowhere, the script flipped. I have to know more. He can't leave this way.

"So what happens now? Do we talk again? Are we really over?" I cover my mouth with my hand to suppress a sob. Saying the words out loud is too much for me. Sawyer drops his bags and comes to me.

Tenderly he cups my face. "I don't have all the answers. Not yet."

I take a deep breath, gathering myself from the inside. On the outside, I lift my chin, pull back my shoulders.

Sawyer watches, his eyes shiny with unshed tears. He touches my chin. "There she is. The indomitable woman I fell in love with."

"You love me?" The tenuous hold I have on my composure is slipping. "I wish you wouldn't have told me that." It takes the pain and increases it ten-fold.

The tears in his eyes spill over. "I couldn't leave without having told you. You've helped me open up my heart. You've shown me how to love again."

Indignation coils in my stomach. The future unfolds in my mind, and I see someone else, a nameless and faceless woman, reaping the benefits of what I did for Sawyer.

I put in the work, and one day someone else might win the prize.

"Just go," I say, my tone harsh. I want to curl up alone with my broken heart.

Sawyer steps back. He picks up his bags, and I turn away. I can't watch him walk out the front door.

I wait until I know he is gone, then take ten deep breaths. Pulling out my phone, I text my entire family, asking for a family meeting ASAP.

The reason for my broken heart is two-pronged.

That second prong is about to answer for what he's done.

33

JESSIE

Everyone is gathered. I've sent Peyton and Charlie to a different room to play with Lyla and Colt.

"What's going on, Jessie?" Wes sounds annoyed. I disappeared around midday to accept the bed and never returned, and now I'm messing up his workday with this meeting.

All three of my brothers are seated on the couch. Tenley and Dakota sit beside each other in the armchairs. Jo is missing. She probably had to stay at Wildflower. My dad, Mom, and Gramps sit on the couch opposite my brothers. And I, the youngest of the family, stand in front of them all.

How many of my siblings already know about Sawyer's mother? Wes, probably. Possibly Warner. Maybe even Wyatt. They were teenagers when the affair was happening. It's likely I am the only one who didn't know.

I hold up the journal. "I came across this today. Sawyer had it, after it was found at Wildflower."

I hand the journal to my dad. His eyes question me,

but I gesture to the book in his hand. "Open it up. Take a peek. It belonged to our neighbors, back when Wildflower was the Circle B."

My dad's eyes darken. So do my mother's. The way she treated Sawyer makes so much more sense now.

He spends fewer than thirty seconds on the journal. I go to stand beside my brothers.

"Kids," my dad's heavy gaze sweeps all four of us. "I don't think we... I," he corrects, sending a swift glance at my mom, "ever planned to tell you this. But it seems like something we should do now, considering what Jessie has found."

My brothers didn't know. I look at their curious but reluctant expressions. A small part of me feels bad for calling everyone together, for forcing this on my dad.

"It was a long time ago, when the Bennett family lived at the Circle B. It operated as a ranch much like ours. Ken Bennett was good for a time, a rancher I respected. But he lowered the cost of his beef, and it was like throwing a stick of dynamite in the market. It fucked up everything and almost made the HCC go broke. I couldn't figure out how he was making enough money to operate, because I certainly wasn't."

"Then you rerouted his water source and forced his land into a drought," Wyatt says. "We know, Dad."

I look at him sharply. "I didn't know that. No shock there, though."

Wyatt meets my gaze momentarily, then glances back to our dad.

"Yes, Wyatt. That's true. But there was something else that happened." My dad sets a heavy, firm hand on my mom's knee and squeezes reassuringly. "I made the worst choice of my life back then, a mistake I will regret until I draw my final breath."

My stomach drops away. I know what he's going to say, yet I can't fathom it. It seems impossible, though I've read the words myself.

"I had an affair with Cynthia Bennett."

Silence from everyone, and then, "What the fuck?" It's Wyatt's outburst.

A heavy breath from Warner.

"I remember that time," Wes says, his voice sounding inside out. "I remember Cynthia Bennett. Coming here. I thought she was friends with Mom." Goose bumps dot Wes's arms. Dakota reaches out, her fingers grazing his forearm. He watches her touch as it flows back and forth over his skin, then he looks up at our dad. I've never seen Wes look quite so... devastated. "How could you do that to Mom? To us? We were all living in this house at that time. How could you?"

"I don't have any excuses, Wes, but—"

"You're goddamn right you don't have an excuse," Warner says. My eyes widen at the venom in his voice. I didn't know Warner was capable of sounding that way.

My dad's head hangs, supported by his hands. I have never, in all my twenty-one years, seen my dad look pathetic. I don't want him to be this person. I want him to be my strong, unflappable father. Who is this fallible man with his chin to his chest?

My mother sits up, pulling back her shoulders, and addresses us. "You know nothing of what was happening back then. It was more than two decades ago. You are allowed to have an emotional response to this news, but you will not dwell on it. We will not be a family who wears this on our chests for decades to come. This will not break us." She points up at the coat of arms on the mantel, the words inscribed on it. *Legacy. Loyalty. Honor.*

"Those words have seen far more than any of us know. Yes, this surprise is hurtful. But it's not the first secret in this family, and it won't be the last."

I am in awe of my mother. Of her strength and poise. Even now, in this moment that can be nothing but painful for her, she is going to pull through and carry us alongside her.

Gramps stands, moving quicker than I've seen in a while. "I'm calling a meeting too. Between me and my grandkids."

34

GRAMPS

My grandkids have had the rug pulled out from under them.

Poor kids.

I look from face to face, from shocked expressions to eyes that reveal the heartache inside. I remember the day each of my grandkids was born. I was at the hospital, waiting to greet them.

They have needed me at various times over the years. Mostly when they were young and required a hand getting up the stairs, or fixing a bike chain. Then again, recently, when each one had to overcome all the damage during the years they didn't come to me for help. Those were the years they needed to make their own mistakes, so that when the time came, they'd know how to make the right choices for themselves. I'd like to believe I had a hand in helping Wes with Dakota, Warner with Tenley, and Wyatt with Jo.

I fear that for Jessie with Sawyer, well, that's beyond what I am able to fix. Right now, my grandkids need me to bandage their image of their parents' marriage.

We're seated out back, the homestead looming tall behind the four of them. They all wait, quiet and watchful, for me to speak.

I call upon words my wife would use, and hope she is sitting beside me in spirit. "I know you're all pissed at your dad," I begin.

Wyatt grunts, as if the word I chose to describe his feelings doesn't even begin to cover it. I expected this of him. He is the most defiant of the four, with Jessie trailing closely behind.

"It's going to take a long time for you to overcome what you've just learned." I glance at Jessie, and she bites her lip and looks away. I'm betting she feels guilty for outing her dad, but the truth is that I saw this coming a mile away. As soon as Sawyer Bennett stepped foot in the homestead, I knew tectonic plates were shifting in our family foundation. Earthquakes have been known to bring up both trash and treasure.

"One thing you need to understand is that every marriage is different." I look at Warner. He's always been the calmest of the four. "Is your marriage to Tenley different than yours to Anna?"

"Night and day," he answers quickly, crossing an ankle over the opposite knee. Wes frowns at Warner's legs taking up his space and inches over.

"That's what I thought. Something else you need to understand is that marriages usually change over the years. The people your parents were back then, even their entire marriage, is different today than it was when the affair occurred."

Pain jumps over their faces at the word *affair*. "You also need to know that what you learned about today is rarely the product of one person's bad choice. It's usually many cracks, many breaks, and various pains that build up over time. Not just from your spouse, but from life. You'd all do well to remember that." I look at them in turn, even Jessie. "You have to know that the only place to solve your problems is in here"—I tap my chest—"and in here"—I tap my head. "None of your problems can be solved externally, so don't go looking. That's what your dad did, and I know that's a bitter pill for you to swallow. Your father is as human as you and me. But he is also a damn fine rancher, a good father, and a loving husband. What he did twenty years ago does not define him. He atoned, he worked on himself, he learned what was broken in himself and in his marriage, and then he fixed it. There is nothing more you can ask of a person but to work on themselves every day until they die."

They are all silent, but it's Wes who's thinking the hardest. I am not surprised by this. He is the oldest and remembers the most. I can still envision a time when he was the only child running around this place.

Wes sits back, one long leg sticking out. "You knew it was happening at the time?"

I look down at my hands, the skin papery and telling of all my time under the Arizona sky. This is where my truth will get sticky. As my dad used to say back when he was running the HCC, *They all deserve to know a little, and none of them should know everything.*

"I figured it out eventually, yes."

"And did you tell him to stop?" Jessie asks this question with a pleading look in her eyes. Everything she knew about the adults who raised her has been challenged today. She needs to believe her gramps is the kind of man who would stop his son from continuing stupid behavior.

"Your father accepts being told what to do about as well as any of you. But I did tell him I disapproved of his choice."

They are quiet again. And honestly? I'm tired. It doesn't take a whole hell of a lot to tire me out anymore. But there is one thing I'm curious about.

I look at my granddaughter. "Where's Sawyer?"

Jessie's eyes flood with tears. She rarely cries. It's a bad sign.

"He left."

"Left your cabin to stay in town?" Wyatt asks.

Her head shakes and she wipes a hand under her eyes. "To return to California. We both agreed that after what we learned," her lower lip trembles, "we don't make sense. He's just as shocked and hurt as the rest of us."

"There's a part of me that wishes he would've burned the journal," Wyatt mutters.

"It was your wife who gave it to him," Wes counters.

Wyatt fixes him with a *fuck you* stare. It's a good thing Warner sits between them.

And on the end, on the other side of Wyatt, Jessie sobs quietly with her fists pressed to her eyes.

Wyatt stands and gently pushes her into his spot. "Come on, Calamity. Don't cry." He sits back down in her vacated spot and puts his arm around her. Warner pats her leg. "I always thought when you cried, the tears would come out shaped like letters and form cuss words, like foul-mouthed alphabet soup."

Jessie's shoulders shake with laughter even though her lower lip juts out and she's still crying.

"I liked him," Wes announces. It's these words that remove Jessie's hands from her eyes. She stares at Wes.

"You *liked* someone? I always thought you merely tolerated other people."

Wes grunts a laugh. "Yeah, well. I'm getting weak in my old age."

I love this. Watching my grandkids argue and love, tease and talk. I think they appreciate each other now, and that appreciation will deepen as they get older. It gives me reassurance that the Hayden name will stay strong, long after I'm gone.

They depart. The boys go to their wives. Jessie leaves after she sneaks into the pantry and does a shot of Macallan 25. I won't tell on her. I've been known to nip at that bottle a time or two myself.

Beau comes to find me on the front porch after they've all gone. The corners of his mouth turn down. Lines gather around his eyes. He sits beside me and looks out at the land we've done countless things, both good and bad, to protect.

"I fucked up, Dad."

"No, Son. You fucked up back then. Today, you were the man they needed you to be. You took responsibility for your choice, and you made no excuse for it."

"I feel like I should do something for Sawyer."

"Too late. He's on his way home to California."

He sighs. "I bet Jessie is heartbroken."

"She is most definitely heartbroken, and hopefully almost drunk by now." I also saw her walk out with a bottle of her mother's wine.

"Good for her." He scratches his chin. "Do you ever think about that day?"

I don't need to ask what day he's referring to. "Not if I can help it."

Beau takes a heavy breath and asks, "Do I know everything about what happened?"

"I don't need to tell you exactly what happened for you to know exactly what happened." I have never, in all the years since that day, provided him with a blow-by-blow account. Doing so would've taken away his deniability.

The look in my son's eyes is unfathomable. "I know. But sometimes when I think about it, I wonder if maybe she would've lived if I'd done something differently. Maybe I could've saved her life."

I stare at Beau. I started out with two sons and a wife. Here I am, nearing the end of my life, and it's just me and my one son. He's old now, and I'm older, but damn do I love that boy. I'd done what I needed to do to protect him. To protect our name and our legacy for him, and Wes, and even Colt.

They all deserve to know a little, and none of them should know everything.

I pat his arm. "She was gone. There was nothing you could've done."

35

SAWYER

I left Sierra Grande immediately, staying the night in some shitty little motel in another town in the Verde valley. I woke up this morning and drove straight to the beach house. On my way out, I called the realtor who sold me the place and asked her to meet me. I might be selling on the upswing, and missing out on additional growth in value, but what about the cost to me? To my heart and my life? I can't hang on to this house for years, the way my dad held on to the Circle B.

Selling the beach house is another way I can move forward. Any step is important right now. My heart feels like it's been carved out with a spork. Might as well go full throttle and wipe the slate clean.

I had the six-hour drive to think about how I ended up in this position. And where I want to go from here. It's easy to look at the events of the past year and a half and see what happened, like data points along a graph. It's more difficult to bring out the magnifying glass and examine the unseen. But that is where I needed to focus, and I did. Through the dry, barren desert, and the spiky-limbed Joshua trees, I forced myself to come face-to-face with facts.

My wife is gone.

I am a widower, and I always will be.

A part of me will never stop loving Brea.

And then, the newest facts, the ones that have torn apart my life for the second time in eighteen months.

My mom was cheating on my dad when she died.

I'm in love with the daughter of the man she cheated with.

It's that last one I can't wrap my head around. The other facts? Data points. But Jessie? She is not data. She is emotion and feeling, warm skin and tender touch. A woman who knows her mind and spirit, and is unafraid of how big both are.

I'm soul-crushingly in love with her.

But how do I reconcile that with who we both are? We've discovered a shared history, and it's ugly and hurtful. How do we come back from that?

I'm twenty minutes early to meet the realtor, so I walk around the home. The entire place needs a good scrub. It's not filthy, but it bears the detritus of a place not maintained. All the pictures are gone, what's left are bones, really. Furniture, rugs, throw pillows. Even so, I see Brea here. Curled up on the sofa with a book, her favorite blanket thrown over her feet because they were always cold.

On the back patio, I kick aside the dried fuchsia bougainvillea leaves scattering the tiled floor. I lift open the stainless steel grill. So fancy, with its integrated smoker and internal halogen lights illuminating the knobs. I prefer the simple grill I bought for Jessie.

Finally, I drag my gaze to the place I've been avoiding. No small task, because it's endless and loud, its presence commanding.

The ocean.

I follow the pavers to the edge of the lawn and stand there. Brea loved the ocean. She didn't need to use sign language to tell me. The first time we stood out here and took in the view, she'd grabbed my arm and nodded emphatically. Her emerald eyes sparkled and she beamed. I'd turned around, met the eyes of the realtor showing us the listing, and given her a thumbs up.

There's a knock on the door, and I answer it. "Anissa, hello." I stand back, welcoming in the same woman who sold me this home. "Come in."

Anissa is around fifty, her corkscrew hair dark as coal. She steps inside, turning to greet me. Her face holds pity I don't want to see. "I'm so sorry for your loss, Mr. Bennett. Such a tragedy. I went to the funeral, but I didn't approach you. Quite frankly, I didn't know what to say."

I accept her words with a simple nod. "Thank you." I walk into the living room and stop. "I'd like to list the house with you. Market value. Don't wait for multiple offers. This doesn't need to become a bidding war. I know it's a sellers' market, but I'm not interested in going along with all that entails. Get a fair price, choose people who will love this home the way Brea did. That's all I ask."

We discuss a few more things, I hand her a key, and leave. The home will always be a part of me, but I want nothing more to do with it.

Still, the finality takes my breath away. I spend a few moments gathering myself in my car.

Before I shift into drive, I glance at my phone. I don't know how many times today I've checked my phone, but it's a lot.

Not once have I found what I'm looking for. Jessie hasn't called, or texted. I don't know that she will. She is as stubborn as she is strong-willed, and she has loyalty in spades. I admire these traits, even right now as I'm coming up against them.

But there is a text from Farley. *I hate to tell you this, but there is nothing to be found about your mother, at least not electronically. No autopsy, like they already told you.*

I think I knew that was going to be the case, but I had to try. I had to be certain. Like I told Jessie, I had to exhaust the possibilities. And I'm relieved the trail was cold. It would be so much more painful if there was something to be found.

A part of me wants to shift into drive and retrace my steps all the way back to Sierra Grande and straight to Jessie's cabin. But I have work to do first. And I have no idea if Jessie will accept me.

I toss my phone back down in my cup holder and pull out. My next stop is my dad's house, for a long-overdue discussion with my father.

* * *

MY DAD IS SHOCKED WHEN HE ANSWERS THE DOOR AND sees me.

He stands back and waves me in. "Come in, come in." There's a napkin balled in his hand, and he uses it to wipe his mouth. "Would you like some dinner?"

I hesitate, and he grins knowingly. "I cooked."

"Then, yes."

Renee and I make small talk while my dad fixes my plate. My indifference to her isn't going to change tonight, but I'll make an effort in the future. I know more now about why he chose her.

They turn their attention to the nightly news while I eat. When I'm done, Renee takes my plate and I thank her. She tells my dad she'll clean up the kitchen. Maybe their deal is that whoever cooks, the other cleans the mess. Or maybe she's giving us time together.

Dad leads me out back. The night is cool. His next-door neighbor is on the phone in their backyard, arguing with someone about something.

It makes me miss Jessie's cabin. I'd never experienced true silence until I sat outside her place.

My dad adjusts himself in his chair. "I don't think my pasta with meat sauce was worth a six-hour drive, Sawyer."

I huff a laugh. "No, it wasn't. No offense."

He holds up his hands. "None taken. Why don't you tell me why you're really here?"

I lean forward in my chair, hands grasped in the space between my knees. "I put the beach house on the market today."

He's quiet for a beat, then says, "That must've been hard."

"It was. But it was necessary."

"Necessary to what?"

I take a deep breath. "Moving on. Something you know a little about."

An empty chuckle rumbles in his throat. "I sure do. I learn a little more about it every day, too. It's not over for me. My guess is that it won't ever be over for you, either. When you truly love someone, I don't think you *get over* them. You simply add them to your heart and keep going. Brea will always be a part of you and your life experience. You don't have to forget her or get over her. But you do need to move forward. Stagnation isn't good for anybody."

"I moved forward with Jessie Hayden." Just saying her name makes me want to hold her in my arms, brush her hair back from her face, kiss the scar on her jaw. "I fell in love with her, even though it confused the hell out of me. It was like it couldn't be stopped."

"Then what the hell are you doing here?"

I shake my head. "Star-crossed lovers, I suppose. A small-town version of Romeo and Juliet."

Dad clears his throat. "That's a cop-out."

My lips turn down at his bluntness. "How am I supposed to be with her now? Mom cheated with Jessie's dad. Mom *died* on the road that leads to town from the HCC. She must've been driving away from Beau. Why else would she be on that road?" My voice catches.

Dad shakes his head slowly. "In life, there are truths we don't get to know. I don't know many details about that day either. I can assume she was driving away from Beau, but I have no way of knowing for sure. And I've had to make peace with that. If you focus on all you don't know, it will consume you."

"I don't know how you lived through all this, Dad." It makes me look at him in a new way.

"As betrayed as I felt, I also knew I wasn't being a good husband. Or even a good person, for that matter.

Your mom and I followed a wild hair when we bought that ranch, and I didn't know what the hell I was doing. I made a lot of mistakes and my pride kept me from owning up to them. I wasn't man enough to admit my limitations, or learn. It took its toll on my marriage. These aren't excuses for what your mom did. Just reasons." He blows out a heavy breath. "I don't want you thinking she was a bad person. Everyone is fallible, given the right set of circumstances."

"That's depressing."

He shrugs. "It depends on how you choose to see it. It can either be depressing, or it can be freeing. As soon as you allow someone to be human and make a mistake, you free yourself from expecting perfection."

I feel his gaze on me, so I look him in the eye.

"What about you, Sawyer? Will you let mistakes made decades ago determine your happiness today?"

Renee pokes her head out of the back door. "Hon, I'm going to sleep. Sawyer, it was nice to see you."

I smile at her and nod. My dad gets up, then looks down at me. "You're welcome to the guest room as long as you need."

I thank him and take him up on his offer. It'll take a bit of time to get the house sold and the papers signed. I have no idea what I'll do after that. Maybe, for right now, I should just take everything one day, one step, one breath at a time.

I take a shower and get ready for bed. When I lie down, I see Jessie. I close my eyes and remember her scent, my hands winding through her silky soft hair, her mischievous grin. There's so much about her I love.

Loved.

Love.

I pinch the bridge of my nose. I have loved and lost. I dared to love again.

But to have it stolen from me once more?

A cruel, cruel punishment.

When I fall asleep, it's Jessie's name on my lips. Her face tattooed on my soul.

36

JESSIE

I've heard time heals all wounds.

What a crock of shit.

It's been two weeks since Sawyer walked out of my life. My heart isn't any less bruised. If anything, all my heart has done is fold in on itself. I think of him constantly. I want him all the time, with a force that frightens me.

I met Marlowe for lunch today. We did some shopping, mostly for home goods. I've been adding to a running list in my head every time I come across something I realize I need and don't have in my house. My back seat is loaded with shopping bags.

I bypass the homestead, where I'm due in an hour for a family dinner that is sure to be awkward. We are muddling our way through, and we'll come out the other side stronger. But the growing pains are, well... painful.

There's a car parked out front of my cabin, and for the briefest second, my brain tricks my heart into thinking it's Sawyer. I don't know why. It's not even the same color as his car.

I know this vehicle though. And I definitely never thought this day would come. I peer into the rearview mirror, checking my reflection, then come to a complete stop in front of my place.

Austin leans against the closed driver door, arms crossed. He is tall, his waist trim, his arms muscled just enough to not be obnoxious. He has not changed.

He'd once seemed so desirable, almost other-worldly. Now I look at him and think of how pathetic he is.

I climb out and spin, facing him over the roof of my car. "Why are you here?"

"Hello to you, too." His smile is cocky.

I shake my head at him. "Don't try that with me."

He taps his thumb against his upper arm. "Don't you want to know how I found you?" There's a trace of pride in his voice.

My chin tips up. It's an arrogant move, one I've seen my dad and brothers do a thousand times. "Not in the least," I say firmly.

"You ghosted me."

Is that hurt I hear in his voice? How rich.

"It was the kindest thing I could do for your wife and baby."

His eyes widen. He blinks and rubs his hand over his mouth. "I didn't realize—"

"That I knew? Yeah. I do." I'm not interested in telling him how I know. I have never been less interested in a conversation in my entire life. "Why are you here?" I repeat, my voice less kind than it was before.

He walks closer, and I watch him warily. He crosses in front of my car and stops on the other side of my open door, so that it forms a barrier between us. "I heard what happened to you. With school. I'm sorry."

I blink and look away. "It was a blessing in disguise."

"How so?" His voice is soft and it draws my attention back to him. It reminds me of how we started in the first place. How he'd invited me to his office hours after I turned in a paper, and told me he thought I could do better. His voice had been soft and caring then, too, and it had felt like a hug when I'd needed one.

I need a hug now, too, but his arms are the last place I want to find myself in.

"I'm running the ranch now. With my brother."

He smiles crookedly. "Your dream came true."

Yes, it did. And yet I've lost so much along the way.

He reaches over the door and tucks a strand of hair behind my ear. His fingers trail over the outside of my earlobe. My shoulders bunch and I move from his reach. "I don't think your wife would appreciate you touching me like that."

He sighs and tucks his hands in his pockets. "I didn't set out to cheat on her. It wasn't my plan. But you, Jessie, you were just," he shakes his head, "you felt like the person I was supposed to be with. You came along too late. Or maybe I settled too early. Does that mean I never get to have you? I have to accept my position, simply because I made the wrong choice?"

I flinch at his words. Considering what I've recently learned about my own father and his infidelity, what Austin is saying packs a punch. "That's the weakest sentence I've ever heard a man speak. Leave your marriage because it's right for *you*, not because you met someone you like better than your wife. For the moment, at least." I close my car door and open the back seat, pulling out bags. "I'm busy. You need to leave."

He stays rooted in his spot, so I cut around him and go toward my house.

Behind me, Austin says, "I spoke to the dean. He's agreed to reinstate you."

I stop and turn around. "Why would you do that?"

"You're smart, Jessie. You have a lot of potential. I don't want to see it wasted."

My arms lift, level with my waist and loaded down with bags. I gesture out at the land surrounding us. "Thanks, but no thanks. I'm happy here."

"You don't seem like you are."

"Fuck off, Austin."

"You liked me, once upon a time. I'm not a bad man, even though I did a bad thing."

"I know good men. I was raised by good men. Just because you're not bad, does not mean you're good." I spin around and keep going. He doesn't say another word, and I unlock the door and step inside. I give it a few minutes, then peek out the front window to see if he's left. He's gone.

My phone chimes with a notification. A text from Austin.

Don't blow this opportunity because you're mad at me.

My fingers hover over the phone, poised as my brain sifts through a snappy response. In the end, I delete the message, block his number, and bring up my last conversation with Sawyer. I read through it four times. A mundane conversation about what to make for dinner.

If only I could be transported back to that time, as recent as it was, when that was our greatest concern.

* * *

THE FAMILY DINNER IS AS AWKWARD AS I THOUGHT IT would be. Where we were once a rowdy, boisterous crew, talking over one another and sending goodnatured barbs across the table, tonight we are quiet. Conversation is contrived. Forced. My dad tries to keep the chatter moving, which might be the biggest, most obvious change of all. A chatty Beau Hayden is unnerving.

Thank God for my nieces and nephews. They provide much-needed entertainment and comedic relief. Just a little while longer and Colt's implants will be turned on. For now, we all use ASL to communicate with him. Every single time someone signs, it reminds me of Sawyer. But in all honesty, almost everything reminds me of Sawyer.

That's what an in-love heart does. It yearns, even when it no longer has a physical target to aim for.

After dinner, my dad asks me for help with dessert. I follow him to the kitchen, knowing this isn't about the pie my mom baked.

He pulls a knife from the block and slices the first of the two pies down the middle. "How are you?" he asks.

I watch him quarter the pie. The scent of apples and cinnamon fills the air.

"Fine," I answer.

He looks at me, his eyes communicating his disbelief.

"I'm not fine," I mutter. I remove a stack of plates from a cabinet, and a handful of forks from a drawer.

My dad finishes cutting the second pie, then places the knife in the sink. He spends a moment gathering his thoughts, facing away from me, shoulders hunched. "I'm very sorry, Jessie." He turns to face me as he speaks. He appears older than he looked a month ago. I thought getting a secret off your chest is supposed to make you feel better, but it doesn't look like the case for him. He's obviously still carrying that weight. Knowing my dad, he will insist he carry it even when everyone has told him he can set it down.

"I hope you know how much I love you," he continues. "How much I love your brothers, and especially your mother."

His love for our family was never in doubt. "I know, Dad."

"And I'm sorry things didn't work out with Sawyer. That's my fault, too."

I nod. My throat feels thick at the mention of his name. "Dad..." I pause, deciding how to word what I've been wanting to say to him. "Sawyer thought it was weird his mom died so close to the HCC, while you were... you know." I cannot say the word *affair*. Not to his face, anyway. "He asked the sheriff for the police report from that day."

I gauge my dad's reaction. There is none. Not even a tic along his jaw.

I swallow past the lump in my throat. "Was there anything weird about it?"

He leans against the sink, folding his arms across his chest. "I can see why he'd think that. If it were my mother, my mind would go there also. But the answer is no. Cynthia's death was an accident. A terrible, tragic accident."

Relief sweeps over me. "That's what I thought."

My dad pulls me in for a hug. His scent is the same as it's been since I was a little girl. It's the first time since Sawyer left that I feel comforted.

37

JESSIE

I rode Titan today, and all it does is remind me of the last person I saw riding him. And also, of the horse I can no longer ride.

Hester Prynne's ashes are ready to be picked up, according to the voice mail left this morning. I'll get them tomorrow. My heart hurts just thinking about it, but it's a familiar feeling. My heart is in pieces anyhow.

Seventeen days since Sawyer left. Not that I'm counting.

After work, I picked up a bottle of wine from my cabin, then stopped at Wes's and requested his pistol. He eyed me warily, asked why I wanted it, then removed the gun from the safe and handed it over. He must think my reason is good enough.

I reach the spot where Hester Prynne broke her leg and get out. I stifle a sob and wipe away a tear. Three seconds before she stepped in that hole, I'd thought my life was perfect. Here I am now, and I've lost my horse and the man I'm in love with.

I unscrew the wine, drink from the bottle because

there's nobody out here to care, and get down on my stomach next to the closest dirt mound. I've done my research. Those rodents like dusk, and a clean shot is the only way to get rid of them. Poison is off the table, because you can't have other animals eating them and getting poisoned as well. Trapping has a low success rate. Enter: the .22.

I wait. And I wait. I am still as can be. A furry little head pops up, and I curl my finger on the trigger. Take a silent breath. And—

Headlights swing my way, a truck in the distance. The gopher drops back into his hole.

"Goddammit!" I'm up on my feet, stomping in the direction of the vehicle. Wes's truck approaches, slows, then turns off. He gets out and rounds the front.

"Thanks a lot, asshole. I had a shot."

He waves me off and opens the passenger seat. Gramps?

Wes grabs two folding chairs from the back of the truck and walks slowly to me, Gramps beside him.

"What's going on?" I ask.

Wes sets up the chairs and tries to help Gramps sit down. Gramps swats at his hands. "Keep your grubby paws to yourself, boy."

Wes grins and backs away. "Thought maybe it was your turn to be on the receiving end of Gramps's words of wisdom. He helped me once—"

"Just once?" Gramps asks sarcastically.

Wes delivers a look to the back of his white-haired head. "He might have something good to say about what you're going through, Jessie. Or maybe not. Maybe he's too old."

Gramps lifts his middle finger in the air. Wes winks

at me and holds out his hand. "Give me back my gun." I hand it over, sheathed in its holster. "Bring him back to the homestead when you're done out here."

"You got it." Wes takes off. I settle next to Gramps.

He looks out at the field and sneers. "Place is full of gophers. Little fuckers. I hate those things."

"Same." If I could snap my fingers and they would all fall dead, I would.

"You shooting them? That's about all you can do."

"I was trying to until you showed up and I lost the opportunity."

"Hmph," he grunts. "Wes came to get me and told me there'd be whiskey."

I walk out to where I'd laid in the dirt and retrieve the bottle of wine. He eyes it distastefully when I hand it to him. "This is a lady drink."

I roll my eyes. "Oh, please. Don't be such a pansy."

He laughs an old man laugh. "Your grandma used to call people that."

"I remember."

He takes a drink of wine, makes a face, and hands me the bottle. "That shit is awful."

"More for me."

"I didn't say I wouldn't drink it. Just that it's awful."

The sun is setting further now, the sky moving from deep orange to purple and pink. I'm not in a position to shoot a gopher anymore, but every few minutes I see a head pop up from a hole. If only I had a rock and a slingshot, David and Goliath style.

"How's that heart of yours doing?" Gramps dives straight into the reason why he was brought out here.

"It hurts, but I'll get through it. At least I have the ranch to keep me busy."

"You better be careful, or you're going to end up like Wes before he met Dakota."

"Wes had PTSD from the military and that's why he buried himself in the ranch. Not a broken heart."

"So? You'll build a wall around your heart and bury yourself in the ranch. Same difference." He taps his knee. "Some broken hearts last a lifetime."

"Aren't you romantic?" I frown at him. "Sawyer had other shit going on too. Like dealing with his grief over his wife."

"Quit blowing smoke up my ass. Maybe he was grieving his *former* wife, but he fell in love with you, Jessie."

I open my mouth to argue, but he stops me and continues. "That boy was spending a lot of time with your nephew and teaching him to sign, in addition to teaching your family. He wasn't just doing it out of the goodness of his heart, even if it started out that way. He did it because he loves you."

I take a big swig of wine and hand it over. "Love doesn't always win, Gramps. Sometimes other problems are too heavy."

He takes the bottle. "Pretend you're on a ship and it's sinking. There are no life preservers. You can either go down with your ship, or jump off and swim, but still risk drowning. What do you do?"

"Jump off and swim, obviously."

"That's what love is like. If you think Sawyer is worth it, jump off the damn boat. Start swimming."

"But our parents'—"

"All relationships have problems to overcome in one sense or another. You give up *this* relationship for *this* problem, you'll only find another one with someone else down the road. What I'm really saying is that if you want to be with Sawyer, you should be. Everything else is details."

I lean back in my chair and draw my knees up and my feet in. "You have anything else to say?"

"Yes," he says. "I'd also like to add that you are a handful and Sawyer likes that about you. It takes a certain type of man to handle a person as strong as you, Jessie. Strong in personality, but also in will. Not everyone is up to the task."

I eye him. "How did you become so wise?"

"I'm old as dirt, that's how. And I pay attention. So, are you going to listen to me and call Sawyer?"

My lips twist as I think. "Maybe. It was a mutual decision though. He left me, too. I think he should work for it a little." I wink at Gramps.

He grins. "That's my girl."

The sun sinks below the horizon. I stand up and reach down for Gramps. "Let's go home."

Gramps shoots me a dirty look and mutters to himself. "Hand to God, if my grandkids don't stop acting like I can't sit down or stand up on my own, I will take a belt to their bare asses."

I scrunch my nose in playful disgust. "I think you can get arrested for that these days. Probably for more than one reason."

He laughs, but he lets me carry both chairs and the wine. I tuck the chairs in the trunk and drive him to the homestead.

He disappears inside and I drive back to my place. I finish the wine, take a shower, and lie down. I look over at the pillow Sawyer used, my hand tracing over the empty space in the bed where his body used to lay.

38

JESSIE

I've stopped to eat lunch at the homestead before heading back out to work. Dakota is here with Colt, and she's just joined me out front. Colt is inside with my mom.

"Are you ready for the appointment next week?" I ask, wiping a smear of my egg salad sandwich from my lower lip. Wes, Dakota, and Colt are going to Phoenix to get Colt's cochlear implant turned on.

"Sure am," Dakota answers, grimacing as she shifts. She's seven months along and says she is officially uncomfortable. "Let's get that device activated so we can move forward. And I can start paying more attention to the next little one." She rubs her stomach. "I feel like I'm so far behind. When I was pregnant with Colt, I was ready months before my due date. This time around, Colt has taken up so much of my time and attention, I haven't been able to focus on his sister."

I pat her stomach. "I'll help you."

She picks at her sandwich. "You're pretty busy these days."

"My evenings are free."

She gives me a knowing look. "Are you ever going to talk about that?"

"It hurts too much." That, and I don't want to give any of it away. Every time I talk about it, it's like breaking off a chunk of my sadness. I want to keep it all together, this hurt I feel about Sawyer, and hold it close.

If I haven't heard from him by the end of this week, I'm going to call him. I'll invent some reason, something he left behind, just so I can hear his voice. He'll see right through me, but that's okay.

She bumps my shoulder. "I'm here if you need someone to listen."

I give a fake smile. "Thanks."

Dakota points at the sky. "Looks like we may finally get some rain. I can't remember the last time that happened."

I follow where she's pointing. In the west, the sky is dark. But all around us, there is nothing but blue sky. "I'll believe it when I see it." It has been only sunny and dry, and every time the forecast calls for rain, there isn't even a stray storm cloud floating by. I'm starting to think the weather forecasters call for rain simply because they are bored with saying the same thing every day.

My mom walks out of the homestead, holding Colt's hand. She hands a plate with half a sandwich to Dakota. "He won't eat a bite for me. Maybe you can get him to eat."

Dakota takes the plate. She picks up his sandwich and offers it to Colt. He shakes his head. Dakota opens her mouth wide like she's going to eat it, and Colt's arm shoots out to stop her. Dakota makes a show of understanding him and holds it out again. He leans forward and takes a bite.

My mom laughs. "Good to know for next time." She looks out. "Oh, look. They didn't even call for rain, but we might get some."

An hour later, it begins to rain. Just a sprinkle, not enough to bother us while we work. We're branding and vaccinating the calves today. Truth be told, I can't stand to be present for either one, but I force myself to do it.

We're in the barn when the rain really starts up. It batters the roof, and Josh runs in, his clothes soaked.

"Is it hailing?" Wes asks, looking up at the ceiling.

"You'd think, by the way that sounds," Josh answers, running a hand through his wet hair. "But it's not. Just raining pretty good."

"Huh," Wes says, eyebrows drawing together.

"What?" I ask. "It's *rain*, Wes. It's what we've been waiting for."

"Rain that comes this fast and hard can lead to a flash flood."

"There's a levee to keep that from happening, remember? Don't be so worried all the time. Just enjoy the rain. Roll out the barrels and collect it."

"They're out, Jessie. Right next to the downspouts, where they should be. The tanks are ready, too." He gives me a long look. It's not unkind, but it's firm. "You're not the only one who's good at your job."

There was a time when that comment would've pissed me off and a snarky comeback would've rolled off my tongue. These days, I'm feeling a little more appreciated, so I say, "Good work, Brother."

Wes glances away, but uses his peripheral vision to

find my eyes and smile at me. I purse my lips and hide my smile.

We finish up for the afternoon, and it doesn't stop raining. It rains and rains, as if the heavens are releasing all they've held back for months on end. Twelve hours later, the rain turned to a sprinkle, and now it is only a mist.

I'm sliding gloves onto my hands to prepare for day two of branding and vaccinating when my mom runs into the barn. She comes to my side and puts her lips near my ear.

"Sawyer is here," she says under her breath.

My heart drops to my knees. "What? He's here? At the homestead?"

She nods. "He pulled up just as I was walking over here. Dakota took Colt to explore around the house after the rain, and I was coming to see if you needed help." She holds up the gloves in her hands, evidence of what she was saying.

I look out the barn doors, but I can't see him from here. I take a deep breath, attempting to slow my frenzied heart rate. It rams against my chest and climbs up my throat anyway.

Peeling off my gloves, I run a hand over my hair and turn to my mom. She smiles at me, and there is nothing but happiness and support in that grin. "Don't live in our past, Jessie. There is nothing for you back there."

"Thank you, Mom," I whisper, kissing her cheek.

I tear from the barn. It feels like years since I've seen him, when in reality it's only been weeks. I turn the corner and there he is, standing beside his car. He's looking down, his hands in his pockets. My God, that man is gorgeous. My heart flips, pivots, stutters. He's wearing the jeans he bought while he was staying with me, and a shirt I don't recognize. The closer I get, the more I see his lips moving. Is he practicing what he's going to say?

I stop a few feet away and clear my throat to get his attention. He looks up. His throat bobs. We stare at each other, the seconds ticking by. Mist dusts our faces.

Sawyer strides across the few feet separating us. He grabs me at the same time I reach for him, grabbing two fistfuls of his shirt.

His lips press to mine, and he kisses me like he is the thirsty land that has been deprived of water. My hands slide through his damp hair. My entire body shivers, and I know it's not the rain.

"Missed you," he says, dragging in a breath and kissing me lightly. "Missed you so much."

The tips of our noses rub together as I nod. "We'll figure it out. All of it. We'll make it work."

"Yes," he breathes, the scent of cinnamon mixing with the smell of rain. "I'm sorry I ran away when it got tough. I was upset and I needed to figure myself out. But the one thing I didn't have to figure out was how I felt about you. You were my constant. I know, no matter what has happened in the past or will happen in the future, that I love you." He kisses me again, and it's the sweetest kiss of my life because his words are still in my ears. "I love you," he whispers again when he pulls away.

I close my eyes and smile. "I love you too, Sawyer. I'm sorry I let you go. I was too shocked to fight, but if there ever comes a time when I need to fight for us, I won't make that mistake twice."

"I—" Sawyer pauses, his expression changing. "What was that sound?"

The sudden change in mood sends alarm bells ringing. "What sound?"

Then I hear it. A rumbling, like a train. Except there aren't train tracks anywhere near Sierra Grande. "Go," Sawyer says urgently, pushing me toward the homestead.

"Sawyer, what—"

Then I see it. And I scream.

39

SAWYER

"Jessie, go," I push her again, just a little harder than before. I have to get her to higher ground.

There were so many things I wanted to say to her, so many things I wanted to do to her, but now making up for lost time is the last thing on my mind.

Someone behind me yells. Wes comes from the barn, arms waving. I can't hear what he's saying. He's too far away, and the thunderous sound is all around us now.

When it appears, it's not what I'm expecting to see. A river of black bears down on us, just a hundred yards out. It looks thick, like sludge, brown and black and full of earth. Sticks, tree branches, and whatever else it picks up as it rolls through. It looks as if it will flow down one side of the house. It will leave a bitch of a mess, but everyone should be fine as long as they get up the stairs and onto the porch.

Jessie is running and pointing, but she's going the wrong way. She's heading toward the flash flood.

I run after her and hear Wes screaming behind me. He's yelling for Dakota and Colt.

I look around, trying to understand, and then I do.

On the other side of the rapidly approaching flood are Dakota and Colt. She lies on the ground on her side, her belly huge, and she's half crawling, half dragging herself. Colt runs in front of her. I look at his little legs, running like hell, but he's smiling. He has no idea the danger in front of him. I don't understand what has happened to Dakota, but I know if she could be running right now, she would be.

There is no way Colt will make it across the yard before the mud and sticks knock him down and very possibly sweep him away. I've seen videos of flash floods and I know this is the beginning. The water is coming.

Dakota, on the ground behind Colt, screams for him.

Wes, sprinting all the way from the barn, screams for him.

He.

Can't.

Hear.

The mud has reached us now, and I sink down to my knees, waving to get Colt's attention. I use my hands to tell him to stay. I sign for *mommy*. He turns around to look at Dakota, who is still crawling on her forearms, using only one leg to propel herself forward.

A sound like a train fills the air again. The ground rumbles. The mud thins, and the water comes, tumbling down from the higher elevation, a river appearing out of nowhere. It branches out, unencumbered by nothing. There aren't any ditches or embankments, no sandbags. The water is free to do to the land what it pleases.

And Colt is swept away.

Over the rush of water, Dakota's wail pierces the air.

My body kicks into gear. I sprint parallel to the flow, my chest burning with exertion. Colt, miraculously, is on his back, but he is spun around and there may only be seconds before the water turns him over. There's a spot up ahead where I can maybe get in front of the water as it surges forward.

I push harder, run like I never have before, and charge into the rushing water. It's more than six inches deep, enough to knock over a grown man. But there's something to be said for adrenaline, and I feel it pulsing through me now. I move quickly, never giving the water enough time to bring its full force against me. I dive in front of Colt, so that he will be stopped by my body, and I wrap my arms around him, pushing his face to the sky. The water rises rapidly, higher and higher, and it takes me and Colt away. I drape him over my chest, and my back takes the scrape of sharp rocks, the stabs of tree branches.

Colt's entire body is shaking, and mine is too.

There's a tree ahead, dead center of the rushing water. I hold Colt tightly with one arm, tucking him into me like an oversized football. I reach out, stretching, and my fingers only brush it as we go by.

I want to sob, but instead of coming from my mouth, it feels like my entire body is sobbing.

Colt deserves to live. That's what I keep telling myself, over and over, repeating it like a mantra. It spurs me on to look ahead, planning for the next tree. And when I see it, I'm better prepared. I cannot control the way the water pushes us, but I can use it. I lean to one side, guiding myself, and when we're close, I grab onto it.

Everything inside me rejoices. With my legs tucked around the skinny cottonwood trunk, I keep Colt to my chest and hold on for dear life.

I take deep breaths in an attempt to slow Colt's heart rate. I want him to feel that we are okay, even if he cannot hear my whispered assurance.

"Sawyer," a voice yells. The sound of water is loud in my ears, but frantically I search the land. An HCC truck, two men on the newly formed bank. *Beau and Wes.* Someone else gets out. Gramps.

The tree was a life preserver, but seeing these men? It's my first taste of hope since I retrieved Colt.

Beau ties two ropes to a tree. He looks down at them, and back to us. Wes takes the ropes from his dad's hands and starts to wind one around his midsection, but Beau shakes his head. I can't hear anything they're saying, but they're in disagreement. Wes points at us, and Beau shakes his head vehemently. Gramps takes the ropes from Wes and loops one around his waist. Beau and Wes tell him no, I can read it on their lips. He ignores them. Gramps ties himself into one length of rope, coils the second, and holds fast to it. He steps into the water.

Beau and Wes's hands press together in prayer position at their mouths. Wes's lips move as he whispers his prayer. If Beau is praying, he's doing so silently.

Gramps widens his stance. He walks slowly, taking each step with great care and purpose. He reaches us, and doesn't say a word. He wraps the rope around my waist and ties a knot. "Do not let go of that boy," he growls, then gives a thumbs-up to Beau and Wes.

Wes yanks the ropes, removing the slack, and then, hand over hand, the two men begin to pull us in. I help as much as I can, but there isn't a lot I can do without risking Colt, and he is the reason for all this.

A fresh torrent of water rips through. Wes and Beau, two strong, healthy, capable men, struggle to pull us across the pressure and force of the running water. Behind them, I see what they don't.

The tree they've tied us to bends, yielding to the weight it's been forced to hold. Gramps's eyes meet mine. He sees it too.

"Hurry," I yell, as if it will help. It won't. It is simply a matter of strength and weight, force and energy.

Gramps stares into my eyes. I cannot read what he's thinking, because the expression doesn't make sense for the circumstance.

He looks at Wes and Beau, struggling despite their combined strength. The water stretches out, encircling the tree, swirling around Wes and Beau's boots. How long before they are swept away too?

Something has to give. If I hand Colt to Gramps, they will be more likely to make it to safety. If I untie myself, I might be able to get myself out of this situation somewhere along the way. But also... I might not.

Gramps reaches underwater, shoulder moving as his arm works at something. His hand clears the surface, and the appearance of the knife confuses me at first. He presses a button, the blade pops up, and it all makes sense.

"No," I yell, but it's too late. Gramps has cut himself away.

Until this moment, everything had been so loud. The water, the yelling, my pulse in my ears. Suddenly, it's silent. I hear nothing. I can see nothing but what may be Gramps's final words. And they don't make sense.

I'm sorry.

The screaming reaches into me. Beau and Wes, their *no's* a piercing howl. Wes shoves his dad's shoulder, shakes his head, points at me and Colt with two fingers. Wes, ever the leader, is directing his dad to act despite their suffering.

We begin to move. Colt, gathered in my arms with his face pressed to my chest, is still silent. I fear that by now, he is in shock.

Without the weight of a second man, Beau and Wes bring us closer and closer to them. I get to a point where I am able to use my own body weight against the current, and I press my feet to the bottom. I am exhausted, my muscles near fatigue, but I walk out of the water.

Wes rips Colt from my arms, and I drop to my knees.

"Son? Son?" Beau says urgently.

My hands are on my thighs, my head bent as relief and agony rip through me in equal measure. Jessie's heart will break once more when she learns about her grandpa.

An arm wraps around my shoulders, hauling me to my feet. "Son, come on." Beau leads me to his truck. I'd thought he was talking to Wes, but he'd been referring to me. *Son.*

Beau is on his phone, telling Sheriff Monroe about his father.

"Beau," Sheriff says, his voice audible in the truck cab. "It's unlikely he'll survive."

"I know." Beau palms his forehead, fingers digging in.

"Get those boys to the hospital. I'll take it from here."

I sit up front. Wes lies down in the back seat with his shirt off. He has removed Colt's wet clothes and they are skin to skin. The heat transfer is helping to ease Colt's trembling. That, and being with his father.

"Sit back, Sawyer," Beau instructs. Tears fall silently down his face. "Try and rest before we get there."

"I can't sit back," I tell him, hinging forward at the hips to show him my back. My skin is as torn through as my shirt.

"Christ," Beau mutters. He reaches across the console, touching the back of my head gently. "I don't deserve what you did for me today."

Maybe he doesn't.

Maybe he does.

I don't care anymore. I can't spend my life allowing other people's past mistakes to dictate my future. I don't want to think about him with my mother. I don't want to hate him.

"I love your daughter, Beau. All I want is to move forward with her."

Beau places his hand back on the wheel. He purses his lips and shakes his head. "You're a better man than I ever was, Sawyer. My daughter is lucky to have you."

We reach the hospital. Colt and I are taken back immediately. They start an IV for fluids, and as soon as the tube is in my arms, I close my eyes and pass out.

40

GRAMPS

A NOBLE ENDING.

That's all a man can hope for.

The flood water throws me about. It hurts. Everything hurts.

Some broken hearts last a lifetime.

That's what I'd told Jessie. I meant it. I broke my own heart a long time ago.

I took the keys from Cynthia Bennett's pocket, rode her horse back to her ranch and took her car. I positioned her car on the road, facing the tree. I placed her in the driver's seat. I laid the biggest rock I could find on the gas pedal.

I watched the car slam into the tree. And just before it did, Cynthia jolted upright, and her eyes opened.

Like Beau, I'd thought she was dead.

She died instantly one second later.

I never told Beau.

Only Sheriff Monroe knew the truth, and he made sure it stayed hidden. Like many of us, the lawman has done a great amount of good, and also some bad.

What I did just now doesn't erase what I did back then. But, dear God, I hope when I get to Heaven, I can look Cynthia in the eyes and tell her I saved her son. I knew what Sawyer was thinking. He would've handed Colt to me and untied his rope if I hadn't cut myself away first.

This is my ending, and I couldn't have written it any better.

41

JESSIE

Sawyer's chest rises and falls, a rhythm I'm profoundly grateful for. When he disappeared from my view, flood water sweeping him and Colt away, I was certain how it would all go.

Flash floods are sudden and powerful, and they often end in heartbreak.

Today, there are two endings.

My heart is overjoyed. It is also broken. Funny how a heart can share such opposite but equally encompassing emotions.

I long to touch Sawyer's face, brush the tips of my fingers over his cheek. I want him to wake up and kiss me.

He lies on his side. The nurse said his back required stitches in multiple places. Where he is not bandaged, he is red. Soon he will be bruised.

His hair flops over, lying against his forehead. He is so handsome, so brave and selfless. My heart, brimming with love for him, spills over, trickling through me.

His eyes open slowly, blinking and adjusting. "Jessie," he whispers.

I'm up out of my chair, leaning down to look him in those stunning gray eyes. In them, I see my future. My forever.

"Sawyer," I whimper, my fear and grief catching up to that all-consuming love I feel for him.

"Your grandpa," he starts, his voice a pained groan. "Is he...?"

My eyes sting. I shake my head. "He passed away, Sawyer."

Sawyer shuts his eyes, and a single tear rolls out, gliding sideways before it soaks into the pillow. "He sacrificed himself."

I nod, the lump in my throat growing. "He died where he was born. On HCC land. He loved that ranch more than anything, and it's exactly where he'd have chosen for it to happen."

Sawyer opens his eyes. He looks so sad. "Right before he cut the rope, he said 'I'm sorry'. What did he mean? Why was he sorry?"

"Are you sure you heard him correctly?"

He nods, biting the inside of his lower lip while he mulls it over.

My fingers drift over his jaw, scraping on the stubble. "If you didn't call me before the week was out, I was going to come up with a reason to call you. I couldn't let it be over between us."

He takes my hand and presses a kiss to the inside of my wrist. "I sold my California house. Everything that was in storage. It will serve someone else now." He sighs, and the heated air streams against my skin. "There was never a chance I was going to stay away from you. I realized quickly that my heart wasn't up to the task."

His words reflect exactly what's in my heart. How many nights did I fall asleep thinking about him? And then wake up the next morning, the thoughts continuing like my brain had pressed pause while it slumbered. Here he is now, in front of me. Bloodied and bruised, but he is here. He came back to me.

"Is Colt okay?" he asks. He doesn't sound too worried though. He saw him all the way up until they were taken to separate bays in the emergency room.

"Perfectly healthy, thanks to you."

He doesn't respond to my recognition. I don't think he enjoys it. Instead, Sawyer studies my hand. "Why are you wearing a ring on your wedding finger?"

The corner of my mouth turns up in a smile. "They told me I couldn't see you unless I was family. So I borrowed Dakota's ring and told them I'm your wife."

"I like how persistent you can be when something gets in your way." He turns my hand over, his finger tickling my palm as he traces the lines. "Is that something you think you could be sometime?"

"Persistent?" I ask the wrong question on purpose. "If the situation calls for it."

He looks up at me through his dark lashes. "My wife?"

His question thrills me, but I'm also devastated. My reaction is watered down, and not representative of how it truly makes me feel inside.

My head bobs up and down, a pleased smile curving my lips upward. "Yes. You're it, Sawyer. There is no one else for me."

"Good." Sawyer smiles, but it's sad too. "Kiss me."

I kiss him gently, because I don't know how he's feeling and he has been through a lot today. He grips the back of my head and holds me close. He is not gentle.

He kisses me like a man who feared for his life today. If he cares about his injuries, he doesn't show it. His fingers curl over my hip bone and his tongue invades my mouth.

Someone clears their throat. We break apart. Wes's head peers around the light blue hospital curtain. He pulls it all the way back. "Sorry to interrupt," he ducks his head in apology, "but—"

Dakota appears beside Wes, her foot outfitted in a walking boot. She'd stepped in a small hole while exploring with Colt and suffered a level two sprained ankle. She'd also narrowly avoided falling onto her stomach, and the scratches on her palms and down her right leg show how she'd awkwardly crawled after Colt.

Dakota steps tenderly across the small space and lines herself up at Sawyer's bedside. "Thank you," she says, gratitude saturating her voice. "I'll never be able to thank you enough for what you did today."

Sawyer waves away her declaration. "I was closest to him. Any decent person would have done the same."

From the edge of the small room, Wes speaks. "That's not true. I've seen plenty of decent people freeze in a moment of crisis. You were a hero today."

Sawyer blinks hard. "I'm sorry about Gramps. For your loss."

Wes bites his lower lip to staunch the overflow of tears that shine in his eyes. "That tricky bastard."

His words make us all breathe out a laugh. "Of course he would do what he did." Wes swipes at one eye.

"That's probably why he insisted on being the one to go out there. He knew it might come to that, and he didn't want anyone else having to make that decision."

"Are Wyatt and Warner coming here?" I ask Wes, who was calling them when I was flashing Dakota's ring to the nurse. I slide it off my finger and hand it back to her, but it won't fit over her knuckles when she tries it.

"Damn swollen fingers," she says, pointing at her large stomach. "Just wear it until we get back to the homestead. I'm afraid I'll lose it if it's in my pocket."

"Wyatt and Warner are meeting us at the homestead," Wes says, answering my question. "I wanted to be the one to tell them about Gramps, but they'd already heard in town. Something like a flash flood on the HCC and the passing of a Hayden makes for good chatter. Once it was called in to the police, I knew it was going to spread instantly."

The metallic screech of hooks being dragged across a rod reverberates through the shoebox-size room. Sawyer's nurse narrows her eyes at the number of people standing around him. Quickly I slide the ring back onto my finger.

"Unless you're Mr. Bennett's wife, you need to leave." She gives Wes and Dakota a once-over. "Please," she adds.

Wes makes a face. "Wife? Who's—"

Dakota shoves him toward the exit. "See you at the homestead, Mr. and Mrs. Bennett."

The nurse gives me a dirty look before she turns her attention to Sawyer. "Are you ready to get out of here and go home with your"—her eyes flicker to me, then back to him—"wife?"

She gives him his discharge instructions, explaining wound care and when to follow up with his doctor.

On our way out, with Sawyer's arm around my shoulder and my arm around his waist, we stop in to peek at Colt. Wes and Dakota listen attentively to the nurse standing at Colt's bedside, so we don't interrupt them. Colt sees Sawyer, and a grin spreads across his small face.

Sawyer waves at Colt, and we walk out of the emergency room.

My mom and dad sit in the waiting room. Everything about my dad is downturned. His shoulders droop, the corners of his lips point at the unattractive brown carpet. My mom runs her fingers through the hair on the back of his head. They see us at the same time and bolt to standing.

My dad does the most shocking thing I've ever seen him do. He *hugs* Sawyer. And Sawyer returns the embrace.

* * *

SOMEHOW, I HAVE JUST WRAPPED UP THE MOST confusing week of my life.

Every night I fall asleep in Sawyer's arms. Every morning he wakes me with a kiss on my neck. And all day long, my heart hurts when I think of who is missing from the ranch.

Sawyer didn't let go of my hand yesterday at the funeral. Not during the service, the greeting afterward, or the reception at the homestead. Sawyer has given my heart a place to go, no matter the emotion.

The Calamity

Warner and Wyatt were, of course, devastated by the news of Gramps's passing, and unsurprised by how it happened. Warner spoke at the funeral, his eloquent eulogy putting tears in the eyes of every attendee. Wyatt, who was not behind a mic, called Gramps a 'slippery sonofabitch' as the tears rolled down his face. Jo consoled him.

Sawyer and I are having a lazy Sunday morning, the kind with creamy coffee and slow stretches. I'm sitting on the couch, reading the local news on an iPad balanced on my lap. Sawyer gets up to refill his coffee, but when he sits down he doesn't have a cup.

"You're missing what you got up for," I point out.

He takes my legs and pulls them across his thighs. Using his thumb, he rubs the instep on my right foot. I smile at him over the edge of the tablet.

"Are you done reading?" Hope lifts his eyebrows.

I slide the iPad onto the coffee table, along with my half-full mug. "I can be."

He grins wickedly. "Good." He crawls up my body, wrapping an arm around my waist and shifting me so that I'm beneath him. He lowers his mouth to my collarbone, nipping along its length. My nails run down his arms, carefully avoiding his back. Just a little more time and he'll be fully healed, with only scars to tell the story of what he did for my family.

His mouth moves up my neck, dragging along my jaw, and then he kisses me.

We stay that way, making out for so long my lips ache. I will probably have irritation around my mouth from his scruff, but it's worth it.

Sawyer's hand trails down my stomach, and finally takes this from rated PG to R. He settles between my legs and buries himself inside me. I feel it through my whole body, but mostly in the center of my chest.

Without thinking, my nails dig into his back. He stiffens and I rip my hands away. "Oh my God, I'm so sorry."

He leaves me, then enters again, looking down at where we are linked. "If this is my prize, I'll gladly take the pain."

I smile at him, my hand trailing over his chest. I draw a heart over his real heart. Sawyer clutches my hand and lifts it, kissing my fingers.

When it's over, he lies on top of me. I love his weight. I love him.

We stay that way as long as we can, and then we are forced to get up. "We'd better shower before we head over to the homestead." Sunday brunch at the homestead feels extra special today. Gramps's passing has reminded us all how precious life is. How quickly it can be taken from you.

We climb into the shower. Sawyer washes my hair, fingers kneading my scalp.

I lean into his hands. "You should give up that fancy job of yours and start a scalp massage business."

He turns me around, guiding my head back into the spray. "What would you say if I told you I was thinking of quitting my job?"

"Why? Your dad said he's fine with you working remotely." Sawyer's dad's only request was that he make an in-person appearance at the office once a month.

He adds conditioner to my hair. "I've been thinking about leaving Tower Properties and forming my own one-man show here. This town is booming, and I'd like to give it my full attention."

I rise on tiptoe to kiss him. "You have my support."

We finish showering, somehow managing to stay on task, and get ready to eat brunch with my family.

I'm on my way out our front door when Sawyer stops me in my tracks with a question.

"How old do you want to be when you get married?"

I stare at him. "Why?"

He shrugs. "Just making plans."

Happiness bubbles up in my stomach, but one thought tamps it down a bit. "Twenty-one seems a little young."

"Perhaps." He slides his hands in his pockets. "Then again, you've always done whatever you wanted without much concern for convention."

He's right. I smile at him. "Ask me your question again."

"How old do you want to be when you're married?"

My arms slide around his neck. "However old I am when I'm asked."

Sawyer beams. He takes my hand and I follow him down the stairs.

The past few months have been filled with tremendous loss.

But also astounding gains.

And the most profound of them all is the man holding my hand, leading the way directly into my future.

EPILOGUE

ONE YEAR LATER

"STOP, STOP," TENLEY SAYS, NUDGING DAKOTA OUT OF THE way. She selects a different lipstick from the various tubes on the side table. "That color is too warm for her." She uncaps the lipstick and applies it to my lips. "There," she says proudly, turning me toward the floor-to-ceiling trifold mirror.

"It's perfect," I declare, smacking my lips. Jo laughs at me. Like me, Jo thinks a lot of this is unnecessary. As long as I'm at the end of the aisle with Sawyer, everything else is just details.

Tenley and Dakota beg to differ. They want the whole nine yards, and I don't mind. Until them, I never had sisters. If they want to dress me up like a doll, well... have at it.

"He's going to lose his mind," Dakota says, looking at me with her head tilted. She smiles warmly at me.

I wiggle my eyebrows and drink my champagne.

"That's the point, right? Honeymoon night, here we come!"

"Oh, please." Tenley bats my upper arm. "You live together. Don't act like that man isn't enjoying the cow whenever he wants." She turns to Dakota. "Is that how it goes?"

Dakota rolls her eyes and laughs. *"He won't buy the cow if he gets the milk for free."*

"Shoot." Tenley shakes a fist. "I tried."

Jo groans and Dakota doubles over in laughter.

I look at my mother, so quiet in her seat. She's been sipping champagne and watching me try on wedding dresses. It's not like her to be silent. I gather the bottom of the seventh dress I've tried on, a big princess-y gown I detest, and make my way over to her.

"Mom? All good over here?"

Her answering smile is thick. "Oh, I'm fine. Just watching my daughter and trying not to cry."

"I think of all days, this would be an acceptable day to cry."

"Yes," she says softly. "It's overwhelming to watch the four of you together. Four Hayden women."

"Soon to be Hayden-Bennett," I remind her.

She touches my leg. I can't feel it through the layers of tulle and silk and beading, but the gesture warms me. "Right, of course."

For the most part, she loves Sawyer. But every once in a while, I sense a twinge from her, a micro-pain.

Sawyer doesn't have a problem with my refusal to drop my last name. I'm happy to be a Bennett, but Hayden is my birthright. The last name, and all that it encompasses, is woven into the fabric of my being.

I joked with Sawyer that he could take my last name.

"We'd be very modern," I said. His response? "A Bennett belongs here."

I cannot argue with that. I'm not interested in erasing his mother. She deserves to be remembered as much as anybody else. She's even represented in town again, with a lemon scone at The Bakery. Few know why it was recently added to the menu, but those of us who know, smile at the secret.

I won't pretend every day has been rainbows and butterflies. It hasn't. My dad and Sawyer had a long talk soon after the day Sawyer returned to the HCC and saved Colt. My dad apologized for his role in hurting Sawyer's family. Sawyer accepted the apology, but he's still working on forgiving my dad. And his own mother. It's a lot for him to take, and he's not alone in that feeling.

Sawyer's dad and his stepmom will arrive a couple days prior to the ceremony. Our dads have assured us their bad blood has long since dried up, but I'm not expecting it to be easy. As long as they are supportive of our marriage, nothing else really matters.

There are moments when Sawyer and I feel hurt and sad, or sometimes indignant, by the choices made by our parents. When those times come, we force ourselves to remember who it was who committed the crime.

Not us.

We are separate from them, and we return to the promise of our love every time we think about what they did. I thank God every day there was nothing for Sawyer to find in his search for what happened to his mother. Sometimes, bad things are simply just bad things.

The shop attendant brings in another bottle of champagne. It's our second, probably thanks to Tenley. When we showed up for our appointment, the woman took one look at Tenley and ushered us back to their private dressing area. Perks of having a famous sister-in-law.

Dakota tops off glasses. Jo declines, and Dakota gives her a hard stare. "You haven't had almost any of the first glass I poured." Her lips purse and her eyes widen. "Do you have news?"

"Wyatt and I are expecting." Jo smiles, but her lips quiver. "I just, um, I don't want to get super excited yet. It's early. I'm eight weeks. And before, you know..."

"Hey," I say, hurrying to her side. "We are *thrilled* for you." My heart twists at the fear in her eyes. Jo has suffered two miscarriages over the past year.

My mother stands up and makes her way over. Of all of us, she understands what Jo is feeling more than anybody. She holds Jo's shoulders and looks her in the eyes. "Everything is going to be okay." Then she folds Jo into a hug.

I throw my arms around both of them. I can't help it. Tenley and Dakota join in, and now it's a big Hayden-women hug.

We pull away, and the saleswoman grins at us sheepishly. "I hope you don't mind, but I grabbed a phone"—she points down at Dakota's phone—"and took a picture. That was just too sweet."

Dakota thanks her and texts the photo to all of us.

Thirty minutes later, I find *the one*. The perfect dress.

We grab lunch and head back up to Sierra Grande.

Later that night, lying in bed with Sawyer by my side, I tell him I chose a dress.

He kisses my forehead. "Don't tell me anything about it. I want to be surprised."

"Ready for another surprise? Jo is pregnant."

He grins. "I know. Wyatt told me today."

While the ladies all went wedding dress shopping in Phoenix, the men went to Warner's house and fished by the river, followed by a barbecue and lawn games. I hear my dad bought a new bottle of Macallan 25 for the occasion, and Wyatt finally got that glass he'd been waiting for.

My brothers have come to love Sawyer. They did the older brother thing by giving him a speech about what they would do if he ever broke my heart, *yada yada*, but it was perfunctory. Sawyer had already sealed himself into the folds of the family.

On my wedding day, Wes, Warner, and Wyatt come to the little room where I'm getting ready. Wyatt hugs me tightly, not shy when he tells me I'll always be his baby sister. Warner kisses my forehead, and tells me I make a beautiful bride. Wes, generally uncomfortable with displays of emotion, gruffly says, "I love you, Cal. That's all I have to say. I'm not good at fancy sentences like these fools." I throw my arms around my oldest brother. His simple words are all I need.

And so, on a cool fall day, with the sun hanging high in the sky and the cottonwood leaves a bright yellow-gold, a Hayden married a Bennett.

"Wife," Sawyer whispers, turning the word into a reverence. His gaze holds warmth and love, and it's only a fraction of what he feels for me.

"Husband," I respond, saying the word for the first time as a married woman.

The pastor tells Sawyer he may kiss me. Sawyer

loops an arm around my lower back, a hand twining into my hair. My face tips, our lips meet, and it's the sweetest kiss of my life.

Our family and friends cheer. Sawyer pulls away, grinning down at me. "You ready to do this?"

I'm beaming so hard it's borderline painful. "I've never been so ready."

Sawyer takes my hand, leading me down the aisle and into our future.

The End

Want more Hayden family? Visit jennifermillikinwrites.com to read a Hayden family prequel novella.

ACKNOWLEDGMENTS

Readers. I have an infinite amount of gratitude for you. The way you make space in your hearts for my stories never ceases to amaze me. The way you've loved the Hayden family and their dynamic brings me such happiness.

Kristan. My sister from another mister. Everyone should know you dropped what you were doing when I called and told you The Calamity was ninety percent done and I was stuck. The story no longer worked. Your words? "Come over. We'll work through it." We changed the entire story that afternoon. Six days before it went to my editor. If it weren't for you, The Calamity would be an entirely different book. And that's not a good thing. So thank you. Thank you forever, for being my hype woman, my shoulder. You're the only person I want to rent a tiny truck and drive two hours on unfamiliar freeways with in Texas.

Jen's Jewels, I love you! Thank you for being a place where I can pop in and say random things, and for spending time in our little corner of the internet.

As always, big thanks and hugs to my husband. I put a little piece of you in all my heroes, especially Wes

Hayden. And Nick Hunter, of course. I love you twice as much as yesterday, and half as much as tomorrow.

Dad. Where would the Hayden Family series be without you? Among these pages lies real-life scenarios, directly from you. Thank you for allowing me to take your stories and adjust them to fit my characters.

ABOUT THE AUTHOR

Jennifer Millikin is a bestselling author of contemporary romance and women's fiction. She is the two-time recipient of the Readers Favorite Gold Star Award, and readers have called her work "emotionally riveting" and "unputdownable". Following a viral TikTok video with over fourteen million views, Jennifer's third novel *Our Finest Hour* has been optioned for TV/Film. She lives in the Arizona desert with her husband, children, and Liberty, her Labrador retriever. With thirteen novels published so far, she plans to continue her passion for storytelling.

Visit jennifermillikinwrites.com to sign up for her newsletter and receive a free novella.

- facebook.com/JenniferMillikinwrites
- instagram.com/jenmillwrites
- bookbub.com/profile/jennifer-millikin

Made in the USA
Monee, IL
23 June 2024